Cold as the Clay

Books by Rod Miller

Rawhide Robinson *series*
Rawhide Robinson Rides the Range
Rawhide Robinson Rides the Tabby Trail
Rawhide Robinson Rides a Dromedary
Rawhide Robinson Rides a Wormhole

Novels
Cold as the Clay
Father Unto Many Sons
Pinebox Collins
Silver Screen Cowboy

Cold as the Clay

Rod Miller

SPEAKING VOLUMES, LLC
NAPLES, FLORIDA
2021

Cold as the Clay

Copyright © 2012 by Rod Miller

ISBN 978-1-64540-632-7

This book is dedicated to my friends
Marc Otte, Mark Henry, and Marc Cameron
who all thought it was a good idea.

And they covered him with clothes, but he gat no heat.

1 Kings 1:1

Prologue

Notes spun gently away from the guitar and entwined themselves with the tobacco smoke drifting through the room. The guitarist sat leaning against a wall, the front legs of his wooden ladder-back chair propped on empty air.

Half a dozen men dressed in cowboy regalia lazed about the room, tired from a long day branding calves and logy from taking on a load of fried beef, biscuits, and beans. And they were yet under the influence of an intoxicating peach cobbler that lingered like a pleasant, remembered dream.

They were young men, mostly. Only the man seated at the head of the table showed any sign of gray, and his full head of hair and thick beard were plentiful with the shade. His supper sloshed in rye whiskey, for while he allowed these men who worked for him only a single shot this evening, he did not likewise limit himself, being firm in the belief that rank has its privileges.

The old man removed his hat and laid it crown down on the table in front of him, raked both sets of fingers through his hair, then, while rubbing the heels of his hands around the lids of itchy eyes, bowed forward until his elbows hit the tabletop to support his head.

He sat stooped and unmoving for some time, fallen asleep, maybe, while his cowboys talked softly and smoked, lulled by the lateness and their tiredness and the music.

The guitarist heard the knife blade hiss as it sliced the air then stuck in the log wall with a hollow thunk, cutting short a chord to leave it hanging in air suddenly turned tense. With held breath, he swiveled his eyes slowly to the left to see the thick-hafted Bowie where it hummed and quivered, spiked some four inches from his shoulder.

"What the hell, Mister Longmore," he finally managed to strangle out. "You liked to kill me with that pig sticker."

All eyes shifted from the thrown knife to the thrower, the old man now upright and pawing through a cubby-hole in a storage cabinet. Once he laid his hand on another heavy-bladed knife he turned back around to face a roomful of hands with eyes wide and jaws agape.

Squinting through whiskey and smoke as he swayed on widespread legs, he found his target. "Damn right I'd like to kill you. You're an ingrate and an upstart and I'm sick of the sight of you. That you're married to my daughter only makes it worse." With that he cocked the knife over his shoulder and let fly.

This time, he did not miss.

The swishing blade pierced the hollow body of the guitar just below the neck. Strings popped and twanged as fingerboard splintered from soundboard and blonde wood became flinders.

The wounded instrument and the chair legs hit the floor together, a mere instant before the door slammed behind the guitarist taking sudden leave of his position as foreman of Longmore's Fishhook Ranch.

There is irony in this situation for those drawn to see such things—for the same guitar shattered at this end of this relationship had started it in the beginning.

Chapter One

The only things Wilson Hayes could claim title to were the clothes he wore and the guitar he held. The tattered attire was hardly worth owning, but the guitar was a beautiful instrument of great value.

Glowing golden wood cut to the classic shape formed the soundboard; the curved sides and back sorrel-colored with a warm polish. The flattop box was his only inheritance from a large, well-heeled family. The boy and the guitar were, in fact, all that remained of that particular Hayes line.

In the boy's practiced hands, the guitar sounded as good as it looked, maybe better. He carried tunes of all kinds in his head and hands, and played practically anything asked. But when the choice was his own, he opted for mournful melodies with a Spanish, maybe Gypsy essence. One such song was the first Jesse Longmore heard him play.

As awash in money as the boy was bereft, Longmore was the wealthiest man for miles around the town the guitarist had wandered into. He owned the biggest mercantile, the busiest saloon, the fanciest hotel, the best-stocked livery, the richest bank, and many of the town lots his competitors in those enterprises occupied.

But none of those businesses interested the man, and he did not even live in what was essentially his town. Cattle made his fortune, the range still held his heart, and a distant ranch was still his home. His brand was the letter "J," first initial of his given name, simple and unadorned. But the ranch took its name from something else the shape suggested—the Fishhook.

Over the man's many years in the country, his Fishhook holdings increased as adjacent landowners abandoned their spreads, unable to withstand the pressure of a bigger, stronger neighbor. The pressure was sometimes financial, with Longmore offering a better price than the owners of choice acreage could refuse, or buying up mortgages and foreclosing when marginal operators couldn't meet their obligations.

Just as often, it was pressure of a different kind. Perhaps a simple matter of Fishhook cattle drifting onto range not their own, no matter how often they were turned back. Sometimes it was the opposite problem of a smaller rancher's stock wandering off repeatedly, no matter how closely herded, to be finally lost among Fishhook herds on the wide range. It might be lack of water, when a previously reliable creek through a nester's place dried up, diverted by Longmore upstream for his own purposes, claiming the right to do so by seniority.

In any event, few ranchers withstood the aggressive Fishhook owner's wish to own everything in sight from whatever vantage point he chose. And the fact is, once they got to know Longmore and see the way he treated the likes of them, most were happy to quit the country at first opportunity.

Only Sam Ballard's Rafter 7, sprawling beyond the Fishhook range, was able to coexist, and that because it was already a big, thriving operation when Longmore arrived. That, and the fact that its owner was every bit as grasping. So the outfits fought for every parcel of land, with blocking moves and flanking strategies and surprise attacks worthy of the best military minds. The two men opposed each other continuously, each bargaining for and buying up any perceived advantage over the other. The fact that the town Longmore owned the most of— Ballard Station—carried the name of his rival irritated like a burr under a saddle blanket. On occasion, disagreements between the two outfits were resolved with blood.

From it all, Longmore had become a cynical, suspicious man. He was ornery, a chronic condition worsened by a fondness for alcohol. His mood was volatile, ranging from despondent to driven. The men and women in his employ avoided him at every opportunity. His children—a son, and a daughter nearly grown—feared more than respected him. They learned to accommodate his sour disposition, mostly by steering clear whenever possible. Their lessons in dealing with their father were learned without benefit of a mother's tutelage, for she had left them years before when a wagon hitched to a runaway team overturned and crushed the life out of her.

And so it was a troubled, lonely, angry, drunken, downhearted, belligerent Jesse Longmore who Wilson Hayes met that night on the streets of Ballard Station.

The rancher, after a long afternoon and evening at a corner table in the quiet bar at the hotel, pulled the slack out of the cinch on the saddle of a leg-weary horse at the hitch rail out front and set out down the town's main street. He soon rode into a quiet drift of song from an unseen guitar. The curious, haunting melody grew louder as he drew even with the dry goods store and lured him off the main street and around the corner onto a side street, little more than an alley giving access to the store's loading dock.

Reining up next to the platform, Longmore searched the shadows for the source of the sound. Finally, he found a pair of spindly legs poking out from beyond a shipping crate. The rider urged the horse forward a few more steps to where he could see past the corner of the crate, and there found a boy with a guitar leaning against the wall.

Whether the player was aware of his audience or not Longmore could not say for the song went on uninterrupted. The boy played with head down, the guitar folded in his arms as another might embrace a loved woman. The man listened quietly until the guitarist relieved the tension in the haunting, unfamiliar tune with a strummed, final chord that rang out softly and slowly into the night.

The man sat entranced, leaning slightly forward in the saddle, one hand resting atop the other on the horn. His mount finally broke the spell, shifting weight from one weary hind leg to the other, creaking saddle leather with the move. The boy looked up at the horseman, but saw only a silhouette against shadow. A voice rumbled out of the darkness.

"What are you doing here?"

"Trying to keep warm, mostly. Am I hurting anything being here?"

"I don't suppose so," Longmore said. "But it's a piss-poor place to shelter up."

The boy said, "I've seen worse. At least it's out of the wind."

"Ain't you got no place to go? Somewhere with a warm fire?"

"No sir. I'm a stranger in this place. And I don't have the means to pay for lodging."

"You try the wagon yard? You could likely bunk up in an empty stall."

"Did that. Hostler there didn't take kindly to my guitar. Said it kept him from sleeping. But I felt like picking some, so I found this hidey-hole. Didn't figure I'd trouble anyone here. I'm sorry if my playing bothered you."

"Come out from there and let me have a look at you."

Will drew his legs up and pushed, his back sliding up the wall until he stood. Neither hand left the guitar. He stepped out of the deepest of the shadows and into the dimness of the loading dock.

The man studied him for a minute or two, realizing the guitar player was both small and young. He guessed him to be sixteen, seventeen years old or thereabouts. It was a good guess. The boy had just turned seventeen, an age at which many of that day and time considered you old enough to make your own way in the world, but young enough that no one would mistake you for a grown man.

"Hell, you ain't but a kid," Longmore finally said. "What's your name, boy?"

"Hayes, sir. Wilson."

The mounted man pondered that for a moment, unable to make sense of it.

"Which is it, Hayes or Wilson?"

"Both. My name is Wilson Hayes."

"Wilson Hayes. How came you to have two last names?"

"Well, Hayes is my daddy's family's name. Ma was a Wilson 'fore she married daddy. They gave me her family name in remembrance."

"So what does a boy with two last names and no first name go by?"

"Mostly, folks call me Will. Short for Wilson."

"What is it you're doing in Ballard Station?"

The boy let the body of the guitar slide out from under his arm. It swung like half a stroke of a pendulum from where he gripped the top of the neck with his left hand, then he let the bottom drop gently to the worn boards of the freight platform and moved his hand to the top of the head to balance it there and the guitar below.

"You sure do ask a lot of questions, mister."

"Hmmph. I got the advantage of you, boy. See, I know who you are and you ain't got no idea who it is you're talking to. If you did, you wouldn't be giving me any of your sass nor bullshit. So let's try this again. If you have any notion of staying in these parts for any length of time, you'd best tell me what you're up to."

"You saying you're somebody important? Like the law, maybe?"

"No, I ain't the law. Around here, I'm more important than that."

Will absorbed that piece of information as he thought about how to answer the man's question. It seemed plain that the man was accustomed to folks kowtowing to him, and he did not doubt the local lawman would be among them. Lacking any reasonable explanation for his presence there, Will decided to simply tell the man the truth.

"Well, I can't rightly answer your question, as I don't know why I'm here. Fact is, I got caught sleeping in an empty cattle car on the train and when it stopped here one of them railroad men kicked me off."

Longmore said, "You on your way someplace?"

"No place in particular. I got run out of Texas and I'm looking to make a new start. Don't have no idea where. I guess I'll know the place when I see it."

"You know how to work, or just play that guitar?"

"Oh, I can set my hand to a thing or two. Most anything around a cow outfit, having been brought up on a ranch."

"Well, Will Hayes, this might be your lucky day even if it is the middle of the night. I happen to own a few head of cattle myself—likely more cattle than you've ever set eyes on at your tender age. There's always work at the Fishhook for any cowboy who can pull his weight. You figure you've got the sand to ride for my brand?"

"I'd sure give it a try. But I don't have much of an outfit."

"What have you got?"

Will lowered his head, shuffled his feet, then looked up again, embarrassed. "You're looking at it."

"Hmmph. Well, the Fishhook's a big enough place that I imagine we can find you a saddle and a rope and probably even a pair of leggings some other shiftless cowboy cast off or left behind."

"I thank you, sir."

"Let's get a move on. We can make the ranch in time for you to get to work first thing in the morning. I'll be damned if I'll pay you to sit around. We'll go wake up that lazy hostler at the livery and get you mounted, but you'll ride bareback to the ranch."

Longmore swung his horse around and headed back toward the main street, then turned in the saddle and said over his shoulder, "In case you was wondering, kid, my name is Longmore. Jesse Longmore. C'mon—and bring that guitar."

Chapter Two

Riding a horse bareback may be the best of all possible ways to renew an acquaintance with your rear end; an acquaintance often ignored since the baby days of severe diaper rash.

Will was soon reminded of this fact as he and Longmore rode through a long, dark, cold night toward headquarters of the Fishhook Ranch.

Without stirrups to balance against and bear weight, dangling legs and feet tingle then burn then hang benumbed like leaden weights, spreading and stretching the hinge of a human being's hind legs well beyond its accustomed position. With no seat between backside and horsehide, the natural side-to-side motion of the equine gait is emphasized, and maintaining stability at (or near) the center as required requires constant shifting, which soon rasps away the outer layers of a rider's hide. At the same time, back-and-forth motion further rubs raw the tender flesh lining one's nether regions, while the up-and-down motion persistently pounds that same irritated skin between the bottom end of the horseman's backbone and the rippled ridgeline of the horse's spine.

Will rode through the pain. Then again, he saw little alternative. His new employer stopped now and then along the roadside to dismount and drain off the leftovers of a long bout of whiskey drinking, and the young cowboy gratefully lit down during the first of these rest stops. But he found the pain of peeling himself off the horse's bare back and the shock of swinging back into the sticky seat worse than staying put. So he remained mounted during subsequent intermissions.

Longmore rode for a good long time in silence. Then, without warning, he peppered Will with a series of questions.

"Whereabouts you from in Texas?"

"What kind of situation was you in there?"

"How came you to get run off?"

"Any law looking for you I oughta know about?"

Will told how his daddy had as a young man from Tennessee emigrated and taken up a ranch between the forks of the Trinity River in the Republic of Texas. He successfully raised a family and horses and cattle, increasing his holdings to become prosperous. But the beginning of the War Between the States was the beginning of the end for the Hayes family.

"I used to have three brothers and a sister, all older than me," Will told Longmore. "I kind of came along late in the scheme of things. Anyway, daddy was too old to go off to war and I was too young. But all three of my brothers was of the age and inclination, and they all joined up right away.

"Thing was, two of them joined with the Confederates while the middle one of the three went off to fight in Lincoln's army. Not a one of them ever came back, and we never even heard what happened to two of them.

"Daddy and what hired hands he could find kept the place going for a while, but there was this mean old sonofabitch—excuse my cussing, but he was—who got up the home guard there and had himself declared captain, run us off the place on account of our having a Yankee soldier in the family. Disloyalty, they called it at first. Treason, later. Daddy fought it all he could, but the lawmen were no help and the courts corrupt.

"One day he just rode back out to our place determined to get that home guard bastard out of the house or die trying. He almost did. They shot him down before he even got through the gate into the dooryard."

Will told how he and his ma and sister had taken his wounded daddy to a small town in the next county to recuperate and wait out the war. Then they went home and took back the ranch and held it for a time. But the carpetbaggers came to town and brought more corruption with them, going so far as to ally themselves with the crooked commander of the old home guard regiment.

"Daddy got a letter from the courthouse saying the ranch had been seized and sold on account of the taxes being unpaid all the years we were away. That was the first we heard of it."

"They showed up at the ranch late one night, masked riders carrying torches, with a warning that we leave within a week. On the way out, they set the corncrib afire just to show they meant it.

"We were laying for them when they came back. There was me and daddy, this old Mexican cowboy who'd been on the place as long as daddy had, and this gaucho from Argentina who'd wandered in during the war. Daddy hired him not knowing what he'd get, but that South American was a hell of a hand, I'll say. Called hisself Miguel, but I don't know if that was his first name or last."

Will squirmed around in an unsuccessful attempt to find a more comfortable—or at least less painful—seat on the bony horse's back.

"Thing is, they never came back," Will continued, "at least not how we expected. Some one of them sneaked onto the place unseen and set the barn on fire. We was all scrambling around trying to douse the flames and get the stock out of there. That's when they came.

"They killed the old Mexican and that Argentina cowboy on the first pass. I shot the horse out from under

16

one of them and daddy shot that bastard captain dead center in the chest, knocked him plumb off the back of a horse running full tilt.

"Daddy took a bad bullet in the leg and another one in his back but he kept fighting. My sister got shot in the face and killed in all the confusion. Unless one of them cowards killed her outright. I don't know.

"Between me and daddy we finally run them off. Ma was trying to beat out a fire they started on the dog run at the house when the roof fell in and killed her. Daddy seen that happen and just laid down in the dirt and bled to death. He might of died anyway. I don't know.

Will squirmed some more.

"I buried them all the next morning and didn't have the stomach to stick around after. The only building that wasn't burned down, or mostly, was the bunkhouse. The only thing there worth saving was this guitar. Belonged to Miguel, but I'd played the thing more than he did since he taught me how. Anyhow, all the saddle stock was run off, so I just strapped this guitar on my back and walked away."

Longmore rode on in silence.

Will rode on in pain.

Chapter Three

The sun had yet to show its face above the sawtooth mountain range in the middle distance to the east of Fishhook headquarters when Longmore and his new hire rode in. But the place was already a hive of activity in the dim dawn light.

Will saw plumes of breath steaming into the chill air from a line of horses halter-tied to the top rail of a corral fence, and from the mouths and noses of swarming cowboys saddling the mounts and hauling tack back and forth across the hard-packed yard.

Sensing the urgency there, Longmore kissed up his tired horse and covered the remaining distance at a brisk trot. Will followed suit, but the jarring gait was more than his tender parts could handle, so he heeled his horse into an easy lope.

On seeing the ranchman's approach, one of the cowboys stepped out to meet him while the others kept to the tasks at hand.

"What the hell's going on?" Longmore said.

"Ballard's got a crew down in Antler Canyon. They're branding every calf they find, no matter the brand on the mother cow."

"We ought to have gathered out of there by now. Don't we have a crew in there?" Longmore said.

"Sure we do. That's how we know what they're up to. Two of our boys caught a half dozen Rafter 7 hands with about twenty head of Fishhook cows mixed with a bunch of their own at a branding fire. Only none of the brands smoking on any calf was a Fishhook."

The country in question, Antler Canyon, was a rugged hunk of range that served as a buffer between the Ballard and Longmore spreads. Both outfits used it for summer graze. More than a single canyon, the area was in reality a broad, relatively flat-bottomed gorge that cut through Curtain Reef and into the Rattle Creek range beyond. The creek, a clear, quick stream that rattled over and around a rocky bed was all that remained of what must have been, in a time out of mind, a raging torrent that gouged the gorge out of the mountains and pushed it through the cliff wall and into the valley.

The canyon, like an antler, branched numerous times from the main stem to cut into the mountains on either side. The side canyons were steep walled, some blind box canyons with no back door. No cowboy liked rounding up out of there in the fall, for the isolation made the cattle uncooperative and the terrain was unforgiving, a combination that led to more than a few wrecks.

Every fall roundup day at Antler ended with branding late calves, born after the herds were moved there in the spring. Stock pushed out of the branches into the main canyon was bunched and held while they mothered up. Each unbranded calf, oversized with the better part of a summer's growth, was roped in turn and dragged to the fire, given a brand to match its mother's, ears notched with the owner's pattern, and, if a bull calf, relieved of its pending manhood.

It was dirty, smelly, smoky labor, and, to make it worse, cowboys doing ground work were likely to get run down and mauled by a mad mama cow. But it was a job to do, and so it was done.

The stock was separated, the Fishhook and Rafter 7 herds held in different parts of the canyon to await the completion of the gather and the drive to their respective winter ranges.

The system usually worked. Oh, no outfit was above burning its own brand onto the wrong calf from time to time. A certain amount of calf stealing was accepted and expected. But when it became a systematic operation, or occurred on a large scale, its discovery occasioned the unholstering of guns and the conversion of cowboy catch ropes into hanging ropes.

"So what did our boys do?"

"Well, it was Jake and Frenchie who caught them. Ballard's boys drew down on them and shot them both. Jake's dead; leastways we expect he is, 'cause he never came back. Frenchie would be a goner too, only his horse spooked and ran off when the shooting started. Even so, he took two bullets and was half dead when he got in."

Longmore swung out of the saddle and handed his bridle reins to one of the cowboys, who led it away.

"What the hell happened out there, do you think, Johnny?" the rancher said. "That Cajun of ours is pretty handy with a pistol and Jake was no slouch."

The man called Johnny said, "Like I said, there were six Rafter 7 hands against two of ours. But that's not the worst of it. One of them was Caleb Short."

While Longmore absorbed that bit of what must have been bad news, Will crawled off his horse and peeled the seat and insides of his pants legs off the skin underneath and winced as he did it, feeling patches of his tender hide come loose, more firmly attached to the fabric than his body. He studied Johnny through watery eyes and detected a resemblance to Longmore—who he was now able to see in daylight for the first time.

Father and son, he decided. But where the father looked to be whittled from a hardwood stump with a dull knife, the son had the appearance of polished marble. Jesse Longmore's face beneath his broad-brimmed hat was weather-beaten and eroded. A coarse black beard, with a hint of roan showing, covered the most of his face, met at the corners of rough red lips by a heavy mustache.

Johnny, on the other hand, was clean shaven. His eyes were the most distinctive feature of his face—the same deep brown as his father's, but brighter, and framed with long, dark lashes and an almost delicate arch of eyebrows, where Jesse's brow was as heavy and tangled as his beard and the hair under his hat.

Johnny's eyes were notable in another respect. In order to see them, Will had to look through the round, clear lenses of a pair of spectacles. And although the man moved with the shuffling gait of one accustomed to being horseback, he looked like a man who might be more at home behind a counter or maybe a desk.

Hmmph," Longmore finally said to break a tense silence. "So Ballard's turned that gunslinger loose, has he. I guess that tells us he's ready to make another run at taking over the Fishhook."

Caleb Short was a weapon Sam Ballard had never before employed in his squabbles with Longmore. But many a nester had been driven off with the barrels of Short's guns, and those who refused to leave alive more often than not shipped out dead. The Rafter 7 enforcer's physical presence belied his name, for he was a tall man, as tall as any in the territory. He was likewise broad and strong. A natural bully, he enjoyed pummeling and pounding people with his fists as well as he liked gunning them down. Many a Fishhook hand had felt the punishment of Short's fists and feet, but the bully had attacked them on a freelance basis, just for fun, and not under orders from his handler, Sam Ballard of the Rafter 7.

"So what's your plan, Johnny?" Longmore said.

"I've got a dozen men riding out, and we're going well armed. We'll find Short and his crew and see what happens. Chances are they've cleared out, now they know we're on to them."

"No. There's no way they'll ride out of Antler and leave any cattle. Ballard will have them back in there in a heartbeat if he thinks there's even one head left behind. You'll find Short and his crew, all right."

Johnny mulled that for a minute.

"You'd best get a move on," Longmore told him.

"We'll be going soon—as soon as we get some grub packed and loaded on the mules. We're working on it."

"Don't wait. Short knows we'll be coming, and the longer it takes, the longer he'll have to dig in so deep you won't be able to dig him out.

"I'll send this kid out with some chuck. He'll bring extra cartridges, too." At that, Longmore turned to Will. "I suppose you know how to run a packstring, kid," he said, then turned back to his son.

"Johnny, meet Wilson Hayes. He's the newest hand on the Fishhook. I don't know what he's good for except pickin' that guitar on his back, but he can damn sure do that."

*****

Antler Canyon was half a day's ride from Fishhook headquarters and Will did not relish the prospect. At least he'd have a saddle under his butt this time. All the same, his backside was worn so raw that the leather would be of little help and would likely make it worse. At least the pain would keep him awake.

Once Johnny and the cowboys rode out, the rancher took his new hire on a brief tour of the headquarters layout. Then Longmore told the boy to stow his guitar in the bunkhouse and go up to the kitchen at the main house for a bite of breakfast. He'd meet him at the supply house in an hour.

All hands at the Fishhook ate at the main house. A trestle table lined with ladder-back chairs had seating for twelve, and, according to the cook, that was room enough most of the time. The place overflowed at spring roundup before the camp men drove their herds off to summer ranges, and again in the fall, between roundup and shipping time. Extra cowboys hired on then to gather the far-flung herds and bring them out of the mountains for the winter, then cut out the yearlings and the culls for market.

If the breakfast laid out for Will was any measure of the chuck at the Fishhook, he knew he'd enjoy eating there. He took comfort from the fact that the cook was a woman, too, for he'd heard enough talk in the bunkhouse back home about the mysterious meals and filthy habits of male dough rollers at some ranches.

The Fishhook storehouse was as well equipped as any mercantile Will had seen. The man running the place, a hobbling old man who introduced himself as Tommy O'Shannon, had already gathered up a set of clothes for the boy, and Will peeled off his tattered rags and donned a new set of togs from the skin out. A bedroll had been assembled, and there was a revolver with a holster and cartridge belt. He hefted the pistol and checked the cylinder to assure it was empty, then tested the action. The Colt would serve, he thought, as he thumbed cartridges into the holes.

The storekeeper had also reeled off forty feet of hemp rope and tied a honda in one end, but said that any other horse gear must be had from the blacksmith. The smithy, he said, also worked leather for the outfit, and kept saddles and tack in a lean-to off his shop. Will strapped on his new sidearm, gathered his bedroll and lass rope and headed out the door.

Longmore was waiting on the porch, with him a black-haired girl who took Will's breath away. She looked to be about his age, maybe a bit older. She was even more beautiful than Johnny was handsome, making him wonder what manner of woman had birthed those two, and how their father had managed to snag such a prize.

"Wilson Hayes, this is my daughter Emma. You're likely to be seeing her around the place so I thought you had just as well know who she is," Longmore said. "But listen to me now. I'll say this one time. If ever I see you any closer to this girl than you're standing right now, I'll kick your ass six ways to Sunday and run you so far off this place you'll be lost for a week. That, or I just might kill you if I take a notion."

Emma smiled shyly and said, "I'm pleased to meet you Mister Hayes. Papa says you go by Will and I hope you won't mind my calling you that. I'd shake your hand, but you don't seem to have one free at the time."

Will shuffled his feet as he tried to find his voice, never once diverting his eyes from the girl's face. He finally managed to croak, "Ma'am."

The girl giggled at that, and before starting back to the house said, "Never you mind what Papa says. I'm sure we'll be seeing a lot of each other." He saw a flush rise in her cheeks as she turned to walk away.

He kept staring as she hurried across the yard to the main house. Longmore jarred him back to reality.

"C'mon boy. Pick your jaw up off the ground and let's go see about getting you a saddle and a horse to put under it."

Three or four saddles in various states of repair sat on rail horses in the lean-to. Two rigs dangled from the rafters on ropes, both double-rigged slickfork Denver-style stock saddles. Will selected the least worn of the two, lifted it off its tether and carried it out over a forearm. He ran the palm of his hand across the smooth leather seat and imagined he could already feel it deep in the bottom of his buttocks.

Meanwhile, the smith had selected a split-ear bridle with a nasty-looking ring bit. A pair of commodious saddlebags were already tied behind the cantle of the saddle. The burly, bullet-headed iron and leather worker looked Will over, pawed through a wooden box and pulled out a pair of buckskin gloves with tall gauntlets of stiffer leather. They fit fine, and the boy stuffed them fingers-first into the gullet of the saddle. He asked the man to stitch a rawhide burner into the honda of his new lariat, then looked around for Longmore.

He found him leaning on the top rail of a horse corral attached to the side of a log barn. Inside the pen, an old man—the wrangler, Will rightly suspected—was leading a dun horse out of a small bunch. Tied to the fence rails between the boss and the barn were three fat mules, each loaded with bulging panniers lashed down under canvas tarps.

Longmore called him over and pulled a folded paper out of the watch pocket of his vest. It was a map he'd scratched out with a smudgy pencil to show the way to Antler Canyon, and a rough map of the canyon showing where Will would likely find Johnny and the Fishhook cowboys.

The rancher looked at the sun's position and said, "I make it about ten o'clock. Johnny and the boys will likely get there by noon. You'll take longer, towing these mules, but if you don't get lost you ought to get there no later than four this afternoon. And you best hope to hell you don't find Caleb Short and his Rafter 7 flunkies before you find Johnny."

Chapter Four

Will heard gunfire and knew he was about to get where he was going long before he got there. The nature of the shooting perplexed him, for it was random and occasional, and seemed to lack any pattern he could associate with a hostile exchange. He also heard shouting, which, drawing nearer, he recognized as taunting, interspersed with loud laughter. Soon, he rode up on a cowboy lazing on a flat rock.

"You the new kid from Longmore's?"

"I guess so," Will said. "We on the same side?"

"Sure enough. Johnny sent me down to wait for you. The boys are on the ridgeline at the top of this draw," he said, pointing the way with his chin. "We got ourselves what you might call a Mexican standoff. Follow me."

The cowboy crawled off the rock, gathered the reins of his ground-tied mount, snugged up the cinch, swung into the saddle, and started up the trail. After a few minutes of uphill riding along a narrow path worn into the side of the ridge through scrub oak and aspen trees, they neared the place where the ridge topped out. Tethered to tree limbs and brush were Fishhook horses.

Will's escort said, "Tie your horse and them mules, then you might as well come on up. The action's just over the top."

At the top, he found Longmore's cowboys sitting around on rocks, making no attempt to conceal themselves. The ground below them fell away gently to the seat of a low saddle, which rose gently again to similar high ground maybe two furlongs away. There, another group of cowboys sat and stood. Partway down the slope of the saddle, maybe fifty yards below the Rafter 7 position, stood a giant of a man. Will suspected it was Caleb Short.

"Come on, you bunch of cowards!" the man boomed, then unleashed a shot in the general direction of the Fishhook hands, obviously not intending—or even attempting—to hit anyone. "Ain't there a man among you?" The question was accompanied by jeers from the cowboys above and behind him.

Will sought out Johnny and asked what was going on.

"We found them in the canyon, down at the mouth of that draw. Still branding, and still burning the Rafter 7 on Fishhook hide. I tried to talk sense to them, but they lit into us."

Will looked around and noticed at least two Longmore riders showing red; one from a shoulder wound and another from his side, just below the ribs. "Anybody hurt besides them two?" he said.

"Oh, yes," Johnny said. "Killed a Mexican named Paco Robles. Short shot him right out from under his sombrero. Damn. His head just sort of exploded. Ford Fargo, a hand who came down from Canada, is gutshot. He's propped up under a tree over yonder, and not long for this world."

"You get any of them?"

"Wounded one guy, is all. Somebody managed to land a bullet in his arm. We backed off to regroup and they took off up that draw. We came up this side to try and head them off and here we are."

"What now?"

Johnny untied the bandana around his neck and unwound it as he spoke. "See that loudmouth down there? That's Caleb Short. He's calling us out. Wants us to come down and fight."

With the bandana in hand, he carefully removed his eyeglasses and used it to wipe them clean.

"Any or all of us, he says. Choice of weapons."

Will said, "So why don't somebody go down and kill the sonofabitch?"

Johnny held the glasses against the sky and scrutinized the clarity of the lenses. Satisfied, he stretched the hooks carefully around his ears. "Will, that's Caleb Short down there."

"I thought as much. But so what? There's only one of him. We got a whole passel of able-bodied men here. Hell, we outnumber the whole bunch of them. We ought to could take them all."

Short continued to hurl nasty slurs and stray chunks of lead into the wind from time to time. Rewinding the wild rag around his throat, Johnny said, "We don't need to worry about the whole bunch of them. Only him."

"Let's get him then, dammit!"

"Take it easy, Will. Like I told you, that's Caleb Short."

"So?"

"That gunfight earlier? The one I told you about? Robles killed, Fargo all but, the other two wounded—Short did that. All of it. There wasn't another Rafter 7 gun even pulled."

"The man's a good shot. That's no call to let him stand down there and sling insults at us like we're a bunch of damn sheep."

"What do you think we ought to do, Will?"

"Like I said, kill him."

"Look around. Who's going to do it? These men aren't stupid."

"Aw, shit!" Will said, pulling his pistol and checking the loads.

"What are you doing?"

"Hell, Johnny, I'm going down there and shoot that rude bastard," he said as he started off down the slope, revolver in hand. The Rafter 7 hands renewed their hoots and hollers, cheering Will, even applauding him, while predicting his impending death.

Caleb Short watched wide-eyed in silence for a moment, then burst out laughing.

"What the hell is this?" he shouted, holstering his revolver and adjusting his gunbelt. "There ain't a man among you, so you send a snot-nosed kid to do the job?"

His laughter rolled uphill toward Will and he imagined he could feel its pressure bouncing off him, almost pushing him backward. But he walked on.

"Hey boy, your mama know you're out?"

Laughter.

Will walked on.

"How long you been wearing long pants, boy? Them look new."

Laughter.

Will walked on.

"That peach fuzz I see on your cheeks? Why, son, you'll be shaving soon!"

Laughter.

Will walked on.

The boy never wavered, never stopped. When he was maybe ten yards from the big man, he hissed softly between clenched teeth, "Why the hell don't you shut up!"

Then, without breaking stride, he raised his pistol and shot Caleb Short dead in the middle of the forehead.

Chapter Five

Whiskey, when swirled around in a nearly empty glass, will cling to the sides for an instant, creating a delicate stain that hesitates before slipping down the surface to be absorbed by the puddle of spirits in the bottom. Longmore seemed fascinated by this trivial truth, for he swirled, waited, swished, waited, and sloshed to wait again, eyes transfixed on the dregs of much whiskey that had passed through that glass on this evening.

He lingered tonight—as he often did—in the communal dining room. He liked it here, where, from his chosen seat at the head of the table, he held court with his cowboys and regaled them with stories of his prowess as a worker, a drinker, a lover, a fighter, a man.

But he was troubled by a budding lack of interest in his yarns. More and more, his tales were upstaged by accounts of the latest escapades of Will Hayes.

Not that the boy was to blame. He seldom spoke a word. Most often, he sat quietly in the corner cuddled up to and caressing that big blond guitar. Longmore liked it when Will's playing accompanied the conversation in the room. The strange, haunting tunes relaxed him, soothing the anxiety stirring in his head and allaying somewhat the vague fears that haunted him.

He knew the guitar helped. He wasn't so sure about the whiskey, but he didn't care to challenge his assumption that it did.

Tonight, the cowboys, Will with them, had long since wandered away to their cots in the bunkhouse. By now they were likely lost in sleep and dreams, snoring and snorting close air redolent with the smell of the sweat of men and horses, and a miasma from malodorous hung clothing stiff with the effluent of livestock.

At least when they're asleep, Longmore thought, they won't be telling stories about the adventures of Wilson Hayes.

He had had a gutful of those tales and did not care to hear more. You'd think the kid was the only one on the place who knew how to ride or rope or shoot, how to hunt cattle hid up deep in the brush, how to cut a cow out of the middle of a bunch and leave the herd undisturbed, how, even, to lay on a hot iron and burn a perfect Fishhook brand.

Hell, the man thought, I was doing all that and then some before that sprout was so much as a twinkle in his daddy's eye. Just 'cause my hair's getting grayer by the day, well, that's no reason to think I still can't out-cowboy that kid.

Then again, he had to admit the kid was a pretty good hand.

His first inkling of that fact had come within twenty-four hours of his meeting Hayes and dragging the foundling back to the ranch. When the boy went out with supplies for the roundup crew he'd sent to Antler Canyon to confront Caleb Short and them rustling sonsofbitches from the Rafter 7, Longmore did not imagine he would come back a hero.

Almost a year had passed since he'd been awakened in the wee hours by shouts and laughter from the yard. He'd put on pants and boots and hat and stumbled drowsy toward the tack shed where he could see in the hazy light of the full moon Johnny and Will and some of the boys unsaddling.

Half mad, he wondered where they had gotten into a whiskey bottle deep enough to fuel such raucous behavior. He knew there had barely been time for Will to ride to Antler Canyon and back; certainly not enough time for him and the others to detour through the swinging doors of the Elkhorn Saloon in Ballard Station on the way home.

Besides which, he wondered why the hell half the crew was back here, instead of tending to business in the canyon.

"Johnny!" he yelled from halfway across the yard, putting a cork in the loud talk and laughter.

Johnny stopped midstride, halfway between the hitchrail and saddle shed door and turned toward his father. Shifting the saddle he carried over a forearm, he said, "Pa?"

"Maybe you'd like to tell me what the hell's going on here."

Johnny shifted the saddle again and searched around in his head for a response, unnerved at the unexpected challenge. Will and the others stood by, clearing throats and scratching whiskers and tracing nervous lines in the dirt with the toes of their boots.

"You can start by explaining why you're not in Antler Canyon keeping the Rafter 7 brand off our calves."

Having been given the benefit of a specific question to which he knew the answer, Johnny replied. "I don't think that's going to be a problem anymore, Pa. At least for now."

"How's that?"

"Caleb Short's passing sort of took the wind out of the Rafter 7 boys. I suspect they'll pay closer attention to how a calf's mama is branded from here on," Johnny said as he lowered his forearm and let the saddle slide slowly down to the ground.

"What? Short's dead?"

"That's right, Pa. Will killed him."

Longmore's jaw dropped, then tried a time or two to close but could not, as though unfinished words were stuck there, preventing it. He removed his hat and scratched the back of his head as he glanced from one grinning face in the group to another. "I guess maybe you boys better fill me in."

He tried to keep up as every one of them tried to tell the story at once. Everyone, that is, but Will, who went back to tending to his horse. As the story unfolded. he stowed his saddle, rubbed the animal's sweaty back with an empty feed sack, then loosed the horse in the small pasture where a handful of Fishhook saddle mounts were always kept.

Longmore watched the kid from time to time, surprised at his nonchalance. Hayes, it seemed, considered the day's events less impressive than did Johnny and the other cowboys.

*****

The next clue that the kid might amount to something had come a few months later in the dead of winter when the Fishhook was belly deep in snow following a particularly nasty storm. Line riders reported that a cougar had been taking cows—an unusual occurrence as the cats preferred elk or deer, owing, perhaps, to the fact that cattle usually lived in uncomfortable proximity to humans. But the cows the lion killed—at first—were weak with age or illness, likely unable to escape or offer much resistance. Now, the cougar had developed a taste for beef and took any critter that was handy, including mother cows carrying calves, which represented a double loss for the Fishhook herd.

Plain trails led from kill sites in the coulees and bottoms to rocky crags in a steep hillside nearby. The cowboys knew the cougar holed up in a cave in the cliffs, but their attempts at catching the cat out or frightening it into showing itself proved futile. Continuing predations were a source of embarrassment to the hands and a growing frustration for the rancher. He organized hunts, even offered a bounty, all to no avail.

Then, one morning at breakfast, Will was missing. When asked, Johnny looked up from the book he was reading and informed Longmore that the kid had gone out after the mountain lion and did not expect to return without it.

Longmore said, "He said that, did he? If he means it, then I guess that's the last we'll see of Wilson Hayes."

"I wouldn't worry about that, Pa. I'm guessing he'll be back before too much time passes, and when he comes, he'll come with a cougar hide tied behind the cantle of his saddle."

"What's the matter with that kid? He so greedy he'll risk his life to get his hands on that reward?"

"I doubt it's the money."

"Why's he out there, then? What's he want?"

"If I had to guess, I'd say he wants to save any more of your cows from being eaten."

"Why the hell should he care that much about my cows?"

"Again, I can only guess," Johnny said, "but if you asked him, I guess he'd say that's what you pay him for."

"Hmmph. That boy gets paid the same as every other Fishhook hand."

"True enough. But what you don't understand yet, Pa, is that's the only way Will's the same as the others."

Johnny's suspicions proved correct when, three days later, the kid rode back into headquarters. But, instead of a pelt behind the saddle, lashed there was a lumpy roll of canvas. Pastured horses stirred as he rode past, heads up, ears sharp, nostrils flared and snorting as they pawed and stomped, finally wheeling away to mill in the far corner of the fenced pen.

A few curious cowboys lazing around the bunkhouse watched him ride by and followed him toward the main house. The smith came away from his forge, dripping despite the brisk winter air, wiping sweat from the palms of his hands onto his leather apron. He, too, followed behind, and Tommy O'Shannon, the storekeeper and swamper, joined the parade as it passed his building.

Johnny and his father were by then already on the porch of the main house, watching the kid's progress across the yard toward them. As they waited, Emma stepped out the door to join them.

"I guess I was wrong, Pa," Johnny said. "He didn't bring the hide. Looks to me like he brought the whole damn animal."

"Hmmph," the rancher said. "Could be. Could be a bad job rolling up his sougans, too."

"Couldn't be that. Will didn't take his bedroll."

Johnny shook out a handkerchief and removed his eyeglasses, polishing the lenses to assure a good look at whatever it was Will was about to show them.

Meanwhile, the rider had reached the porch and dismounted. Without speaking, he slapped a bridle rein against the crosspiece of the hitch rail and watched the free end spin itself around for a loose tie. He stepped back beside the horse's flank and worked the saddle strings on the rear skirts loose and gently patted his mount's rump as he crossed behind to repeat the task on the off side, freeing the awkward load.

The kid grabbed canvas with both hands, hefted the roll off the horse and dropped it to the dirt. He bent over and rummaged around to find the end of the sheet and lifted, the load inside tumbling over and over as the wrap unrolled. Will had, as Johnny predicted, brought back the entire cat.

And it was alive.

Cowboys backpedaled instinctively as the trussed-up cougar strained at its fetters. Emma stood as if riveted to the porch, eyes frozen wide. The horse, previously resigned to its strange load, reawakened to the predator's presence and shied away, skittering sideways and pulling the wrapped rein free of the hitch rail, then left in a high-headed gallop across the yard and away from the lion, neck cranked around to keep wide eyes on the lion the whole way.

The cat's front legs were lashed to each other with several wraps of whang leather, as were the hind legs, then all four were bundled together and bound with rope that looked to be cut from the end of a lariat. But the security arrangement that drew the most scrutiny—and curiosity—from the onlookers was on the animal's head.

Around and around the neck wound a leather strap, snug enough that it couldn't slip over the head. Tight in the animal's mouth was a snaffle bit, presumably bor-rowed from the bridle on Will's horse, the rings on either side of the jointed mouthpiece lashed tight with whang leather to the neck wrap. The pressure and presence of the snaffle bit stretched the cat's lips back and wide and kept the jaws from working and the mouth from closing, effectively rendering it useless as a weapon.

"Hayes, what the hell do you think you're up to?" Longmore said.

"You wanted this critter, so I got him for you."

"You damn fool. You know good and well I wanted it *dead*. Not wrapped up like a Christmas package and left on my doorstep."

Will stood over the mountain lion and said nothing. Johnny stepped down off the porch and toed the cat's belly. "Why *did* you bring it in, Will?"

The boy lifted his hat by the front of the brim and tipped it back on his head. He looked at Johnny, looked at Emma, looked at Longmore. "Truth is," he said, shifting his gaze back to Johnny, "I don't know. Seemed like a good idea at the time." He looked down at the cat. "I guess killing him seemed too easy. Besides, I never seen one up close. Not even a dead one."

Will squatted down next to the cougar. "Look here," he said, poking the cougar's left hind paw with his forefinger. The cat flinched and let loose a moaning growl. "Something wrong with this foot. Got broke and didn't heal, maybe."

He said it likely kept the cat from its usual bounding and leaping, possibly explaining why its tastes changed from fleet deer and elk to lumbering cows. Then he peeled back the lion's lips, revealing several gaps where teeth should have been.

"That bridle bit didn't break them teeth, they were already gone. I'd guess this is a pretty old tom. Not much time left to him."

"Hmmph," Longmore said. "If it weren't for my cows being such easy pickings, he'd probably be dead already." Then he said to one of the gawking hands, "Clancy, you and Pete drag this cat somewhere out of the way and kill it. Then peel the hide off real careful like. I'll have it tanned. Make a nice rug, I reckon. Hell, Will, maybe I'll give it to you."

The boy did not volunteer any information as to how he managed to capture alive a cougar that no one else had managed to even lay eyes on. Will had to be badgered into relating the tale.

He said that finding the lion's lair was not difficult; many of the Fishhook hands knew of the cave in the cliff. Figuring the animal wasn't likely to come to him, he decided to go to the cougar.

Will lashed his lariat to a length of sapling in a way that affixed the loop firmly to the pole but still let him take up the slack. He figured the arrangement would allow him to snag the feline and keep it at a safe distance for both the catching and the keeping.

Shoving the staff ahead, he wormed through the narrow cleft in the cliff and into the cave. He could see the cat's eyes glowing with reflected light as soon as he crawled into the cavern. It was more a crack in the rock, really, no more than two feet wide at the floor and narrowing to a six-inch slot four, maybe five feet above.

The ceiling angled downward and the slit narrowed as it moved toward the back of the chamber, ending in what looked to be a compact hole just large enough to accommodate the recumbent cat. Whether the cave continued beyond, he could not tell.

The cougar did not take kindly to his presence. It commenced growling as soon as Will darkened its door, and the deeper the man crept into the lair, the more agitated the cat became—hissing, spitting, hunched up with hair on end and bunched up as if ready to spring.

Despite the winter chill, sweat runneled down Will's forehead, and as the struggle with the lion stirred up the dust, it forced him over and over to wipe the sting out of his eyes. The stink and the close quarters likewise irritated his nose, causing an annoying itch and labored breathing.

Manipulating the long pole with the loop dangling from the end proved more difficult than anticipated, and early attempts to snare the lion were parried by swatting paws. Others failed when the cat ducked away before the loop settled, or simply pulled its head free before the boy could secure the loop.

But once the loop was on the lion and drawn snug, Will didn't hesitate. He took a dally around his end of the stick to keep the rope taut and scrambled backward out of the hole, dragging the scratching, spitting cat along.

Fresh air renewed Will's strength, but the prospect of leaving its den invigorated the cougar, too. Will double half-hitched his end of the rope around the pole, then slid down the rocky face and, despite its writhing and yowling, forced the lion along by main strength assisted by gravity.

Bottoming out on flatter land, Will rested a moment to catch his breath, checked his knot, then set off again downhill with the cat in tow. Doing its utmost to scramble backward as the boy dragged it forward, the lion's claws scratched furrows in the crusted snow when it hung back, and ripped and flung icy chunks in all directions when it got on the fight. The catch was a good one, though, and the length of sapling served its purpose of keeping the angry animal at a safe distance.

Once the boy reached a sheltered area in a thick stand of aspen trees, he moved on to part two of his plan. He sat on a downed tree, freed his end of the catch rope. He drew it tighter with steady pressure, reducing then eliminating the cat's ability to breathe. He played with it for a time, testing the amount of time it took the animal to lose and regain consciousness.

Finally feeling confident, the kid choked down the cat, secured the rope to the log in case the cougar regained consciousness sooner than expected, then approached quickly but cautiously to further disable it.

Unsure which weapon presented the most danger—tooth or claw—he arbitrarily decided to hogtie the cat's legs first. Besides, he wasn't sure if his plan to put a bit in the cat's mouth would work and figured having those risky feet out of the way would allow more time for experimentation.

It didn't take much. He tied lengths of whang leather in the rings of the snaffle bit then threaded it through a snug collar of leather wrapped and lashed around the lion's neck. Shortening the tie between bit rings and collar until painfully tight forced the jaws apart and kept the cat from either opening or closing its mouth, rendering the fangs useless.

Bound and gagged, the mountain lion eventually realized the futility of struggling. Wrapped securely in the dark of a sheet of canvas, the conquered cat offered little resistance and suffered that indignity and the lengthy horseback ride that followed without incident.

The horse, while less cooperative, soon enough settled down and hauled cowboy and cargo home to Fishhook headquarters.

*****

The swirled whisky looked a thin shade of orange for the brief instant it stained the side of the glass before slipping down into the puddle in the bottom where it took on a deeper tinge. A pleasant enough color, Longmore thought. But the stuff isn't made to look good. He tipped up the dregs of the drink and drank it down. Hell, he told himself, it ain't even made to taste good.

The chair scraped across the plank floor as he pushed back from the table and left the room on unsteady legs. He dropped heavily onto the bed, dragged his feet one at a time by the pantlegs onto his lap to work off the boots. Pitching his hat onto the bedpost, he wiped drool from loose, heavy lips with a forearm before tipping over and clawing a pile of bedding over his fully clothed body.

The last thought he thought before dropping suddenly into sleep was a question, the answer to which would be the work of another day:

What the hell was Wilson Hayes up to?

Chapter Six

Some niggling annoyance worried Longmore's sleep but it was not, as yet, anything he could identify. His hand rose involuntarily and swatted it away and he sank back into the depths of slumber.

But not for long. Whatever it was, there it was again. And again, he pawed at it unconsciously. But the aggravation was persistent in luring the man into wakefulness.

First to reach the level of awareness was pain. Longmore imagined, initially, that Will Hayes had the back of his head gripped in a pair of blacksmith tongs, applying a steady, bone-crushing pressure. Then he wondered in his dreamy state if, instead, the boy had a stranglehold around the top of his head with a lariat, for the hurt encircled his throbbing skull.

The annoying itch returned, teasing its way through the headache, and he imagined Hayes bearing down on the rope and tickling him with a feather or blade of grass at the same time. Again, his hand swatted at the itch and lifted him further out of sleep.

Sound drifted into focus. He heard a buzz, a wandering drone that was somehow familiar but still swaddled unrecognizably in the confusion of interrupted slumber. The drone stopped and soon after the itch returned.

The man dredged up the realization that his tormentor was not Will Hayes, and, in fact, wasn't even human. Rather, he was being troubled by a fly.

He kept still for a moment as the insect waded through drool pooled at the corner of his mouth, slurping and siphoning at the foul brew. Instead of repeating earlier sleepy swats, he used his growing awareness to purposefully brush the fly away, then, with the back of his hand, smeared away the slobber. He wished the pain in his head could be pushed aside as easily.

Hesitantly cracking open one crusty eyelid, he slammed it shut when assaulted by the harsh light of full day. Mustering courage, Longmore dared another peek, this time managing not only to keep that eyelid peeled but to skin back the other as well. He lay there for a moment and twitched his various extremities as if to reacquaint himself with his parts. His bladder made its presence known, but while the need was urgent it did not constitute an emergency, so he did not stir.

The lazy fly soon returned, circling above its chuckwagon as if contemplating a landing, and Longmore used the annoyance to push himself fully into the morning. Shoving wadded covers aside, he dropped both feet over the edge of the bed and dangled his legs back and forth to locate his boots. Once shod, he stood, bent slightly at the waist by the stiffness of sleep and the added weight of his hung-over head.

He creaked himself upright and shuffled the few steps to the washstand, sloshed a few handfuls of water out of a china pitcher into the matching bowl, scooped it up and slapped it over his face, drying wet hands by sliding them through his thick hair. He wondered at his image in the filmy looking glass while unbuttoning his shirt, which he then used to towel off his face. His once black hair was now a blue roan hue, with as many white strands as black mixed together to create the shade. The white hair was outgrowing the black nowadays, and he suspected his head would soon fade from roan to gray.

His face in the hazy mirror was further blurred by weak eyes. Longmore, like his son Johnny, needed eyeglasses to bring the world into sharp focus. Unlike Johnny, vanity prevented his wearing them.

He tossed the shirt onto a pile of soiled clothing in the corner and pulled another from a peg on the wall. Emma, with help from the cook, kept the Longmore house spotless except for the owner's bedroom. He discouraged their visits here, allowing them in only when the boar's nest got too rank even for him. Buttoning his shirt as he went, the man shuffled out the back door toward the outhouse, thinking he might just remove his head and dump it down the hole if the damn thing didn't quit pounding.

The hands had long since abandoned the dining room when he finally mounted his accustomed chair at the head of the long table. Sipping at the coffee he'd poured from the battered pot kept warm on the potbelly stove—topping it off with a slosh of whiskey—he awaited breakfast, but only picked at the eggs, bacon, cornbread, and molasses when they arrived.

Still fretful over whatever had troubled his sleep, the rancher slid the plate away and hunched forward, fore-arms and elbows on the table, both hands wrapped around the warm mug. Grimacing with the pain in his head, he wished the cure swirled into the coffee would kick in. Lingering anxiety, attached to something he couldn't quite put his finger on, contributed to the wrinkled forehead.

He knew it had to do with Will Hayes, but couldn't decide why.

The boy, somehow, some way, was a threat. Nothing the kid had said or done in the year he'd been on the Fishhook could be chalked up to evil intentions. Hell, truth be told, it was just the opposite.

The kid was a hard worker, and a skilled one at that. After that business with the cougar, Will had settled back into winter ranch work. He never shirked his turn at riding a long circle to check the whereabouts of the stock, no matter how bad the weather. Longmore had long ago realized the boy had a sixth sense when it came to caring for cattle, and about the time the rancher decided it was time to push one herd or another to fresh winter range, he'd find out the move was already under-way, at Will's instigation.

Come calving time, Will spent more time slogging on horseback through the herds than he did hanging around headquarters. Most ranchers and their cowboys were content to let critters fend for themselves, but the boy was determined that every cow, every first-calf heifer, and the issue of every one of them survive and thrive.

Cowboys reported finding him ankle-deep in mud and slush, shirt stripped off with bare arm shoulder deep in the back end of a cow straining unsuccessfully to birth a backward calf. Others told the rancher of watching Will neck an uncooperative mother cow to a cedar tree and help a hungry calf find its first meal. Every tight-bagged cow he encountered constrained the boy to search up and down every gully and under every brush for a calf too sick to eat or too weak to hunt up its mother.

All in all, Longmore's throbbing head thought, the kid takes care of the stock like he owned it. Hell, he thought, he takes better care of it than I do and I *do* own it.

The old man realized, too, that his uneasiness about the boy was his alone. No cowboy on the place ever complained about him. The other hands seemed to recognize and respect the kid's abilities, and, much to the rancher's surprise, often deferred to this boy who was barely dry behind the ears.

Even his own family liked the kid. Johnny, the theoretical foreman and cow boss of the outfit, asked Will for advice and ideas. And he detected something in Emma's manner that suggested she was sweet on the boy. Hell, even the cook was under his spell, never once complaining and even volunteering to fix the kid a meal when he came or went at odd hours. *Hmmph*, the old man thought, *she whines if I want a fresh pot of coffee boiled.*

The kid's heroics with Caleb Short and the excitement he stirred up bringing that cow-killing mountain lion in alive had established his rep. His willingness to lend a hand whenever and wherever necessary didn't hurt. Even the guitar playing that made evenings more enjoyable—*hell, even I like that*, Longmore thought—added to the kid's popularity around the place.

But it was spring roundup and branding time that clearly demonstrated Will's cowboy credentials.

Being a newcomer, Will was naturally assigned to ground work. It was a dirty, dangerous job no cowboy liked. Aside from being afoot, the work required more brute strength than smarts, and swallowing a half-pound of dust was all part of a day's diet.

Cowboys with seniority rode into the herd and roped the calves, then dragged them to the branding fire. Depending on whether it was caught by neck or heels, one of the ground crew would flank or tail the calf down, then drop to his knees on the bawling animal's neck and ribs and get a hammer lock on the front leg. Another crew member, backside in the dirt behind the calf, grabbed a handful of one hind hock, braced a bootheel against the other, and scissored the legs apart.

With the calf thus disabled, someone came running with a red-hot stamp iron to burn a Fishhook high on the ribs, while another hand holding a sharp knife notched the ears with Longmore's mark then squatted in the smoke to slice the bull calves' scrotum and squeeze out the budding testicles to cut loose the cords that held them.

Will took his place without complaint and did more than his share of the dirty, stinking, bloody work. But, early the first afternoon, an inattentive instant on the part of one of the mounted cowboys resulted in his catching his hand in the dallies, rendering him useless for the work. When invited to replace the roper, Will eagerly saddled a horse and shook out a loop.

Roping, as Longmore knew, was a skill common among cowboys; competence, for that matter, was required for the job. He fancied himself, in fact, a better-than-average roper. But he, along with everyone else at the Fishhook, saw in Will an ability with a lariat that surpassed proficiency to become artistry. He seldom missed a conventional head or heel loop, and could thread his twine into tight places and still hit his target.

But it was the unconventional loops, most of which had never been seen on the Fishhook, that set the kid apart as a roper. The rancher, his role as boss allowing him the leisure to watch the boy, saw forehand loops that stood on end, backhand loops that rolled over, shots that wheeled over the back of a calf to wrap around the legs on the opposite side, catches from every angle of the three hundred and sixty available, and even occasions when the young roper released a loop then whipped and snaked it around in the air until, like it had eyes, it would fly over several animals in a bunch to drop suddenly around the neck of the intended critter.

The rancher could see the fancy catches weren't meant to show off, but, in fact, allowed Will to put his loop on more cattle than the other ropers while disturbing the herd less than they did. But while the kid did not intend to show off with his rope, the other hands could not help but take note. More than once, Longmore looked around to see every cowboy on the job standing flatfooted or sitting idle in the saddle to watch the kid at work, and yelled at them to get back to work.

The boy's ability to handle a rope became a continuing topic of conversation among the cowboys around the place. Many attempted to mimic the skills, and the kid willingly schooled them in the techniques. When asked, he claimed to have learned from the old Mexican *vaquero* his family had long employed on their Texas ranch.

Even though the rancher shared their admiration, he soon tired of hearing about the kid's roping and the accolades were added tinder in his smoldering distrust of Will.

But, Longmore realized as he pondered over his long-since-empty coffee mug, he had been barely aware of the budding distrust and dislike at the time. That realization would come later, and would grow stronger as the admiration others heaped on the youngster increased.

In no hurry to face the day, the old man decided to refill his mug and sit some more. This time, the whiskey went in first, leaving room for barely enough coffee to flavor the mix. He took to the chair again, realized his headache was mostly gone, and gulped down a mouthful of the fresh mug, hoping it would complete the cure. His thoughts, as was more and more the norm, turned again to Will Hayes.

*****

With the branding out of the way, the Fishhook herds had moved to summer range. Far from headquarters, the camps would be largely self-sufficient for the season, each operating like a smaller ranch—which many of the cow camps were, having been built by other ranchers whose outfits Longmore had taken over, some of whom were willing, others not.

The last herd moved was the one bound for the mountains in and above Antler Canyon. While nearer the Fishhook than most of the other camps, the grass came later to the high country. Three hands drifted the herd toward the canyon. The cowboys—Will, Clancy, and a rawboned man called Rib—simply allowed the cows and their calves to graze in the general direction of their destination. They would spend two weeks on a trip that a well-mounted man could cover in half a day.

They'd been gone just over a week when Clancy came riding into headquarters one sunrise at a high lope. Longmore and Johnny heard him coming and rushed out into the yard. It was not unusual to see one of the drovers coming in—being nearby, the Antler Canyon herders did not go out with a wagon, instead riding back regularly to the storehouse for supplies—but to see someone coming in such a hurry signaled trouble.

"Rib's dead!" Clancy shouted as his winded horse slid to a stop in the packed dirt of the ranch yard.

"What happened?" Longmore said.

"Shot. Rustlers," came the reply between gasping breaths.

Johnny said, "Where's Will?"

"Gone after 'em."

Longmore grunted angrily and threw down a pair of gloves he was carrying.

"What the hell does that kid think he's doing?"

Clancy had no reply.

"Who is he after? Where are they headed?" Johnny said.

"You know damn well who he's after," Longmore said. "It's that sonofabitch Sam Ballard. He's the one behind it."

"Not this time," Clancy said. "We reckoned it's them desert bandits. Y'know, that Amos Parker bunch."

Parker, headquartered over the mountains in Cane Valley, had moved into the territory just two summers ago. He ran a typical band of ne'er-do-wells whose members came and went as opportunity for mischief and pursuit by the law required. Given mostly to robbing stagecoaches and trains and freight wagons, it was rumored that the band had knocked off a couple of banks up north somewhere in the Dakota country and had felt the heat of pursuit all the way here.

Like most outlaws, this bunch wasn't above rustling cattle or horses when the opportunity presented itself. Until now, their thieving had been limited to the few smaller outfits still in the area, the Fishhook brand being too well known over too wide an area to allow the stolen stock to be easily sold. But the brand was simple to alter, too.

"Why do you think it's Parker?" Longmore said.

"Hunch, mostly. That, and they turned the part of the herd they cut out toward the desert before stampeding them and ridin' hell for leather after 'em."

"Step down and tell us how it happened," Johnny said. "Start at the beginning."

"They showed up around three, maybe half past, this morning," Clancy said after dismounting. "We's all asleep and the fire had burned down. They rode through the edge of the herd away from where we was camped, scared up maybe two hundred head. Most of the calves got left behind. Didn't even try to take 'em and they couldn't keep up anyhow.

"Anyways, by the time we woke up enough to figure out what was goin' on the whole thing was damn near over. Rib had a night horse saddled and lit out after 'em.

Me and Will saddled up to follow but it was so damn dark you couldn't hardly find your hat if'n it was on top of your head."

"Get on with it!" Longmore said.

"Will and me followed best as we could. When it finally got light enough to see, we found Rib riding the same way we was, only about a quarter mile off to our right. We couldn't see no cattle, but their trail was plain, soft ground all tore up and all. It looked like by the time they got that far they was slowing down and them riders was starting to bunch 'em up.

"We kicked up our horses and Rib was ridin' at an angle to join up with us. Then he keeled off the back of his horse ass-over-tea kettle like he'd been pole-axed. About the time he hit the ground we heard the shot. Another piece of lead came whistling past my ear, so we ducked down into a little coulee to figure out what to do next.

"Will figgered one of 'em had held back to scare us off. But Will thought he wasn't likely a good enough shot to get both of us if'n we lit out in opposite directions. Sent me back the way we came so I could hustle back here for help. He rode right at where we figured that gunman was. Last I looked, he's still ridin' but I don't know for how much longer."

Johnny said, "You're sure Rib was dead?"

"Didn't wait around to check," Clancy said. "But he hit the ground like a sack of shit and bounced like no live man I ever seen would do."

"We ain't doing no good standing around here jawing," Longmore said. "Clancy, you go catch up a fresh mount and saddle my horse while you're at it. Johnny, roust out anybody still in the bunkhouse and tell them to get mounted and let's get moving."

"I'm on the way," Johnny said. "But I think Pete's the only one here. Everyone else is out with the herds."

Longmore said, "He'll have to do. I don't suppose we'll have much to do by now, anyhow, outside of burying Rib and seeing if we can find Will's body. The headstrong little bastard!"

*****

Longmore swirled the remnants of his whiskey coffee around the bottom of the mug. He remembered as if it were yesterday his surprise at topping a rise to see Will riding drag behind a spread-out herd of some two hundred bawling cows mixed with a few tuckered calves. He and Johnny, Clancy, and Pete had passed the big herd a few miles back. So it wouldn't be long, Longmore knew, until the cows Will was pushing caught wind of the hungry calves they'd left behind and would be off and running.

As usual, Will didn't volunteer any information about what happened. The rancher practically had to threaten him to learn that the kid had ridden down the shooter, homing in on the smoke from his rifle with lead whistling by on every side, bowling the man over, then doubling back to finish him off with a bullet. He wondered how the man had ever managed to hit Rib, poor a shot as he was.

Will rode hard, putting a low ridge between himself and the rustlers and the herd. Once beyond the cattle, he dismounted, topped the rise afoot, and holed up in jumble of rocks just below the skyline. From his sniper nest there, he managed to shoot three of the outlaws off their horses before they knew what hit them. The fourth bandit took two shots to stop, as he'd bailed off his horse and was running for cover.

Then, Will told them, he chased down the last of the bunch and shot him out of the saddle with his pistol. The downed man was still alive and likely to live. The kid learned from the wounded outlaw that the rustlers were, as Clancy suggested, part of Amos Parker's bunch. Will disarmed the man, bound up his wounds, and sent him back to Parker's hole across the mountains with instructions to stay away from the Fishhook—or he'd personally hunt down and kill every one of the thieving bastards.

*****

Hell, Longmore thought as he drained the dregs of the whiskey and coffee gone cold, the kid could probably do it.

Somehow, he did not find that a comforting thought.

Chapter Seven

The dust hung heavy and thick in the round corral. Will led in another mount, a cow-hocked appaloosa gelding with a white blanket over its rump speckled with blue roan spots the size of hen's eggs that matched the hide covering his neck and front shoulders. Experience handling this colt before warned him to be cautious. He dropped the halter, worked a bit between the horse's jaws and slipped the headstall over its ears. A few ranch cowboys sat the top rail, watching the youngster work his magic with horses.

Before Will's arrival at the Fishhook, the hands were more likely to ear down a colt, fight a saddle onto its back, climb aboard, get pitched, and climb back on again and again in a test of wills until the horse admitted defeat and submitted to the man on its back.

Horses thus broken were turned out with the saddle stock, considered ready for cow work. It didn't always work that way. Many a hand, finding himself in a tight aboard a skittish colt, would hoof it back to headquarters after picking prickly pear thorns out of his eyebrows or backside. It took a lot of wet saddle blankets to finally calm these skittish, green-broke colts until they were reliable, and often involved a lot of buck offs along the way.

So the cowboys showed undue interest when Will became the breaker in the pen. As many as were around headquarters would line up, perched atop the round corral fence. His approach was slower, more methodical, and easier on man and mount. He rubbed the horses all over, hoisted their hooves one by one, talked softly to them, got them accustomed to the touch of his hand and the feel of the rope, the bit, the cinch, and the saddle.

Horses being horses, there was still plenty of pitching in the round pen when finally he swung into the saddle, but the colts bucked more out of a sense of duty than mad panic, and when they quit bucking and lined out in a trot under Will's tutelage, more often than not they had little more inclination to try to unseat a rider.

The appaloosa skittered a few steps sideways when Will laid a saddle blanket over its back, but a firm tug on the bridle reins settled him down while the cowboy swung the stock saddle aboard and gave it a good shake to settle it into position. Once he snugged up the cinch, Will threaded the latigo back through the d-ring on the saddle and looped it around into a tight cinch knot.

With bridle reins in hand, Will grabbed the cheek piece on the bridle and bowed the horse's neck toward him as he reached the stirrup and lifted into the saddle.

When the appaloosa tried to sidestep away, pressure on the headstall turned his motion into a tight circle. After a couple of turns, Will turned loose of the cheek piece and hauled in the reins, pulling the gelding's head straight.

The horse sat trembling for a few seconds, then squatted on his hind legs and exploded upward. When gravity got the best of him, he dropped back down, landing on stiff legs that jolted Will's spine and made him catch his breath. Almost the instant he hit the ground, the colt lunged, snapping the cowboy's neck back, which whipped forward again when the colt hit ground and sucked back into himself, then repeated the whole bone-rattling process. Will weathered the storm and settled into the horse's rhythm, then tightened the reins jump by jump, lifting the colt's head and dampening his ability to buck.

"Ride 'im Will!" came a shout from atop the fence.

"Put the spurs to him," said another.

And another, "Hang tight! He's a snaky one!"

The lunging and jumping eventually smoothed out into a stiff-legged trot around the pen. Will worked the reins, turning the appaloosa one way then the other through the dusty haze, turning figure-eights in the round corral. Finally, as the winded colt slowed to a walk, Will reined him into ever-tighter circles, reversing direction from time to time, letting the horse grow accustomed to the demands of the bit. He dismounted, loosened the latigo, dropped the cinch, pulled the saddle, stood it against the fence near the gate, and replaced the bridle with a halter.

Will led the colt out of the pen and nearly ran into Emma, water bucket in one hand and dripping dipper in the other, held out toward him.

"I thank you, Emma," he grinned. "I could sure use a drink. Turn some of this dust I've swallowed into mud."

"That was quite ride, Will."

"You saw that?"

"Every jump."

"Ah, well, he's just a colt. Not like he's big enough to do a fella much damage."

"Still," Emma said, "you sure impressed the other hands."

Will looked at the railbirds atop the fence, every one of them with eyes on the young couple and silly grins on their faces. One puckered his lips with a resounding smack.

Another said, "Think you can handle that filly like you did that appaloosie, Will?"

That brought a laugh, and another cowboy followed up with, "Nah. Them girls is a lot more likely to fight their heads."

With face and neck burning red, Will handed the dipper back to Emma.

"Thanks again," he said. "Better get back to work. Got more horses to ride."

She dropped the dipper into the bucket and watched him tie the sweating colt to a fence rail. "Be careful," she said before starting toward the house.

Leaning against a post propping up the shed roof in front of the blacksmith shop, Longmore watched the whole thing. Big as it was, the Fishhook Ranch couldn't put enough distance between Will and Emma to suit Longmore. Fully aware of his daughter's beauty, not to mention the attraction the family's wealth would hold for suitors, he had high hopes for a suitable match. And, to him, "suitable" did not include a cowhand working for forty a month and found. A powerful politician, wealthy financier, or the like was more in keeping with his plans.

Sweating beside his boss in leather apron, the bull-necked smithy said," I do believe them young'uns is sweet on each other, Mister Longmore."

"I sure as hell hope not."

"Oh? And why might that be?"

"No girl of mine is going to settle for some fiddle-footed saddle tramp."

"I don't think you need worry about young Will. He ain't no ordinary cowboy. Unless I miss my guess, that boy's goin' far."

"Hmmph. You can take that guess of yours and pound it out on that anvil into a horseshoe nail for all I care. That kid is nothing more than trouble brewing." Longmore shouldered himself away from the rail and started for the house. "I ain't paying you to watch no rodeo nor give advice, either one. Get back to work."

Emma dumped the water from the bucket into a flower bed lining the front porch, climbed the steps and went in the front door. The smithy watched Longmore fast-walking toward the house and wondered what was in store for the girl once the door shut behind her father.

Chapter Eight

The front door banged shut and Longmore's boots clomped into the house.

"Emma!"

The skin on the back of her neck tingled and her muscles clenched as she slid the water bucket into its place next to the sink and wiped her hands on a dish towel. "In the kitchen, Papa."

He filled the door and lit into his daughter.

"I've told you before, girl. You're not to be keeping company with that boy."

"But Papa! It was a drink of water!"

"Will knows how to quench his own thirst. He don't need you looking after him like some kind of wet nurse. Stay away."

The bloom in Emma's cheeks spread, coloring her face and creeping down her neck. She wadded the dish towel and threw it into the sink. "I'm not a little girl anymore. Why can't I do as I please?"

"You're still my daughter. And you ain't old enough yet to know what's best."

"What's wrong with Will, anyway? You brought him here."

"That was my mistake. This family don't need any more mistakes where that kid's concerned."

"Answer my question, Papa. What's wrong with Will?"

"Emma, I don't rightly know. But there's something about that boy that don't sit right with me. He's nothing but a saddle bum. He came here with nothing but the shirt on his back."

"Same as you."

"Difference is, girl, I'm still here. And I've got a hell of a lot more than the shirt on my back to show for my time here. That boy, he'll leave the same way he came. You watch your step, or he'll be leaving sooner than you think."

"You won't send Will away, Papa! Will you?"

"That's up to you, Emma. I catch him sniffing around you, he's gone. I catch you fawning over him again, he'll be walking down the road kicking horse turds faster than you can say goodbye."

The catch in her throat kept Emma from saying more, but the tears welling in her eyes said enough as she pushed past her father and rushed to her bedroom, brushing Johnny aside as she went. He had been doing bookwork at the desk in the dining room and heard every word.

Johnny joined his steaming father in the kitchen. He retrieved the dishtowel Emma had thrown in the sink, leaned against the table, removed his spectacles and wiped the lenses.

"You know, you're wrong about Will," he said.

"Hmmph."

"It's true. If you could see past your nose, you'd admit he's far and away the best hand on the Fishhook," he said as he threaded the hooks of the eyeglasses around his ears.

"That's not much in the way of praise," Longmore said.

"Maybe not. Sometimes. But the boy knows horses. He knows cattle. He knows the land. He's accomplished everything he's set his hand to here, and unless I miss my guess, he'd accomplish anything he set his mind to."

"Including stealing my daughter?"

"Aw, hell, Pa. Stealing isn't any kind of word for it. Especially if Emma is willing, which I believe she is, or will be. More willing than Will at this point, I'd say."

"She deserves better. I deserve better."

"Well, you won't find better in this country."

"Bullshit." Longmore said.

"You think? Like who?"

"Hell, I don't know. She's so young I ain't give it much thought."

"You best start thinking, Pa," Johnny said. "She's not as young as you think. Emma's a grown woman. Or will be, next time you open your eyes."

Longmore massaged his eyes with the heels of his hands. "How about that young feller I got helping run the bank?"

Johnny laughed. "Glen? Glen? Emma wouldn't give that dolt the time of day. To quote Hotspur, 'He's as tedious as a tired horse'."

"Hotspur my hind end. Glen's got a lot better prospects than Will. Besides, I'd think his fancy-ass diploma from that St. Louis college would count for something, with you."

Again, Johnny laughed. "How many times have I heard you say that education doesn't equal smarts? If that pot-bellied banker isn't the proof of that, I don't know who would be. Besides, Will's prospects aren't as limited as you seem to think."

Longmore's eyebrows shot up.

Johnny said, "I'm thinking we ought to make him foreman of the Fishhook."

This time, it was Longmore who laughed. "Ain't a man on this ranch with hair on his ass who'd take orders from that snot-nosed kid. You're dreaming."

"Not so. I've been out with the hands day in and day out. There isn't a one of the men who hasn't come to admire Will and his ways."

"Still, they'd resent taking orders from him. If not right away, soon enough. Then they'd leave. I can't afford to lose good cowboys."

"And yet you seem perfectly willing to run off the best cowboy you've got."

"Maybe he does make a hand. I'll give you that. But that's a long throw from foreman. Besides, that's your job."

"I'm ready and willing to give it up, Pa, if it means putting Will in charge. I'm a lot better suited to management and bookkeeping, buying and selling. You know that as well as I do. And you're not getting any younger."

Longmore laughed again. But there was no humor in it.

He said, "I might not be young anymore but I damn sure ain't past it yet. In my younger days, that boy would not have been able to wipe the dust off my boots."

"Maybe. Maybe you're not past it, as you say, but you must admit you're well past your younger days."

"I ain't got to admit no such thing."

"No, Pa, you wouldn't. And I think that's the real problem here."

"What do you mean?"

"You don't like Will because you see too much of yourself in him, what you used to be."

"Hmmph."

"I must say, though, that he's a hell of a lot better natured than you are, or ever were. Come to it, as cranky as you are these days, I think the men would rather take orders from Will than from you."

"That day won't ever come."

"Maybe. I wouldn't bet on it, were I you."

"It's still my ranch. And I won't stand by and watch you hand it to that guitar-strumming orphan sonofabitch. And I won't let him marry Emma to get it, either."

"You may not have a say in the matter. I hate to say it, Pa, but you won't live forever. And Emma will do what she will do, sooner or later."

"I ain't dead yet. So there ain't no use acting like I am."

"No, Pa, you're not dead yet. But Will and Emma have time on their side. And it won't do them or you—or the Fishhook—any good to make them outlast you."

"Hmmph."

Chapter Nine

Rattles and squeaks, creaks and clatters accompanied the buckboard along the road from the Fishhook to Ballard Station.

Will held the lines, but, lost in thought, he allowed the horses to follow the hardpan road of their own volition, which they did. Beside him on the seat, Johnny studied the pages of a well-thumbed book.

The more road they left behind, the more Will's eyelids sagged, hanging over his eyes like roller blinds on a window. After feeling his chin bounce off his chest a few times, jarring him awake, he decided it would take conversation to fend off sleep.

"What's that you're reading, Johnny?"

With a sidelong glance at Will, Johnny closed the book, using a thumb to mark his place, and showed the cover. "It's called *Leaves of Grass*. Poems by a fellow from back East name of Walt Whitman."

"Seems like you're a-readin' something or other all the time."

Johnny fished a scrap of paper from a vest pocket and it replaced his thumb as a bookmark. He set the book in his lap and said, "I reckon that's true. It seems like there's never enough time to read everything I want to—especially with books like this one, that I keep reading over again."

"Why's that? Seems like once you've read it, you've read it."

"That's the thing about a good book. It's familiar like an old friend, but every time you read it you find something new. Or maybe things just look different, depending."

"On what?"

"Oh, I don't know. Maybe the mood you're in. Something else you read, or something you saw or heard. You know, things just seem different, different times."

"Yeah," Will said. "I guess I sort of know what you mean."

"You read much?"

"Oh, no. Not hardly ever. Maybe something in a magazine now and then, or a page from the mail-order catalog while sitting in the backhouse. I've tried to read the Bible a time or two but couldn't make nothing of it. I guess I just ain't got the head for book learning."

Johnny rode along in silence for a few minutes, the only sound the groans and whines of the wagon. "Tell me something, will you, Will?"

"Sure. I guess. If I can. What d'you want to know?"

"Emma."

Now it was Will's turn to ride along in silence for a time.

"What about her?" he finally said when overwhelmed by the quiet.

"What are your intentions where she's concerned?"

Will laughed. "Isn't that something Mister Longmore ought to be asking?"

"Probably. But I think he thinks his not saying anything means there's nothing to talk about."

After gnawing on that for a minute or two, Will said, "I guess I sort of knew your Pa wasn't too keen on the idea of me and Emma keeping company—what little of it we do. But seeing as how he never said anything . . . "

"Well, you were right the first time. He's none too happy about it. Fact is, he's downright unhappy about it. Told Emma he'd run you off if she didn't stay away from you, and you from her."

"I swear to God, Johnny, there ain't nothing at all between us. Not that there might not be, someday, but I ain't never even held her hand, let alone kiss her. Or anything like that."

"Think you can stay away from her?"

Again, silence.

Finally, "Truth is, I don't know. I sure like the look of that girl. And she seems to me sweeter than molasses in her ways. And unless I miss my guess, she wouldn't chase me off with no broom handle."

"I suspect you're right. But Pa might."

"I reckon you're right. What might Emma have to say about that, do you think?"

"She's not too pleased with Pa's views on the matter. And she's made no secret of it."

The wagon bumped and bounced along.

"I ain't sure what to do. I sure don't want to lose my job. And I sure don't want to lose out on no chance with Emma. If there is a chance. What would you do, Johnny?"

"It's not my place to say. There's something about you that rubs Pa the wrong way. Never mind there's no rhyme nor reason to it. It's just the way it is. I more or less told him Emma would make up her own mind, no matter what he thought. And I told him he was way off base where you are concerned."

"You did?"

"I did."

"I don't know what to say. Thank you, I guess. I'm obliged."

"That's not the half of it. I told him I thought we should make you foreman of the Fishhook."

The wagon rattled along.

"What do think about that?" Johnny said after a time.

Will struggled for a response. "I . . . I don't know. No such thing ever occurred to me."

"Think you could do the job?"

"I don't know. I can do the ranch work, certain sure. Whether or not I could get the men to go along with what I wanted to do—well, I don't know if I could or not, me being so much younger and all."

"I don't think they'd mind."

"I don't know."

"You underestimate yourself, Will. There isn't a hand on the Fishhook who doesn't respect you as a cowboy. They've seen for themselves that you're a man to ride the river with."

"I don't know . . . "

"Like I said, Will, you underestimate yourself." Johnny picked the book up from his lap. "Listen to this," he said as he thumbed through the pages. "Old Mister Whitman has something to say about that in a poem called 'Song of Myself.' " He found the page he wanted, and ran his finger down the lines and stopped at the one he wanted.

"Listen to this," he said. " 'I am large, I contain multitudes.' "

Will looked perplexed.

"It means you are more than you think—bigger than you think—big as anybody—big as everybody, in a way.

Not really, you understand. It's just telling you not to sell yourself short, to be as big a man, as big a person as you want to be, or ought to be."

"You really think 'I contain multitudes' or whatever?"

"I think you've got it in you. It's up to you if you want to become such."

By now the buckboard was rolling into Ballard Station.

"You think about it, Will. Drop me at the bank. After you've picked up the supplies at the mercantile, meet me over at the Elkhorn and I'll stand you to a drink."

After driving past the bank, Will wheeled the wagon off the main street and down a narrow alley, pulling up next to the loading dock where he had first met Jesse Longmore. After wrapping the lines loosely around the brake handle, he pulled the tether weight from under the seat and clipped it to the headstall of the horse in the nearside harness.

Inside the busy store, he handed the clerk his list, then took a chair near the stove in the corner to watch the shoppers come and go, gnaw on a dill pickle, and pass the time with the two old men who held court there most every day.

The store belonged to Longmore, so his sizeable order took priority over the walk-in shoppers. Ben White, who managed the store on shares and spent his days clerking there, bustled around pulling items off the shelves, rolling kegs and shifting crates, and packing items likely to break in boxes, cushioning them with peanuts.

Will wandered over into the corner where yard goods, lace and ribbons, and sewing notions were on display. He fingered a bolt of ivory-colored fabric dotted with light blue flowers.

"Ben, you reckon a young lady like Miss Emma could find some use for cloth like this? You know, to make herself a dress or apron or some such?"

"Don't ask me," the storekeeper laughed. "Lucille!" he hollered into the back of the store. "Customer needs your help."

Ben's wife set aside the box she was filling with various goods and bustled to the front of the store, the carpet slippers she wore for comfort whispering her progress across the board floor.

"Oh! It's you, Wilson Hayes! What can I help you with?"

"Miz White, I'm just a-wondering if some of this cloth with flowers on it would be useful for miss Emma out at the ranch."

"Oh, yes, indeed it would, Will. It's beautiful fabric. Just came in on our latest shipment from Massachusetts. How much do you suppose she'll be wanting?"

"Can't rightly say, ma'am. Don't even know as she would want it. I's just thinking of doing something nice for her. You know, like a present or something."

Lucille arched her eyebrows and said, "I see. This particular print would make a lovely dress. Especially if you trim it up nice—with something like this, I'd say," holding up a thick roll of lacy ribbon pulled from a nearby shelf.

"Yes ma'am. Just fix me up with whatever's proper."

Will looked on as Lucille rolled fabric off the bolt, stretching it from her outreached arm to her nose for a measure. She scissored off the desired length and loosely folded it, then did the same with the ribbon. Two spools of thread from a drawer, a paper of pins from another, and a packet of needles topped off the stack.

"Will you carry this with you, or shall I have Ben put it with the supplies?" she said as she wrapped the bundle in brown paper and tied it up with string.

"In the wagon, please," Will said. "But not in the back—up front in the jockey box, if you don't mind."

"I'll see to it," Lucille said, giving the knot on the tie string an extra tug. "Emma will find this a thoughtful gift, I'm sure. What's the occasion?"

"None, so far as I know."

"That makes it all the more thoughtful. Let me know how it turns out," she said with a wink.

Overhearing all this was a Rafter 7 hand who had stopped at the store for a box of cartridges for his Colt's pistol. He snorted and snickered as he walked out the door, leaving a fading trail of laughter behind.

When Will and Johnny walked into the otherwise empty Elkhorn Saloon a few minutes later, that same cowboy sat at a table with two other Rafter 7 cowboys. The room being dim at the best of times, and more so when coming in out of the sun, Will did not see him or pay much attention to the quiet laughter coming from the table.

"Two mugs of your best beer, if you please, Karl," Johnny said as they stepped up to the vacant bar.

"Ain't got no best beer. Ain't got no worst beer. Only got one kind of beer, and it's just plain beer."

"Well, draw us off a pair. The only beer you've got is, by definition, your best. I'm sure it will go down smooth on a day like this."

"Sure enough, Mister Longmore."

"Johnny. Mister Longmore, if there is such a person, would be my father."

"As you say, Johnny," the bartender said as he knifed beer foam off one mug and filled the other from the tap.

Will studied the saloon. It was typical of many such places in Western towns—a long, narrow room half of whose length was occupied by the bar, with a few tables near the opposite wall, a pair of felt-covered card tables in the back, and, finally, an out-of-tune piano that, at this early hour, sat silent in the corner near a door that opened onto the alley.

The wavy walls were covered with peeling wallpaper up top, skirted with wainscoting of rough-sawn pine. The pressed-tin ceiling, like the walls, was uneven, and both were smudged with smoky film from the lamps that lined the walls, rendered mostly useless for illumination because of their sooty glass chimneys. The floor of rough-cut pine planks was as irregular as the rest of the room, the edges of the boards warped and knots rising from the softer wood around them, worn down by years of boot traffic.

Will sipped his beer, then turned his attention to the cowboys at the table.

"Taken up needlework, have you, Will?" said one.

The others laughed.

"Sorry?"

Another replied. "We hear you been shopping for cloth. Pretty stuff, with flowers. Lace and all that."

More laughter.

"What of it?" Will said.

"Oh, nothing. Just didn't know you was a seamstress, is all."

Again, laughter. For some reason unclear to Will, the three cowboys saw something seriously funny in all this.

Said the third cowboy, "No, no, no! You fellas got it all wrong,"

Will realized he was the one who'd been in the store.

"I told you it was a present. For the boss's daughter, so she can make herself a pretty dress!"

Once more, laughter.

Will turned back to his beer and took another sip.

Said another, "Maybe he figures it will be easier to get that girl to lift her skirts if he's the one put 'em on her in the first place!"

Before this round of laughter even got started, it withered in the fire of Will's anger. He jerked the offending cowboy to his feet and, with the other hand, landed a shattering blow to the point of the man's chin. He crumpled, and Will let him drop slowly as far as the length of his arm, then released his grip to let the cowboy fall to the floor with a hollow thump.

The other two cowboys jumped to their feet, upsetting chairs and scraping table legs across the floor.

Johnny grabbed Will's elbow. "Will," he said.

"Let me go, Johnny," Will said as he pulled his arm free.

"Just want you to know I'm here."

"Thanks. But even though Emma's your sister, this ain't your fight."

Backing slowly toward his place at the bar, Johnny pulled off his eyeglasses and laid them next to his beer mug, just in case circumstances required him to step in.

Deciding to leave the man from the store for last, Johnny started around the table toward the other. Unwilling to wait his turn, the neglected cowboy grabbed the whiskey bottle from the table by the neck and swung it in a hard arc toward Will's head.

He sensed the impending impact and ducked, so the blow was a glancing one—not hard enough to knock Will down or out, but it staggered him. That his target was still on his feet rattled the Rafter 7 cowboy, and he turned for the door. But Johnny stepped away from the bar, blocking his path.

"Not a chance," he said. "You stay put."

Meanwhile, Will was fending off a vicious attack, the other cowboy deciding his best hope was to get it over with before the kid got his wits about him. Three, four, six roundhouse blows landed on Will's head and shoulders before he shook it off. He managed to grab a fistful of the cowboy's shirtfront and bandana and jerked him off balance, then immediately pushed him backward.

As the man backpedaled, trying to keep his feet, Will pressed forward, keeping the man reeling with another shove. It took the wall to keep him upright, and the instant he hit it, a punishing blow to the midsection bowed him over. Then the force behind Will's uppercut lifted him off his feet, and did the same for the man whose mouth it landed on. The cowboy snapped upright, and any consciousness left in his head was knocked out when it left a bloody smear on the wallpaper. Will stepped out of the way as the man's body crashed to the floor like a falling tree.

Wiping blood from a split lip with the back of his hand, Will finally turned his attention to the cowboy whose smart mouth had started this whole fandango.

"Didn't mean no harm, mister," the Rafter 7 cowboy said.

"Like hell. You could have shut your mouth anytime, anywhere from the store to here. But you three decided, instead, to taint the repute of an innocent girl. A girl you ain't even fit to breathe the same air with."

"I'm sorry. Really, I am."

"I know it. You are one sorry sonofabitch."

With that, Will stepped up to cowboy with the warped sense of humor and turned his nose into a mushy, bloody pulp. If the Rafter 7 hand felt the blow at all, it wasn't for long. He was out before he hit the floor.

But he would feel it when he awakened. And for weeks afterward.

Johnny fetched his spectacles from the bar and put them back on his face.

"Mind if we finish these beers, Karl?"

"Holy shit," the bartender said, barely above a whisper. "That boy whipped them three and didn't throw no more'n five punches!"

"Four, by my count," Johnny said, and drained off his beer.

"Buy you another one, Will?"

"No thanks. I ain't thirsty anymore. If it's all the same to you, I'd as soon get back to the ranch."

"I'm right behind you. Karl, we owe you any damages?"

"No, sir, Mister Longmo—Johnny."

And so the two climbed aboard the creaky buckboard and rattled their way back to the Fishhook, leaving Will's growing reputation behind them.

Chapter Ten

The cool air in the copse of cottonwood trees enclosing the clear, cold spring that provided water for Fishhook headquarters often lilted with birdsong. But songbirds fell silent with the setting sun, so the only music in the grove in the gloaming came from Will's guitar.

He did not mind, and often enjoyed, playing for the Fishhook cowboys in the bunkhouse, or for the Longmore family and the hands as they relaxed after dinner in the ranch house dining room. But sometimes he wanted to be alone with the music. He found his time caressing the strings relaxing; it allowed him the peace to ruminate on his growing relationship with Emma, the suspicions of her father, and contemplate what the future on the Fishhook might hold.

Somehow, it all seemed more manageable with music.

Johnny understood. In fact, he put it into words, written, he said, way back when by some long-dead writer of plays from England: "Music has charms to soothe a savage breast." It seemed Johnny had words for any occasion or eventuality, borrowed from all those books he read. It made Will wish, sometimes, he had a head for reading.

Soft footfalls interrupted his thoughts and his fingers froze on the frets.

"Please. Don't stop."

"Emma!"

"Play, Will. I'll be quiet and not bother you, I promise."

Will laughed softly. "There's no way your being nearby couldn't bother me, Emma. Anytime you're around, I . . . Well, I . . . Nothing ever seems normal when you're near. My heart pounds so hard I fear it will punch right through my ribs and I can't hardly catch my breath."

Now it was Emma's turn to laugh, and Will found the music of it sweeter than any sound from his guitar.

"I'm awful sorry, Will. Maybe I should just stay away."

"Not a chance, Miss Emma. That would be even worse."

"Play, Will. Please."

As the last note of the tune rang out, Will muffled it with his palm on the strings.

"Does your Pa know where you are, Emma?"

"No."

"You think it's a good idea for you to be out here? With me, I mean?"

"I don't care, Will. Papa doesn't need to know everything. And he doesn't need to treat me like I am still a little girl."

"But you are his little girl. Always will be, I reckon."

"What about you? Do you think I'm a little girl?"

"Oh, you know better than that, Emma. You're as full-grown as a woman gets. I ain't got a way with words, like Johnny does, to say it, but I think—I hope— you know how I feel about you."

"And what do you propose we do about that?"

"I wish I knew, Emma. I wish I knew."

"I used the word 'propose' on purpose, Will. I guess you didn't get the hint."

Will set the guitar aside. "Your father, Emma. He won't have it. He don't like me much as it is. He'd send me packing—maybe worse. Hell, he might even cut my throat."

"Are you afraid of Papa? You? Why, I've seen you stick to wild horses like a cocklebur—horses most men wouldn't even get on. The very day you got here, you braced Caleb Short when no one else would! My goodness, Wilson Hayes, you even captured a mountain lion! Alive! And you're afraid of Papa? An old man?"

Will sat for a moment and let the air between them cool down.

"Not afraid. Not exactly. But he is you father, Emma, and where I come from that's deserving of respect. Not only that, he picked me up off the street and gave me a chance when no other man between here and Texas would. I figure I owe him."

"You figure you owe him more than you want me?"

"No, Emma. It ain't that. I want you more than anybody knows. More, even, than I know. But I don't know, either, what to do about it."

"Well, I do."

"What d'you mean?"

"Like you said, I'm his little girl. Sooner or later, he always gives me what I want."

Longmore sat in the dark living room keeping company with a whiskey bottle and a glass. The only light drifted in from the dining room where Johnny worked over the ranch's books by lamplight. He heard the back door close as Emma slipped in, then heard her bedroom door click softly shut. Through the window, he saw Will crossing the dooryard, guitar in hand, toward the bunkhouse.

He poured off another heavy splash of whiskey, swallowed it in a long gulp, and followed it up with another the same way.

"Johnny!" he called.

In a moment, his son's shadow entered the living room, followed by Johnny himself.

"What is it, Pa?"

"Sit."

Johnny did. "What is it?"

"It's that damn kid again."

"Will?"

"You know damn well it's Will."

"What is it this time?"

"Hmmph. I guess you didn't hear Emma sneaking in the back door just now."

"I heard her come in," Johnny said. "Didn't think anything of it."

"About that same time I saw Will making his way back to the bunkhouse. He had that guitar with him, but I don't think that's all he was keeping company with this evening."

Johnny lowered himself into a spindle-back rocking chair and waited.

His father downed another drink and said, "You know that don't set well with me."

Johnny rocked.

"Well, hell, Johnny! What do you think we ought to do about it?"

"I've told you before, Pa. I'm not inclined to do anything about it. And I don't think there's anything you can do about it, even if you are so inclined."

"She's my daughter."

"In more ways than one."

"What the hell's that supposed to mean?"

"It means that when it comes to being stubborn and bullheaded, she's every inch a match for you. The same thing's true in terms of being relentless in getting what she wants."

Longmore poured off another drink and slugged it down.

"I never expected you'd take sides against me, Johnny. My own son."

"Nobody's taking sides against anybody here, Pa. Unless it's you. Thing is, you've got a blind spot a mile wide when it comes to Will. The boy's done nothing but good since he got here. In fact, bringing him here is one of the best things you've ever done for the Fishhook."

"Hmmph."

"Face facts, man. He's got more horse sense in his little finger than all the other hands on this outfit combined. And when it comes to handling cattle, the only person on this ranch that's half the cowboy he is, is you. The way you used to be, that is. Before you started spending so much time crawling inside that whiskey bottle, hiding from something no one else can see."

"Aw, shit. Don't you start lecturing me, Johnny. I can still handle myself. Even half drunk, I'm more man than most others are stone cold sober."

"True enough, Pa. But I'm not comparing you to other men. I'm comparing you to yourself. You may be better than most, still. But you're making up the difference fast, every time you take a drink. Every time you let yourself get wound up tighter than a lasso rope over every little thing. Or nothing. No matter how much man you still are, you're not half the man you were. Or ought to be."

Longmore leaped from his chair with unexpected agility and arced a hard backhand against his son's cheek. Johnny's glasses flew off, skittering across the floor, sliding to a stop against the mopboard.

Matching his father's speed, he rose from the rocker and grasped a handful of beard on Longmore's cheek, giving it a hard twist like a twitch on a horse's lip. The effect was much the same.

"You're still my father, and I will not fight you," he hissed through clenched teeth. "But I am telling you now, for the first and only time, do not ever lay a hand on me again. If you expect respect from me, or from Emma for that matter, you had best be worthy of it. Our father is not a frightened drunk who thinks the whole world has turned against him. You had best remember who you are, or we are likely to forget."

Johnny turned loose, retrieved his spectacles, and went back to the desk in the dining room. He sat down and held the glasses up to the light to check for broken lenses.

His hands were shaking so uncontrollably he could not tell.

Chapter Eleven

Somewhere in Longmore's tortured dreams a bell chimed. Relentless in its ringing, he squirmed under the disturbance, struggling toward wakefulness. Finally, he recognized the sound—it was not a bell at all, but the ring of a hammer on an anvil. He wondered what the hell the smithy was doing shaping metal in the middle of the night. But a slight parting of one eyelid informed him it wasn't nighttime at all, and he squeezed his eyes shut to fend off awareness of the glaring light.

He wriggled his cramped and knotted body and realized he sat, more or less, upright, and his searching hands found him seated in a chair. Another brief peek put him in the front room of the ranch house. The intensity of sunlight in the room said the day was well underway.

Longmore straightened up in the seat, trying his best not to jar his throbbing head, and massaged his numb face with the palms of both hands. He winced at a tender spot on his left cheek, and last night's quarrel with Johnny flooded his memory. The bad taste in his mouth intensified with the thought and he looked around for a whiskey bottle, thinking a drink would cut the foul film.

But he thought better of it. When you've gotten your-self into a hole, he decided, you'd best stop digging. Besides, there'd be time enough for drinking later. He had all day.

He wandered the still house. The rolltop desk against the wall of the dining room was closed, so Johnny must be out with the hands. He wondered for a moment what they might be doing, and shook his head at being so out of touch with goings-on at the Fishhook. The kitchen was empty, the breakfast mess long since cleaned up and the cook off to her own devices somewhere. An ear against Emma's bedroom door heard nothing, but then he heard rustling in the room down the hall—the room that had been his wife's.

Pushing the door slowly aside, he saw Emma, delib-erately working the treadle on the sewing machine under the window. Sunlight streamed through the glass, creat-ing a halo around her face and hair and he was reminded of his daughter's remarkable beauty. More beautiful even, he realized, than her mother. With the tip of her tongue poking out the corner of her mouth and a furrow between her eyebrows, her involvement was so intense she did not sense her father's presence in the doorway.

He knocked gently on the doorjamb, startling Emma out of her concentration.

"Papa!" she said, raising a hand to still her pounding heart.

"Sorry, darling. Didn't mean to startle you. Sitting there like that, you remind me of your mama."

Emma studied her father for some clue to his mood.

"You look a mess, Papa," she said.

"Yeah, well. Last night was a little rough. Didn't sleep well at all."

"Likely you'd have been more comfortable in your bed."

"Likely."

The furrow reappeared above the bridge of Emma's nose. "Can I fix you something to eat, Papa?"

"No. Thanks. I don't think my stomach could face food right now. Maybe later."

She continued to study her father.

"I would like to talk to you Emma," he finally said. "If you can spare the time."

"Certainly, Papa."

He lowered himself into the chair his wife had used for reading and took a minute to collect his thoughts, wondering how to have this conversation; how to keep it from deteriorating into the usual argument.

"I'm worried, Emma. About you. And Will."

"Not again, Papa. We've been over this before."

"I know that. But nothing's been settled."

"There's nothing to settle."

"Maybe not yet. But I know you were out with him last night."

"He was playing for me on his guitar. That's all."

"It ain't proper for a young girl—lady—to be out alone with a young man."

"Nothing happened, Papa."

"Maybe not. But you never know what such things will lead to. Gossip, if nothing else."

Emma laughed. "Gossip? There's no one around here to gossip except a bunkhouse full of cowboys. And they know, even if you don't, that where Will is concerned there won't be anything to gossip about."

"I was young once, Emma. I know what a pretty girl like you can do to a man. I'm telling you it ain't proper for the two of you to be sneaking off like that."

"It's not that way. I know sometimes Will takes his guitar up by the spring to be alone. I wanted to see him, so I went up there. It's not like you give me any choice, Papa. You'd have a cow if I invited him to sit with me in the front room or on the porch like 'proper' folks would do."

Longmore sat massaging his temples, letting what his daughter said sink in, trying to formulate a reasonable response.

"Maybe it's time we changed that," he said, ending the tense silence.

*****

Longmore bit his tongue through the long summer, trying not to think about Will Hayes sitting in his favorite chair in the front room, talking softly and giggling with his daughter. Try as he might to ignore it, it grated on him like a burr under a saddle blanket, leaving him raw most of the time.

He consulted with Johnny about when and where to drift the cow herds, riding out to the camps from time to time to check range conditions, resupply the camp men with grub, and help move cattle now and then. An attempt to get Will out of the way and off his mind failed when he sent the young cowboy out to one of the camps; a distant ranch he'd forced a small-time operator off of years ago.

But Emma sulked so, and thoughts of the boy never left him anyway, so he brought him back to headquarters. Fact is, Will was much more valuable in the round corral breaking horses than following after cud-chewing cows.

Fall works came and went, and a big herd of fat yearlings trailed to the railroad in Ballard Station swelled

Fishhook coffers at the bank. Johnny's management of the money added to the assets column in the ledgers.

Wintertime meant more time snugged up indoors, and it was all the more difficult for Longmore to steer clear of Will. And, if he were honest with himself, he found the guitar music that often accompanied Will's visits with Emma calming as it drifted through the quiet house. But, on balance, it did not outweigh his dislike of the situation. Johnny, on the other hand, seemed pleased with the arrangement and even joined the young couple many an evening. To Longmore's surprise, Will and Emma invited his presence. It did not occur to him, that he, too, would be welcome.

All in all, winter at the Fishhook was more enjoyable and uneventful than ever. And that, too, made Longmore nervous and added to his suspicions. Trouble, he thought, must be brewing. But he couldn't put his finger on it. Try as he might to avoid doing so, he sought refuge in whiskey. Of everyone in the house, on the ranch, even in Ballard Station, he alone could not see that the drink intensified his fears and increased his paranoia.

Late one afternoon Will washed off the corral dust, donned a fresh pair of britches and a clean shirt and knocked on the front door of the ranch house. Johnny answered the knock.

"Come in, Will. Have a seat. I'll fetch Emma directly."

"No, Johnny, it ain't her I want to see. Is Mister Longmore here?"

After a moment, Johnny said, "Sure. Follow me. Let's see if he'll talk to you."

Will followed him into the dining room, entering through the house rather than the outside door he and the other hands normally used. Longmore sat at the head of the table, his accustomed place at mealtime, nursing a whiskey. He lifted the glass so the cook could swipe the tabletop under it with a wet rag, tracks of which grew increasingly faint down the length of the table as they dried.

"Pa," Johnny said. "You've got a visitor."

Longmore turned toward the door, squinting to find focus.

"Wilson Hayes," he said. "You sure he's not here to see Emma? Again?"

Will said, "No sir, Mister Longmore. It's you I want to see."

"Hmmph. Leave us alone for a minute," Longmore said, sweeping Johnny and the cook from the room with a wave of his hand.

Will stood, hat in hand, waiting.

"Don't stand there with your face hanging out, kid. Take a seat."

"Yes sir," Will said, scraping a chair back from the table. He sat, elbows on knees, working the brim of his hat through his hands, turning it in a circle. He cleared his throat. Shifted his seat in the chair. Repositioned his feet. Cleared his throat.

"What? Spit it out!"

"It . . . It's about Emma, Mister Longmore. Me and Emma."

"What about you and Emma?"

"Well, sir, I'm asking you for her hand."

"You mean you want to marry her?"

"Yessir."

Longmore laughed. "I can't believe you'd even ask me such a thing. What makes you think you're any kind of match for my daughter?"

"I'm not, sir."

Longmore, perplexed, took a drink of whiskey.

"I don't think any man is worthy of Emma. But, I reckon I'm as good as the next guy."

Another laugh. Another drink.

"Not in my book, you ain't. You're nothing but a shiftless ranch hand."

"I'm a hard worker. I've been here on the Fishhook for a good long time. Haven't I proved myself, sir?"

"You've proved you're a hell of a cowboy. I'll give you that. But that's all you are. A cowboy, with not another thing to your name. You work my cattle. You ride my horses. You eat my chuck. You sleep in my bunkhouse. Hell, kid, you ain't got a pot to piss in or a window to throw it out of. How and where do you suppose you and Emma are going to live?"

Will continued wearing out his hat brim.

"Here's what I thought, Mister Longmore. You could make me a camp man at one of your places. Maybe the old Hawkins outfit. If you'd stake us, we'd work the place on shares. Pay back what it takes to set us up, then keep on working for shares to buy out the place. We'd pay you a fair price."

"Emma go along with this?"

"Yessir. We've talked it over. A lot."

Longmore refilled his glass, emptied it, refilled it again.

"Sounds pretty dicey to me. One hard winter, one bad crop of calves, and you wouldn't be able to keep up the payments."

"We're willing to risk it, sir."

Longmore tipped the whiskey down his throat and slammed the glass to the table.

"So you two lovebirds have it all worked out, do you? Well, I'm not willing to risk sending my only daughter off to wear her fingers down to nubs on some hardscrabble greasy-sack excuse for a cow ranch!"

A few turns of the hat later, Will spoke again.

"I'm awful sorry to hear that, Mister Longmore."

"I'll bet you are. Now get back to the bunkhouse where you belong."

"That ain't what I mean. I'm not sorry like you think I mean."

"What the hell are you talking about?"

"Well, sir, Mister Longmore, Emma wanted your blessing, even your help. But the truth is we intend to get hitched, like it or not. We'll make our own way. It'll just be somewhere else."

Tipping his chair over in the process, Longmore sprang to his feet and slammed the heels of both fists onto the table. The whiskey bottle rattled, and the glass jumped into the air then landed on its side, dribbling whiskey as it bounced, rolled around its rim, and finally settled.

"Damn you, Will Hayes! Damn you to hell!"

He turned and kicked the fallen chair, tumbling it out of the way as he bulled out of the room and stomped out back door.

Chapter Twelve

A pitchforkful of manure-laced straw sailed out the barn door and tumbled down the side of the pile in the buckboard. Tommy O'Shannon, the broken-down cowboy who kept the Fishhook stores in order, milked the cows, tended to the barnyard chores, and generally tidied up around headquarters, worked the business end of the fork. He stepped out the barn door and sponged off his forehead, runneled with sweat despite the fact that the plume of his breath was visible in the late-winter air.

The swamper was the first person at the ranch to lay eyes on Jesse Longmore in more than a week. He wiped the back of his neck, shook out the bandana, and tucked it into a back pocket as the rancher rode up.

"Tommy, will you see to my horse?"

"Sure thing, boss."

Longmore handed him the reins and started toward the house. Tommy caught the scent of sour whiskey in his wake, and thought the man had aged a year in the days he had been away. He pulled the bandana from his pocket, lifted his hat to again mop his head, stuffed the clammy rag back into his pocket, and led the steaming horse toward the saddle shed as Longmore hobbled across the dooryard and up the front steps.

"Pa! Are you all right?" Johnny said, shortly after the front door slammed. "We've been worried."

"Fine. I'm fine. Just had to get away for a while. Things closing in on me got a little too tight. How's things here?"

"'Bout average. Nothing to report, really."

Longmore continued on to his room, not to be seen again the rest of the day. The cook carried him a tray when he didn't show for supper, but the knock wasn't answered and the food still sat at the door untouched come morning.

But, breakfast time found the rancher at his accustomed place at the head of the dining room table and his appetite seemed healthy enough. He exchanged small talk with the hands about the state of things on the Fishhook.

All, save Will, who he pointedly ignored.

When the cowboys pushed back their chairs to go to work, Longmore asked Will to stay behind.

"I don't suppose you and Emma have come to your senses."

"No, sir, I suppose not, not from your way of looking at things."

"So you're determined to steal my daughter."

Will mulled that a moment, and said, "That's one way to say it. Not my way."

"I think what you really want is the Fishhook. And you see Emma as the way to get it."

Will thought that one over even longer.

"No, Mister Longmore. Much as I've come to like this place, and working here, such thinking never crossed my mind. I figure this place is yours, until it becomes Johnny's. The Fishhook ain't got nothing to do with me. Other than a job, like I said."

"Hmmph. So the wealth of Emma's family means nothing to you?"

"Not a thing. I don't know how things work around here, but where I was raised a father passes down what's his to his sons."

Longmore refilled his coffee mug from a pot kept hot on the potbelly stove that warmed the room.

"How bad would you say you want my Emma?"

"Sir?"

"What's it worth to you to have my blessing?"

"Everything I've got, Mister Longmore."

The response drew a laugh. And, "Hell, boy, you and I both know you ain't got a damn thing. Except a guitar, which I can't use."

"Then I'm not sure what you mean."

"Maybe the Indians have the right idea. A brave wants to take a woman to wife, he gives gifts to her family until they approve."

"Like you said, I've got nothing to offer."

Longmore laughed again, but there was more sarcasm than humor in it.

"Suppose I asked ten ponies for her, like the Indians do. That's a pretty steep price, in Indian terms. But Emma's no ordinary Indian maiden, either."

Will stood, put on his hat, and headed for the door.

"Sit down, boy. Where you going? We ain't done yet!"

Will opened the door, stopped, turned to Longmore. "I'll be back," he said. "I'll be back with your damn horses."

*****

The stiff, steady wind blew through Will like cow's milk though cheesecloth and ricocheted off the rocks in front of him to chill again on the rebound.

Had he been able to wend his way through the rock pile and put it at his back, it would have offered shelter, but then the herd of mustangs he watched would have sensed his presence. They were skittish enough already.

For three days he had watched the herd, studying their pecking order and habits, identifying the lookouts and leaders. The stud horse, of course, was easily identified. But such herds were led as much by a dominant mare as a stallion, and it was she who disciplined them, stirred them to flight when threatened, led them to safety.

That mare, it became clear, was a heavy-boned bay with three white socks; both forelegs and the right-side hind. A blaze marked her face and muzzle, the top of it visible only in glimpses through a long, thick, tangled forelock.

He'd located the herd six days' ride south of the Fishhook, deep into the desert where forage was scarce, but where incessant winds scoured the snow, exposing the yellow, sun-cured clumps of bunchgrass that sustained the mustangs through the winter. The herd wandered a long valley hemmed in on either side by bare mountain ridges outcropped with rocks like the bones of the earth breaking through.

The rugged ranges were some two miles apart, and the horses favored the mountains to the west. Will had seen the horses water there, from at least two seeps at the base of the ridges, one tucked into a cove that offered safe harbor from the biting wind.

Will crawled backward from the concealing outcrop at the spine of the ridge until he dropped well below the skyline. He walked to the bottom of the draw and scrambled his way up the other side, occasionally grabbing rock ledges for balance and to pull himself up the steep ridge. He topped out again, then walked down a gentler slope to where he'd ground-tied his saddle horse.

Tightening the cinch with a firm tug, he found the stirrup with his left foot, swung aboard, and turned the horse uphill, crossing over a low saddle to the other side of the mountain range that defined the eastern edge of the valley where the wild horse herd roamed. He picked his way down, the horse sliding on his hocks in steep places; sometimes turning switchbacks where the fall was too long or too steep.

Partway down the slope, the little canyon broadened and leveled out some, forming a bowl too small to count as a valley. It was sheltered enough to allow a fire, and a hole Will scooped out of a muddy spot between rock outcrops filled with water often enough to quench his thirst as well as that of his mount and the packhorse, left there in hobbles while he'd made his scouts of the opposite valley. Grass wasn't abundant, but with the oats he'd packed in, the horses were more than getting by.

A big batch of pan bread, curled bacon, and boiled coffee later, Will crawled into his bedroll to await the morning.

With the first faint silvering of the sky, Will reached to the bottom of his bedroll for his boots and pulled them on. He crawled out, brushed the frost from the bed's cover tarp, glad it wasn't snow, folded it twice and slid it into a large hollow under a ledge. He kindled a fire in the rock circle he'd laid and as it gained strength enough to bring last night's coffee to a boil, he checked the hobbled horses and poured each a small bait of grain. Today, he'd leave both horses behind.

He submerged his canteen into the puddle at the seep and watched it bubble full. He wrapped leftover bacon and pan bread in an oilcloth sheet and stuffed it into the belly of his shirt. He fastened on his canvas coat and contemplated strapping on his chaps for warmth, deciding, instead, in favor of freer movement. The last of the preparations for the day was to hang a length of whang leather around his neck, attached to which was a leather tube with leather caps tethered to each end, and inside of which was a brass telescope borrowed from Johnny.

With that, he started his hike up the mountainside, topping out and starting down the opposite slope in full daylight but ahead of the sun, still waiting to rise in the east.

He found a sheltered spot in a rock reef, booted aside the bigger stones underfoot, sat and wallowed out a depression for his backside. He uncapped the telescope, stretched out its sections, and methodically glassed the base of the mountains across the valley. Within an hour, he identified two places that might suit his purposes; places he'd noticed in passing earlier, while watching the horses, but now merited a closer look.

By the time Will hiked halfway down the mountain, he'd worked up enough of a sweat to want to shed his canvas coat, but he thought better of it given the wind. The last thing he wanted to do out here in the high, wide, and lonesome was catch a chill. He had an idea where the horses were, having fixed their location in his mind while up on top. As low as he was now, they were out of sight, and that meant they wouldn't see him, either. And, being afoot rather than horseback, his presence in the valley would be less disruptive.

Bottoming out in the valley, the cowboy set a course for the first possibility he'd picked with the telescope. He'd chosen to visit the most distant first, so that later in the day, when he knew he'd be leg-weary, home—camp, that is—would be closer at hand. As much as possible, he followed dry watercourses to stay below the horizon and reduce the risk of revealing himself and upsetting the mustangs.

He reached the mountain slopes west of the valley just north of his destination. Working his way around the point of a ridge as it met the basin, Will kept to the edge of the slope and followed it back into the wall of the range. As he had seen from his lookout, the gap between the ridge he followed and the one to the south narrowed and their slopes steepened, forming a narrow gorge. Not far ahead, the small canyon took a turn, and Will followed, hoping to see the kind of place he needed.

But it was not to happen; not here. After the bend, the canyon walls squeezed together and met in a jumble of scree and boulders tumbled down from the slopes above. He sat on a shaded rock out of the wind and fortified himself with a bit of bread and bacon and a long drink of water before setting out again.

The next site looked promising, even before he got there. It, too, was a narrow defile in the mountainside. The ridges on either side, steep enough for his purposes, rose from the valley floor and grew ever higher as they approached the mountain proper. The dry gulch between them lost elevation as it followed the ridges down from the range, growing wider as it met the valley until blending into the surrounding plain. Will worked his way up the wide ravine, pleased to see it narrow and nearly pinch off as it passed between twin rock outcrops rising some twenty or thirty feet.

Beyond, the dry watercourse widened again, unraveled into sandy threads through the sage and rabbit brush, then rejoined as the canyon narrowed some fifty yards along until the sides met at a ledge. A steep, narrow draw cut its way from there up the mountainside. He could almost see a muddy waterfall pouring off the rocky shelf during spring runoff.

Will had work to do, so he shed his canvas coat and set to it. He stomped and yanked woody branches off the sagebrush, some of the plants nearly as tall as he, and piled his plunder on either side of the bottleneck exit from the compact box canyon. That done, he rolled and carried the biggest boulders he could manage and stacked them nearby.

Even in the cold, the labor was enough to wet the back of his shirt with sweat, so the rock he chose for a seat this time was in the shade. He finished off the bread and bacon, quenched his thirst from the canteen, rested for a time to dry off, then set off afoot across the valley and up the opposite slope to spend his last night at the campsite.

Tomorrow night, he hoped to bed down somewhere near here.

Chapter Thirteen

The pounding hooves of some forty mustangs rolled across the valley like distant thunder. Will rode the wave, crouched low over his horse's neck, peppered with dirt, twigs, and other debris tossed airborne by the running herd.

Leading the charge, the bay mare with three white socks pounded over the plain, always with a white-rimmed eye on the mounted cowboy. Will rode to stay close to the mare, reining his horse in subtle moves that drove her, hence the mustang herd, ever closer to the box canyon. The horses ran in a mindless panic, surprised by the rider that came over a rise and into their midst at a dead run, unannounced and undetected in the gray light of dawn until the whistling and whooping and shouting started.

As they neared the low gorge, Will had maneuvered the herd until their track ran almost parallel with the base of the mountain range rising from the western edge of the valley. Just ahead of the entrance to the small canyon, he reined up a bit and took a turn, quartering into the herd, splitting off the leaders and turning two-thirds of the horses into the funnel and up the sandy wash. Will braked and brought up the rear, pushing the herd ever forward. The confused horses kept running until forced to slow as they reached the defile.

Screaming horses, churning hooves, and clouds of dust created chaos as the colliding mustangs piled up trying to push through the slot. A few stragglers wheeled around and raced back to the valley, but Will paid them no mind as he shouted and whistled, slapping a coiled lariat against chap leather, pressuring the herd ever forward and through the bottleneck.

Will bailed out of the saddle and hurled brush from his piles into the gap like a cork in a bottle while the confused horses milled in the narrow confines of the box canyon. They wheeled this way and that, looking for a way out, but avoiding the unfamiliarity of the man in their midst. By the time he finished the brush pile, it would make an effective, if flimsy, barrier. Rocks came next. Will humped them into place against the heaped brush and across the face of the slot, strengthening the illusion of impenetrability.

Satisfied with the job, Will wormed around one edge of the barricade. He would let the mustangs cool down and grow accustomed to their surroundings without the additional stress of his presence.

He checked the cinch and climbed aboard his horse, sweat already drying and breathing back to normal, but still excited from the chase. Uncorking the canteen for a much-needed drink, he rode down the sandy wash and into the valley. Near the ravine's end, he veered up the side of the ridge and stopped the horse on top. Dust from the chase had long since settled, but Will could still detect a smudge to the south, satisfied that the remainder of the herd had run far enough south to be out of sight from his vantage point.

Lighting out on a long trot to the north, he angled across the valley to fetch his packhorse and camp goods. Then, back across, with a watering hole in sight. The packhorse drank slowly, raising from time to time to blow and shake his head. But Will's mount buried his muzzle in the water sucking long drafts. He had cooled enough, by now, that a bellyful of water would not hurt him.

Back at the entrance to the box canyon, he again rode a ways up the ridge to look for the mustangs. He spotted them in the far distance, herded up, heads down, foraging in the brush as if nothing had happened. All but the bay mare. She stood on a slight rise, neck outstretched and nose in the air. Will could almost feel her eyes boring holes through him. Back down in the mouth of the canyon he made camp and settled in for the night.

The morning sun was late making its way into the canyon's mouth, and when it arrived the cowboy seemed to be waiting for it. With nothing to hurry him, he scraped a depression for his backside next to a rock that afforded a comfortable backrest and sat, out of the wind, and nursed a cup of coffee—one in a long line he'd enjoyed since rising. The horses—the ones that came here with him—were content nibbling at the piles of oats he'd poured for them. There wasn't much forage on the sandy ground, so he'd have to move them out to grass sooner or later. For now, it would be later.

When the indolence finally got to Will—he was never given to laziness for long—he hiked up the draw and pawed his way around the side of the brush barricade. Every one of the horses was alert, ears sharp, nostrils flared, all eyes on him. He stood for a moment, allowing them to get used to his presence before walking out into the hollow. Again, he stopped, and watched the nervous horses as intently as they watched him.

The animals were flighty, but knew, by now, there was nowhere to go. As Will moved slowly toward them, they backed away, occasionally turning as a flock of birds and trotting a short way before again wheeling to face him. For hours he stayed among them, and with each passing minute his presence proved less upsetting. He counted twenty-seven horses; four, maybe five, were too long in the tooth to be useful. But the rest of the band, including seven colts—yearlings come spring—

suited his purpose just fine. He left the band to its own devices.

Will saddled up and rode, leading the packhorse with him, to the waterhole, filled his canteen and coffeepot and let the animals drink their fill. Balancing the pot carefully on the saddle horn, he returned. Just outside the canyon's entrance, he hobbled the packhorse to let it graze, stowed the coffeepot on a rock, and rode south to locate the bay mare and what was left of the mustang herd. He made no attempt at concealment, keeping to higher ground when possible.

When he was a half mile or so from the horses, they started moving, keeping the distance between them consistent. Arriving at a playa that stretched some distance ahead of him, Will put the spurs to his mount, leaving a rooster tail of alkali dust in his wake. The bay mare likewise stretched into a run and urged the mustang band along. After pressuring them for a mile or so, Will reined up, reversed course, and rode back to the canyon, unsaddled, led his saddle horse out to graze, and hiked back up the canyon.

Come morning, Will fetched his saddle horse and rode to the slot. Pushing just enough brush out of the way, he led his mount around the edge of the brush pile. The mustangs were still skittish, but not as much as the day before. They had long since cropped off the scarce forage in the sandy bowl, and were feeling the want of water.

Unsure of the mounted man, the horses avoided Will as much as possible in the confined space, but, soon enough, he was riding among them, splitting the herd into smaller bunches, letting them regroup, and riding through them again. At times he would simply stand, watching the animals, and letting them take his measure. By day's end, they seemed accustomed to, if not comfortable with, his presence, and that of his horse.

The next day he brought both his horses to the camp and tethered the packhorse to a stout sagebrush at the edge of the ravine. Action inside the box canyon was a repeat performance, only today Will was more aggressive, applying more pressure and forcing closer contact. Increasing hunger and thirst helped calm the horses. Late in the day he loosened his lariat, shook out a loop, and rode as close as he could to one of the older horses. Will tossed out a houlihan and the loop dropped over his target's head. He reeled in the slack as soon as it settled, set the loop tight and high, and took a hard dally.

He expected a fight, but the mustang put up more of a fuss than he anticipated. By relieving and tightening the slack, dragging and driving the horse, shortening the distance between his mount and the mustang, he worked ever closer to the bottleneck. After stopping there for a moment's rest, he towed the recalcitrant old bronc around the edge and through the concealed gap he'd created between the canyon wall and brush pile. Once clear, he worked the loop over the mustang's ears, battling its fighting head every minute, then shooed the tired, winded, hungry, thirsty horse down the canyon. It ran past the camp and the tied-up packhorse to freedom.

He repeated the process with three other horses, all too old to be of any use. Then, back to camp for a night's sleep to rest up for what tomorrow would bring.

Tomorrow came early, with Will up and around, boiling coffee, frying bacon and panbread, warming the beans he'd let simmer overnight, and packing up his camp equipment in the dark. He ate and drank as much as he could comfortably contain, wrapped up a sizeable package of leftovers, and stowed them in his saddlebags. There would be no stopping for a time.

Will pushed the brush aside and led both his horses into the enclosure with the mustangs, by now standing with heads drooping. He ground-tied the saddle horse and packhorse near the barricade, long since gone dry and brittle. After hefting the boulders out of the way, he flung the brush off to the sides, revealing more than half the opening. Tying the packhorse's lead rope to the lash ropes on the packs, knowing the horse would follow, he checked his cinch and swung into the saddle.

The mustangs perked up as he rode among them, bunching them up and pushing them through the slot in as tight a crowd as possible. Once they were all through, he spurred up his mount and rode past them, taking the lead. He turned northward as they cleared the canyon's mouth and the mustangs followed at a trot. The fact that he was leading the thirsty horses toward water worked in his favor. Though miles in the future, the mustangs knew the water was there.

Keeping close to the verge of the mountain range, he led the horses into the sheltered cove and allowed them to nudge and shoulder each other and push their way to and into the shallow spring-fed pond. Will hung back to prevent escape, but the mustangs were too intent on slaking their thirst to try.

Once all the horses had a chance to drink at least something, he spooked them through the roiled water, turned them toward the open country, then hustled into the lead. Standing on one stirrup with neck craned around, he watched the band trail behind, with the pack horse in the thick of the bunch, encouraging them to follow Will's tracks northward toward the Fishhook.

All day long he kept the horses on the move, occasionally dropping to the rear to hurry them along with fear, letting the packhorse take the lead. And so it continued into the night, with the only accommodation to darkness moving at a walk rather than a trot.

With first light, Will spooked the band into a high lope, alternately riding point and flank to maneuver the herd in his intended direction of travel. They reached a broad watercourse at midmorning with narrow threads of clear water wending their way through a sandy bottom littered with cobble rocks. The horses spread out along the narrow streams, sucking up water as fast as they could. But before they drank their fill, Will spooked them into action again. By nightfall, he hoped to reach an old cattle trap he knew of, still many miles ahead. On the way out he'd noticed it was in sorry state of repair, but it would serve to hold the horses for a while, particularly with darkness concealing the weaknesses in the old pens.

Well past sunset, but before full dark, the fatigued rider led the horse herd into the wings of the trap, dropping back when the entrance to the big corral came near, driving them through the wide gate. At the last minute, a young sorrel stallion sensed trouble and pivoted to escape, but Will, lasso rope at the ready for just such an eventuality, front-footed the horse as it tried to slip by, took a tight dally and set up, spilling the horse in a tangled heap. The little stud soon caught his breath and clawed his way to his feet, and willingly headed for the pen at Will's urging.

With the gates in place, Will pulled the now-slim packs and lifted the sawbuck saddle off the packhorse, stripped the kack from his saddle horse, poured each a ration of grain and, as they ground it hungrily, wiped down their sweaty backs with a rough burlap sack. He dined on cold bacon, beans, and panbread, but kindled a small fire and boiled coffee in a tin cup of canteen water. His eyelids barely lasted the length of the cup, and he stretched out atop his bedroll and slept without dreams.

By morning, Will's horses were rested. The mustangs, on the other hand, were worn down. Grain made the difference—oats made a more nourishing meal than the sparse, dry grass the wild horses searched out in the overgrown brush in the pen. That, and the ranch horses were hardened by work, rather than moving about only enough to stay fed and watered and out of danger.

Rather than risk a hard turn out of the trap, Will pulled down a few rails off the far fence and drove the herd through the hole, already headed north toward home. He again rode to the lead. By now, the tired, hungry, thirsty mustangs had little inclination to do anything but follow.

Will rotated his shoulders and flexed his back as he rode at a trot.

Tonight, he would sleep in his bunkhouse bed.

Chapter Fourteen

The only sound in the dining room came from knives and forks clattering against plates, jaws working on fried beef, coffee splashing into china mugs, and platters and serving bowls sliding around the table. A late-winter day in the saddle and cold chores around headquarters left the Fishhook hands with a bigger appetite for eating than talking.

Heads down, hands and elbows flying, mouths working, the cowboys were slow to awaken to the rising rumble. But, as the sound of pounding hooves grew stronger, questioning looks passed around the table like a plate of biscuits. Chairs slid back and the men poured out the door like coffee from a spout to see what was up. Trailing the herd was Emma, who had just entered the room with a fresh bowl of gravy, and her father, bringing along a mug of steaming coffee seasoned with a splash of whiskey.

Down the ranch road came Will Hayes, riding point ahead of a herd of galloping mustangs, trailing wispy clouds of steam blown from wide nostrils and rising from sweaty hides. The band of horses entered the yard, and Will circled them in front of the ranch house. He finished the loop, reined up in front the gawking cowboys on the porch, and let the skittish mustangs mill and fidget behind him.

He sought out Longmore, caught his eye, said, "Ten horses, you said. I make this bunch to be about twenty-three."

Longmore's blank stare widened with realization, then narrowed in anger. His coffee mug missed Will, but painted the leg of his chaps with scalding coffee when it bounced off the fork of his saddle.

"You sonofabitch," Longmore said, and stomped back into the house.

Emma looked on, perplexed.

The bareheaded cowboys helped Will haze the herd into the horse pasture with the saddle stock, then hurried back to the warmth of the dining room and their unforgotten supper. After ridding his horses of saddle and packsaddle, Will turned them into the pasture and headed for the ranch house, mouth watering in anticipation of the first real meal he'd had in days.

He hung his canvas coat and hat on a wall peg, slid into his accustomed place at the table and loaded his plate.

Longmore, it seemed, had lost his appetite—chair empty, plate going cold.

"What's with the wild bunch, Will?" a cowboy said around a mouthful of pie.

After finishing a forkful of food and following it up with another, Will answered. "Oh, just a deal I had with Mister Longmore. Something he wanted done."

"The boss didn't seem none too pleased."

Will broke open a biscuit and drenched it with brown gravy as the cowboys looked on, expecting more. But Will did not offer it.

Emma gathered an armful of soiled plates, thought it a poor substitute for arms full of Will. Knowing this was neither the time nor place, she headed for the kitchen to help the cook with cleanup.

The cowboys drifted away, the lingering tension driving them out of the room, until it was just Will and Johnny.

Johnny polished the lenses of his spectacles on a napkin. Wrapping the hooks around his ears, he said, "What the hell, Will? You've been gone for days without telling anybody where or why. Now you come back with a bunch of bone-tired mustangs. Are you going to tell me what's going on, or do I have to wonder like everybody else?"

Will poured another mug of coffee and served himself a slice of dried apple pie.

"Like I said, it was something your Pa wanted."

"You're going to have to say more than that."

Savoring every bite, Will swallowed a mouthful of pie. Johnny watched.

Will said, "You know, I suppose, that I asked him about me and Emma getting married."

"Not exactly. I knew the two of you talked about it. So you're telling me you broached Pa with the idea?

"I did."

"So, what, did he run you off? That why you've been gone?"

"No. What happened was, he laughed at me. Got my dander up. Then he said maybe I ought to show I was serious, like Indians do, and give him ten horses for her."

"You're kidding! And you thought he meant it?"

"Oh, I know he was funning with me. Trying to get my goat. Like I said, it made me mad. So I decided to show the ornery old bastard he ought not be messing around where I'm concerned. Especially when it comes to Emma."

Will forked up another mouthful of pie. Johnny watched.

"Besides," Will said, washing the bite down with a drink of coffee. "Now that I done what he asked, how can he say no?"

Johnny laughed. "I guess you've got a point there. Pa might be a lot of things, but a welcher he's not. But if he said ten horses, why twenty-three?"

"Well, I figured if he thought his daughter was worth ten horses, I'd show him I thought she was worth a hell of a lot more."

Elsewhere, Longmore leaned on the dresser in his room, staring at the reflection in the mirror and cussing it for its stupidity. "Damn!" he said, slamming both fists so hard the clutter on the dresser top bounced. "You fool! That cagey little sonofabitch. He's got you over a barrel, now."

He stomped out of the room, leaving his reflection behind, and burst into the kitchen. "Emma! Come with me." And he stomped away.

"Don't worry about that, girl," the cook said of the shattered coffee mug that hit the floor with Longmore's shout. "I'll clean it up. Best go see what your daddy wants."

She tossed the dishtowel onto the drainboard and made her way to the front room. Her father, already burrowed into his overstuffed chair, was sloshing whiskey into a filmy glass.

"Yes, Papa?"

"Sit," he said, waving the glass toward the rocking chair.

An uncomfortable pause later, he said, "So, Emma, what about you and Will?"

"What about us?"

"He says he wants to marry you. Says you've talked about it, serious-like. That so?"

"Yes, Papa. I have a question for you—may I?"

"Ask it."

"Where has Will been?"

"Don't know, Emma. Down on the desert chasing horses, looks to me like."

"Can you tell me why? It seems like you and Will are the only ones who know."

He emptied the glass and refilled it.

"He came to me. Said you two wanted to get married. Asked for your hand. He wouldn't listen to sense. So I said to him—joking, mind you—that if he was serious he'd make me a present, like Indians do. Ten ponies, I said."

"You offered to sell me to Will!"

"No! No, girl, it's not like that. I only wanted him to understand that he had nothing—and, nothing to offer you."

Emma lifted the tail of her apron and wiped away the tears dampening her cheeks and upper lip.

Longmore said, "So, what about it, Emma? You really want to marry this boy?"

"He's not a boy anymore, Papa. He's a man. More than most. If you could see past your spiteful nose, you'd know that."

"Maybe. But you can't deny you're both young. Too young, I say."

"Mama was my same age when she married you. And you weren't all that much older than Will."

The whiskey swirled as Longmore spun his glass mindlessly. "True enough. Things were different then."

"Things are different now, Papa. And things are the same. I love Will. He loves me. We'll find a way. Without your blessing, if need be."

Longmore swirled his whiskey. Emma wiped her tears again.

"Besides, you made a deal with Will. You've got your ten ponies. Twice over, it looked to me like. Now what?"

Slamming the glass to the table, Longmore stomped out of the room.

*****

Come morning, Longmore's anger had wound down some. But his frustration had ratcheted up enough to offset it. With a pounding head fronted by a flushed face, he stomped into the kitchen.

"Emma! Come with me. Bring Johnny with you. And Will. And coffee."

Emma had nothing in hand to drop this time. But she flinched when her father yelled and scorched the heel of her hand on the edge of the skillet in which she stirred cream gravy. The cook nodded her go, and took up the spoon herself.

Will and Johnny carried their own coffee-filled mugs into the living room; Emma handed the one she carried to her Father. Much to the relief of everyone else in the room, he did not sweeten it with whiskey from the ever-present bottle on the lamp table.

Johnny sat in the rocker; Will and Emma on the settee.

"Unless I miss my guess," Longmore said, "Nothing's changed overnight. You two haven't come to your senses about marrying."

Will cleared his throat. "No sir. Leastways I haven't. Emma?"

Emma shook her head.

"Johnny, what's your mind on this?"

"Like I told you a long time ago, Pa, I don't see anything wrong with the idea. Fact is, I kind of like it."

Longmore shook his head, reached for the whiskey bottle, thought better of it.

"Well, I can't see it," he said. "But I can see that it don't matter what I think. So; Johnny—you once said we should make Will foreman of the Fishhook."

Will's eyes widened and he turned to Johnny.

Longmore said, "You still think that's a good idea?"

"I do, Pa."

"Well then," Longmore said as Will turned back to look at him. "Much as it pains me to say so, we'd best do it."

"But, Mister Longmore, Sir . . . "

"As of now, kid, you're in charge of day-to-day operations on the ranch. Until you screw up, that is. You work with Johnny. I don't want to know what you're doing or see your face if I don't have to."

Try as he might, Will had nothing to say.

"Pa," Johnny said, "why the change of heart?"

Longmore laughed. "Nothing changed. I still think it's a damn-fool idea. But no daughter of mine is going to marry some forty-a-month-and-found cowpuncher."

Emma used the tail of her apron to mop her eyes. Will struggled to find his voice.

Finally, "Mister Longmore, I don't know what to say."

"You don't have to say a damned thing, kid. My giving you this chance ain't got nothing to do with you. I'm doing this for Emma. Just don't screw it up."

"No, Sir, Mister Longmore. I won't. Leastways, I'll try not to. I'll give it my best."

"Then get to work. Go on. All of you."

As the three left the room, Longmore reached for the whiskey bottle. This time, he did not stop.

Out in the hallway, Emma spun around and threw her arms around Will's neck. "Will!" she said. "Oh, Will!"

Will wrapped his arms around her waist and squeezed. Then, realizing Johnny was behind them, he reached up and pulled her hands away from his reddening neck. "Emma," he said, and whispered, "your brother!"

Johnny laughed.

"Not to worry, Will. 'Her passions are made of nothing but the finest part of pure love,' as the great Bard of Avon once wrote."

"I swear, Johnny, you've got fancy words for everything. I don't know where you keep them all."

Longmore uncorked the whiskey, thought better of diluting it with coffee. He pulled a long draught directly from the bottle, swallowing as fast as he could suck it through the narrow neck.

Chapter Fifteen

The wedding was a simple affair. Emma Longmore, daughter of Ballard Station's most prominent citizen, stood before the circuit judge, hand in hand with her chosen mate, Wilson Hayes. They spoke their respective vows in a matter of minutes and boarded an outbound train, watching Johnny, waving farewell on the station platform, fade into the distance.

Johnny walked to the Elkhorn saloon to celebrate with a drink or two and whatever company was available. Jesse Longmore attended the wedding, but rather than accompany Johnny to see off the newlyweds, took a seat behind a corner table in the hotel bar. He preferred the quiet of the hotel to the saloon, not wanting anything or anyone to interfere with his drinking.

The happy couple's honeymoon tour took them to Salt Lake City, Cheyenne, Denver, and Santa Fe. The trip was an education for Will, not only in learning every detail of Emma in ways that surpassed his imagination, but also a newfound knowledge of traveling in style. Riding the new Pullman railroad cars, sleeping in hotel featherbeds, dining in restaurants, attending the theatre— it was all a revelation to Will, and he found he enjoyed it.

Emma, too, enjoyed their adventure, as she and Will melted together until she could no longer tell where she ended and he began. Nor did she care.

As much as they relished their time together, freed of all responsibility save making acquaintance and forging a relationship as man and wife, both eagerly returned to the Fishhook and a new, if familiar, life of normalcy.

By the time they got back to the ranch, their new home was already rising on cleared ground on an angle across the yard from the ranch house; just far enough away to afford some semblance of privacy. Johnny supervised the job, taking advantage of the slack season before calving to put some of the ranch hands to work assisting an experienced home builder from Ballard Station. Emma and Will walked among the rising walls, seeing their rough sketches come to life. But until the house was habitable, they took up residence in the house where Emma grew up, squeezing into her small room. Neither minded the tight quarters.

Will took up his duties as Fishhook foreman. He supervised the positioning of the ranch's cattle herds into sheltered areas to protect the calves that were soon to drop, and where there was sufficient graze to keep the cows strong and producing milk. Rather than leaving the animals to drift and fend for themselves, crews rode the bed grounds day and night, keeping a careful eye on the calving cows, with extra attention paid to first-calf heifers, who sometimes needed help to expel their offspring when the time came.

From time to time, cabin fever drove Longmore out of the house and he saddled a horse—or, more often than not nowadays, had one saddled for him—and rode over his ranchlands. He seldom found anything amiss. But even that had him tugging at his beard and raking fingers through graying hair.

The attention the mother cows were getting perturbed him. No cow on the Fishhook had enjoyed this kind of attention before, and he cussed and cursed the hours of manpower babysitting the herds. But when the crop of surviving and healthy calves was noticeably larger than years past, the ornery rancher could see the profit those extra calves would bring when they grew to market size, or started producing calves of their own.

Still and all, the furrow in his brow seemed permanent and his grip on the whiskey bottle nearly so.

Come branding time, he showed up now and then and sat in the saddle watching the work. This spring, Will had the cowboys divide the herds into smaller bunches, more closely held, allowing for less cutting, less chasing, less commotion during the chore of applying the hot iron to the calves. One morning while the irons heated, Longmore said to Johnny, "The little bastard can't leave anything alone. To his way of thinking, we never did anything right on this ranch before he got here."

"What are you complaining about, Pa? Look at the calves. There are more of them, and they look better than ever. That's going to put money in your pocket."

"I can see that. But I don't give a damn how much money he's making us. The Fishhook was making money while he was crawling around in the Texas dirt in diapers. Damn kid ought to show some respect for the way we do things around here."

"Nobody ever said there was anything wrong with the way you've always done things—no, change that—the way you used to do things around here. But that doesn't mean it's the only way, or even the best way. I can't see why you're complaining, Pa, or what it is that's bothering you."

"I'll tell you what it is. I feel like Will Hayes has crawled up my butt and is eating me alive from the inside out."

"You've got no call to feel that way. Hell, most any man alive would give his left eye to have what you've got. But whatever it is that's eating at your insides isn't going to drown in whiskey, no matter how much you pour on it."

Longmore practically pulled the bit from his horse's mouth when he jerked his head around and spurred him into a high lope toward the house.

And that's where he was when the cowboys came home for supper. He sat at the head of the table, still wearing hat, chaps, and spurs, fingering a glass of whiskey. No one knew how long he had sat there, or how many times he'd refilled the glass. The weary cowboys took their seats and concentrated on filling their mouths and bellies. Longmore did not acknowledge their presence or partake of the meal.

As the hands scraped the finish off their plates so as not to miss a single taste of the peach cobbler dessert, Johnny suggested a serenade from Will. "Say," he said. "A little music would go down pretty well right now. Will?"

The young foreman took up his guitar, propped his chair at a comfortable angle against the wall and fingered a soft melody to accompany the lazy conversation among the cowboys around the table as they rolled and lit smokes and enjoyed their one drink of whiskey. As Will played, the rancher roused once in a while, but mostly sat, head in hands, and may as well have been asleep as not—and may well have been.

And so no one noticed when the old man sat upright, drew his Bowie knife from its belt scabbard and sent it flying along a hissing path toward Will.

Perhaps it was too much drink. Maybe bleary eyesight. Whatever the reason, Longmore's aim was slightly off and the knife buried itself in the pine log wall mere inches from Will's ear. He eyeballed the quivering knife without turning his head, swallowed hard.

"What the hell, Mister Longmore," he finally managed to strangle out. "You liked to kill me with that pig sticker."

Longmore, now on his feet and pawing through the shelves in a wall cabinet said, "Damn right I'd like to kill you. You're an ingrate and an upstart and I'm sick of the sight of you. That you're married to my daughter only makes it worse."

Another knife came to hand and this one, too, cut a trail through the smoky air on a straight line toward Will. Had not Will been holding the guitar, the blade would have struck somewhere near where ribs ended and belly started. Instead, the knife buried itself up to the haft in the body of the guitar, shattering the soundboard, breaking the fret board, and sending strings twanging in every direction. Before the discordant sound died, Will dropped the ruined guitar and lit out the door.

"Pa! What the hell?" Johnny yelled. "Have you lost your mind?"

Nervous cowboys pushed back from the table and crowded the hat rack in their hurry to leave the dining room for the safety of the bunkhouse.

"Hell no, I ain't lost my mind. That's the first sensible thing I've done since that kid got here. Bringing him here—that's when I lost my mind!"

Johnny watched Longmore stomp out of the room, brushing Emma aside as she rushed in, wiping her hands on her apron. "Johnny! What happened? Where's Will?"

"Don't worry, Emma. He's all right. Pa tried to kill him, but he's fine.

"Kill him? How? Why?"

Johnny peeled off his glasses, snatched his napkin from the table, and wiped the lenses as he pondered an answer. "I don't know why, Emma. It's like he went crazy all of a sudden. Threw a knife at him. Twice."

Emma's hands flew to her face as she saw the shattered guitar on the floor, and gagged at the sight of the knife buried in the wall. "Oh my God! Where is he? Where's Will?"

"I don't know. He left in a hurry. I don't suppose he'll be back until he thinks it's safe. Try not to worry. Will can fend for himself. Besides, I think Pa's shot his wad, at least for now."

*****

A few hours huddled and shivering in a corner of his unfinished house were enough to convince Will to risk a visit to the bunkhouse. He did not intend to stay, fearing his presence might endanger the hands should Longmore's rampage drive him there in search of his prey.

But a quick trip yielded Will a borrowed coat and a blanket—enough to get him through the rest of the night. Fitful sleep saw him wide awake well ahead of dawn. He wanted to be gone before work started on the house, so at first light he rolled his blanket and headed for the hill behind the ranch house and the grove at the spring. This place, he believed, afforded the best opportunity to see Emma, for here they shared many private moments and his wife would likely be drawn there, just as Will was.

He guessed right. It was mid-morning, well after the hands had ridden out to work and the breakfast mess cleared and cleaned up, when Emma came up the path. The trees had yet to leaf out so the seclusion at the spring wasn't what it was during the green of summer. Will stayed hidden for a time, making sure Emma wasn't followed, before revealing himself.

Emma rushed to him, nearly tipping him over as she threw her arms around his neck. They embraced without words, Emma's sobs mingling with the music of spring-time songbirds and rippling spring water.

Will grasped her shoulders, stepped away to hold her at arm's length, and watched her wipe away tears with the tail of her apron.

"Oh Will, whatever will we do?"

Will again pulled her to him, and said, "I don't know, Emma. I don't know."

After a few more minutes locked in the embrace, they joined hands and took familiar seats on a fallen cotton-wood log. Words were hard to come by.

"Did you talk to your Pa this morning?"

"No. He did not come to breakfast. He is still in his bedroom, so far as I know."

"What about Johnny? You talk to him?"

"He's as flummoxed as everybody else. We talked for a time after he got the men lined out for the day. He has no idea what's got into Papa. Well, whiskey is what's gotten into him. But why he flew off the handle like he did is, well . . .

"Thank God you're all right, Will!" she said, again throwing her arms around him and nearly tipping them both off the log. "I don't think I could live without you—not anymore."

After a moment, she said, "I can't believe it. My own Papa trying to kill you. Oh, Will, what's going to happen?"

Another helpless pause. Then, "Emma, I think I need to talk to Johnny."

"But he's gone. After we talked, he rode out to help with some job or another."

"I know. I saw him go. But tell him I need to see him. I need to know which way the wind's blowing with the old man. Your Pa won't tell you the truth. And I don't dare talk to him myself, for fear he'd come at me again and I'd have to kill him. I just couldn't do that, Emma— so I won't do anything that might make it happen. Please, have Johnny talk to him, see if we can't smooth this over. I don't know what I ever done to make your Pa hate me so, but if there's something I can change, I'll sure do it."

Emma agreed with the plan, feeble as it was. Johnny would meet Will atop Sheep Rock, an outcrop on a ridge some three miles down range from Fishhook headquarters, tomorrow afternoon.

Named by trappers wandering the vicinity in days gone by, Sheep Rock was said to resemble the head of a Desert Bighorn ram bursting out of the mountainside. Will couldn't see it, but enough others did that the name stuck, and the landmark was known throughout the area.

The meeting spot was well chosen, for while Will could not see Fishhook headquarters from his nest in the rocks atop the ledge, anyone coming from there would be visible within minutes, once they cleared the ridge beyond which the ranch buildings sat.

He watched Johnny pass the point of the ridge at an easy gallop, towing a saddled horse behind. He watched as he reined up into a trot, watched as he slowed the horses to a walk and rode into a draw at the base of the ridge downhill from Sheep Rock.

Johnny loosened the saddle cinch on his horse, then tied the other horse's lead rope to a juniper limb. He slung a canteen around his neck, untied the saddle strings to free a bedroll and saddlebags, which he shouldered and started climbing. By following the draw up the ridge, he skirted the side of the cliff that was Sheep Rock, scrambled up the side of the narrowing gully once he was above the landmark, and picked his way through the boulders strewn about.

"Will?"

"Here, Johnny," Will said, rising from his nest not ten yards away.

Taking a moment to catch his breath and take in the view—especially along his back trail—Johnny joined Will and selected a suitable rock for a seat.

"How you holding up?" he said, using his bandana to clean his spectacles, then mop his forehead and the sweatband of his hat.

"Nights are still a mite cold," Will said.

"Here," Johnny said, tossing the bedroll out onto the ground between them. "This ought to take care of that. And here's something to fill your belly," he said, slinging the saddlebags and canteen atop the bedroll.

"Thanks. I am hungry," Will said as he pawed through one of the pockets, pulling out a hunk of jerky to gnaw on.

"I suppose you noticed I brought you a horse."

Will nodded as he chewed.

"It's not your saddle, but it will do. I didn't want to rouse Pa's suspicions, so I told him Luis's horse rolled out at the Hancock camp. Broke the saddle tree and sprained the horse's leg, so he needed both replaced."

"I guess that means I won't be coming home."

"Not anytime soon, unless you want another run-in with Pa. Not ever, if you want his views on the subject."

"Damn."

"Emma and I will keep working on him. But I fear the whiskey is working harder."

Will chewed on the information along with the jerky. Neither proved easy to swallow.

"Well, hell. I can't stay up here. Or anywhere around here, for that matter, without your Pa finding out about it sooner or later. I suppose come nightfall I'll ride out and find someplace else to be for a while."

"That horse has a full belly and had a drink before we left headquarters. He'll be fine where he is until you're ready to go. Damn it, Will, I wish there were some other way. Emma's a wreck. But she can't see any way around it, either. She says once you settle in somewhere, let her know where and she'll come running."

The men stood. Will offered his hand and Johnny shook it, then pulled Will into an awkward embrace, slapping him hard on the back.

"Good luck to you, Will. Ride easy. Let us know where you land. We'll get you back on the Fishhook as soon as we can talk some sense into Pa."

Will said, "I guess you'll know I'm back when you see me coming."

Chapter Sixteen

Riding into Antler Canyon always bristled the hair on the back of Will's neck. Memories of the killing of Caleb Short permeated the confines of the defile. Shooting the scourge of the Fishhook had been his introduction to the place, establishing his reputation on the ranch as quick as the hammer fall on a revolver.

Only Will was aware of his fear that day. But he had learned as a child that surprise and bluff went a long way toward coming out on top in a brutal encounter, and his walking downhill directly into Short's challenge was both—bluff on his part, surprise on Short's. He had no doubt, then or now, that the oversized gunfighter could have killed him as easily as swatting a mosquito. But defiance from a boy barely able to produce a whisker put Short off his guard, and that put a bullet between his eyes.

Will rode up the main branch of the labyrinth and took a side canyon that led to the saddleback pass where the fight with the Rafter 7 hands took place; the place where Caleb Short breathed his last. The scent of sage and juniper hung heavy in the spring air, tickling Will's nose and scratching his eyes, but the air thinned out once he left the confines of the canyon.

He crossed over the seat of the saddle and started down the back side of the range cut by Antler Canyon. Gentler in slope, less riddled with outcrops and reefs, canyons and cliffs, it proved an easy ride down the mountain to Cane Valley. The way would have been easier still had he foregone the canyon to ride farther on to where both the railroad and a wagon road crossed the mountains on their way to and from Ballard Station, but, just now, Will wanted to avoid anyone who might know him so as to keep his whereabouts unknown.

Although aware of Cane Valley, Will's study of the basin's landscape as he made his way downslope was his first look at the place. It was much like the valley he'd left—the mountains bordering this side mostly dry and barren, while on the opposite range snowmelt and springs fed small streams and creeks that tumbled out of the mountains to water fertile meadows and grasslands that stretched well out onto the valley floor. Each drainage sprouted at least one homestead, with the bigger streams supporting a string of small ranches. Here, no Fishhook or Rafter 7 dominated the region; small landholders and larger ranchers managed to coexist.

Rio Largo, long river, snaked down the center of the valley in a low, rocky gorge. A town of the same name bordered the river and straddled the railroad farther down the valley. It served the same purpose as Ballard Station—a supply point for ranches and a shipping point for cattle. But the town was larger and more prosperous, as it also hosted office operations for a coal mine. The mine supplied the railroad, and excess fuel was shipped from a tipple at the mine, where locomotives also tanked up on water before taking on the grade that led out of Cane Valley and on to Ballard Station.

With no prospects and no particular place to go, Will decided Rio Largo was as good a destination as any. But the sun already brushed the western mountaintops, so he opted to make a dry camp and go on in the morning.

*****

With the sun already on the downward slide after his long ride down Cane Valley, Will tied up at the hitch rail on the street out front of a likely looking eating house. A hot meal washed down with scalding coffee would sit pretty well after days in the saddle living off stale biscuits, beef jerky, and tepid canteen water. Fortunately, Johnny had packed a handful of double eagles in a pouch in the saddlebags, so Will was well fixed for funds for the foreseeable future.

Following the welcome dinner, he rode slowly through the streets of Rio Largo, getting the lay of the land and a feel for the place. Then to a livery stable, where his jaded horse could fill up on oats and grass hay and rest up from walking on tired legs.

The whump of saddle bags on the hotel desk roused the clerk from an afternoon nap. Will booked a room, ordered up a hot bath, and, while the water heated, crossed the street to a dry goods store for fresh clothing. The pants he wore could probably stand on their own, and the shirt had long since lost the salutary effects of laundry soap and water.

Refreshed and revitalized, Will followed the board-walk down the block to a saloon he'd spotted on his tour of the town. He carried the foaming beer mug the bar-tender drew for him to a back table, took a seat against the wall and dragged a chair around to prop his feet. Nursing that beer and three more to follow, he watched the comings-and-goings, the first of which outpaced the second as afternoon turned to evening. The crowd seemed convivial enough; a couple of friendly card games occupied nearby tables, a tinkly piano added to the atmosphere. Will sensed no hostility toward himself, a stranger, but, outside of a friendly nod or greeting, the other patrons seemed content to leave him alone. And that suited him just fine.

Half a beer before Will intended to take his leave to get an early start on a good night's sleep, two cowboys pushed through the batwing doors. Like a bucket of water dumped on a branding fire, their entrance washed the warmth out of the saloon. Will watched several poker players fold their hands, drinkers empty glasses, and talkers turn silent and join a general exodus from the barroom.

While dressed the part, Will could tell the men were not cowboys. No manure decorated their boots, nor did the usual complement of bovine shit, snot, slobber, and blood adorn their chaps and shirtsleeves. Not that the men were clean, by any means, but he had the feeling the grime wasn't associated with cow work or any other kind of honest labor.

The pair tossed off their first whiskeys in short order, poured another, turned their backsides to the bar and leaned against it, propped on elbows with glasses in hand, looking as alike as twin pictures for a stereoscope. A mixture of contempt and belligerence burned in their eyes as they surveyed the room, taking stock of the patrons still there. They settled on Will for a moment, but soon dismissed him and moved on.

He set the empty mug on the table and started for the door. As he drew even with the prickly pair, one of them stopped him with a question.

"Hey city boy, where'd you get them new duds?"

"I declare," said the other, "that shirt looks clean enough to eat off of."

A snigger, then, "I swear you're right, Earl. That shirt's shinier'n a china plate. Fella could suck gravy outa that thing 'thout swallowin' a single speck of sand."

Will waited.

"Ain't no shirt ought to be that clean, Mendoza. It just don't seem right. 'Specially when we gotta wear these rags. Reckon we ought to fix that?"

"What you mean, Earl?"

"Well, I'm just wonderin' how that pretty new shirt would look with a glass of cheap whiskey poured over it."

More laughter.

"Only one way to find out," the one called Mendoza said.

He lifted the whiskey glass in his right hand and reached out toward Will with a stupid grin all over his face. Earl laughed. Before the glass had a chance to tip, Will's left hand struck like a snake, grabbed Mendoza's wrist and kept going, smashing the drink into his face, crushing his lips and nose and releasing a stream of blood that dribbled off his chin with the whiskey and onto a spreading stain down the front of his filthy shirt.

Will took a step back to watch what happened next, and when Earl started pawing at the pistol on his hip he pulled his own and shot the man in the chest at such close range the flame scorched his shirtfront.

Mendoza, still sputtering and spitting blood, drew his revolver, but Will rotated slightly and put a bullet in his throat while the dying gunfighter's shot kicked splinters out of the floor halfway across the room.

Both men slid down the bar and collapsed on the floor, mixing spilled blood with the spilled whiskey and beer and spit that already stained the planks. Once they were down, Will slid his Colt into its holster. The bartender slowly lifted his head above the bar down the way, saw he was safe, and stood.

"Where will I find the law in this town?" Will said.

"Oh, don't you worry none about that. You can count on him showing up soon as the shooting stops. What you do need to worry about is what Amos Parker's likely to do when he finds out you killed two of his boys."

"Parker, you say? Never met the man. But this isn't the first run-in I've had with his bunch."

"Ain't likely to be your last, either. You'd be well advised to beat it over to the railroad station and buy a ticket on the next train to anywhere."

"No, thanks. I think I'll just wait here for the marshal and make sure this mess gets cleared up. Then I suppose

I'll hang around a while, seeing as I don't have anywhere else I need to be."

The swinging doors squeaked open and a man with a badge on his vest walked through, followed by half a dozen or so other men, some of whom had been in the saloon until Parker's men showed up. The lawman squatted down and examined the dead men, stood up, looked at Will and said, "You the man shot these two?"

"Yes, sir. I did."

"Who are you?"

"Name's Wilson Hayes."

"Where do you hail from, Mister Hayes?"

"Will. Folks call me Will. I come from over around Ballard Station. Worked on a ranch there."

"And what brings you to Rio Largo?"

"Nothing in particular. Lost my job over there. Just looking for something to keep me occupied for a while till I settle in somewhere."

"You make a habit of killing folks?"

"No sir. Not unless I have to."

"These men here—I guess you 'had' to kill them."

Will did not offer a response, figuring the less said the better.

The marshal looked around the room at the few other patrons and settled on a man in town clothes leaning against the end of the bar. "You see this shooting, Carter?"

"Sure did, Marshal."

"Want to tell me what happened?"

"Them two came in, started slugging back drinks. Hadn't been here but a few minutes when this here feller took a notion to leave. They set in to razzin' him about his clothes, and that Mexican-looking one went to pour whiskey over his shirt. So he—him, I mean," Carter said, nodding toward Will, "shoved the glass right back in his face. Then that other one went to draw on him. But this feller was faster; shot him dead. By that time, the Mex was fixing to shoot him, so he shot him, too."

The marshal looked around the room again, said "That sound about right to the rest of you?"

The question prompted nodding heads and grunts in the affirmative.

"Well, I guess that about wraps it up, then," he said. Then, to the bartender, "I'll get the undertaker over here with his cart to haul these two off."

Will said, "Am I free to go?"

"Sure. And if I was you, I'd keep on a-going. Amos Parker don't generally take too kindly to folks shooting the stuffing out of his men."

"So I'm told. But right now, I'm going to bed. See you around, Marshal," he said with a nod and left the saloon.

Chapter Seventeen

Once a day on the two days following the shooting, the town marshal tracked down Will and encouraged him not to linger in Rio Largo.

"Soon enough, if he hasn't already, Amos Parker is going to hear what happened. And I can guaran-damn-tee you he'll come looking for you."

Will pushed his supper plate away and sipped at a fresh cup of hot coffee. He'd taken all his meals at the little café he'd stopped at upon arriving in town. Far from fancy, the eating house still put on a good feed and he doubted he'd find better.

"Maybe," Will said. "If he does, I'm not too hard to find. You seem to have sorted out my habits easy enough."

"You don't want to take the man lightly," the marshal said, massaging his face with the palms of both hands. "He's filled more than a few graves in his time. Most men I know would as soon avoid him."

"You're probably right. But I never did cotton much to men who shove other people out of the way to get where they want to go. He pushes me, I'll have to push back."

"That's if he gives you a chance. Parker ain't known for staging a fair fight."

"All the more reason to stand up to him. I'm obliged for your concern, Marshal, but I guess I'm willing to take my chances. I got no other reason to leave town, and worrying about this outlaw ain't reason enough."

The marshal lifted his hat from the table, where it had sat on its crown during the conversation. He stood, squared the hat on his head and walked away without saying more, realizing he was wasting his breath.

Pondering the situation over the rest of the coffee, Will came to the conclusion he was more concerned about Jesse Longmore than Amos Parker. With all the drummers and other travelers making their way from here to Ballard Station, word of the killings was likely to make its way there. And, once it did, it would not be long before Longmore heard it. And the crazy old man may well come after him.

So, he decided, if he wanted to avoid killing his wife's father, maybe leaving Rio Largo was a good idea, after all. He had no idea where he would go, or what he would do when he got there. He decided to sleep on it.

Morning found Will sitting at the same table, sipping coffee, awaiting his breakfast. He'd just started on his second cup when a disheveled man walked into the café like he owned the place, looked around the small room studying the customers at the other tables, looked Will over, then walked across the room and helped himself to the chair across the table.

"Mind if I sit here?"

"Looks to me like you're already sitting there."

The man laughed. Will judged him to be a decade older than himself, somewhere in the neighborhood of thirty years, or getting close. He wore store-bought clothes, a little pricier than what a cowhand could afford; more like a prosperous rancher might wear. They were well worn and badly in need of a wash, and you could say the same thing of the man who wore them.

"Do you know who I am?" he said.

"Can't say as I do. I don't believe I've had the pleasure of your company up till now."

He laughed again. "Well, maybe you've heard of me. Name's Amos Parker."

The name did not surprise Will. He'd suspected that's what it would be the instant the man stepped through the door.

"I have heard the name," Will said.

"And you, unless I am mistaken, are Wilson Hayes."
Will nodded.

"You're the man who gunned down two of my best hands a few nights ago."
Will nodded.

"I suppose you're going to claim they had it coming."

Will nodded.

"I can see how that could be possible. Earl and Mendoza were prone to forget their manners every once in a while."

A platter heaped with curled bacon, scrambled eggs, fried spuds, and biscuits slathered with milk gravy slid onto the table between Will's elbows. He hefted his fork and knife and dug in, not paying much attention to the man opposite.

Parker watched him eat for a moment, then said, "I got a feeling them two ain't the first of my men you've done away with."

Will paused, fork halfway to his mouth, and stared at Parker.

"You're the kid went to work for the Fishhook a few years ago, ain't you?"

Will nodded.

"It was you that shot the hell out of a bunch of my men rounding up cattle over there."

Will nodded. "They weren't their cattle. Every last hide of them was clearly marked with Jesse Longmore's Fishhook brand."

"That's likely true enough. Thing is, though, Longmore's got more than enough cattle. If a few of them wander off here and there it won't hurt him none."

Will stared for a moment, then turned his attention back to his breakfast.

Parker said, "I take it you don't agree."

"Those were Fishhook cattle. I worked for the Fishhook. It was kind of my job to look out for Mister Longmore's interests."

Parker reached across the table and took a strip of bacon from Will's plate. He bit off a mouthful, chewed on it for a while, said, "You say you *worked* there. That mean you don't work there anymore?"

"Not just now. I reckon I'll be back on the Fishhook one of these days, but it might be a while. Mister Longmore and me, we're kind of on the outs just now."

Parker chewed and swallowed another bite of bacon. "So what is it you're doing these days—outside of killing my men, that is?"

"Truth is, not much of anything."

Another mouthful of bacon went down, then, "You know, kid, I can always use another good man. Especially seeing as how I'm down two just now."

"Good?"

"Good with a gun. Which you are."

"What is it you've got in mind?"

"Well, I put my hand to any number of things as the occasion arises. Livestock. Banks. Trains. Most of the time, nowadays, you could say I'm in the cattle business.

Sometimes I'll put together a herd to fill an order, other times I gather a bunch to sell wherever I can."

"I take it your customers ain't too particular about what brand these cattle of yours are carrying."

Parker laughed. "You got that right. Most of them end up down on the Rio Grande, or south of there. Brands don't mean too much down in that country."

Will pushed the plate away and drained his coffee cup. "What's this kind of work pay?"

"Strictly on shares. I get a triple share for settin' up the deals and runnin' the outfit. The rest gets divided up equal among the hands."

Will thought it over for a minute. "Those two in the saloon. They didn't look to me like they'd been spending any time with cattle."

"True enough. But like I said, them shit-smeared leather bags of grass is only one part of my operation. Earl and Mendoza, they . . . Well, I guess you could say they worked security for me."

"Security? How's that?"

Parker talked on at some length about how Cane Valley was different than where Will came from. That there were no big operators like Longmore and Ballard pushing out and gobbling up smaller outfits. That, he said, was no accident. Among the services Parker offered was protecting the small ranchers from predatory practices at the hands of neighbors driven by greed. It was simply a matter of convincing any rancher with a notion to strong arm a smaller outfit over grazing, water, or anything else, that it was not in his best interest to force the issue.

Of course that wasn't the only danger Parker protected the ranchers from. There was always the risk of rustlers or something else chasing off cattle, a range fire could happen anytime or a haystack might burst into flames, horses could pull up lame or wander off—any number of things could happen and Parker made it his business to see they didn't.

"And you do this, I suppose, out of the kindness of your heart, or sympathy for the little man, or some such?"

Another laugh. "Hell no. I get paid for it. I sell insurance, you might say."

"More like a shakedown, sounds to me like."

"You could look at it that way, I guess. But them ranchers are happy to pay it, so what's the harm?"

Will thought that over, and said, "What about the bigger ranchers?"

"Not the same deal, but they pay, too. Most of them sort of agree not to notice if a few cows turn up missing now and then."

"So that's where you get the stock to fill your orders."

"Some. The Rafter 7 over your way, they've chipped in a few head over the years. So has your Fishhook. Lots more than Longmore knows about. 'Course them ranches across the mountains over there—hell, cow outfits in every direction—they don't do it under any kind of arrangement, like the ranchers here in Cane Valley. Most times, they don't even know when it happens."

"Rustling, plain and simple," Will said.

More laughter. "That's one way of putting it. But that's such a nasty sounding word. Like I said, I'm in the cattle business. My way of doing things ain't a whole lot different from what your Mister Longmore does. Only difference is, he pays off the law to make it all seem legal-like. Me, I'd as soon pocket that money as hand it over to some lard-assed judge or tin-star lawdog."

Neither man said anything for a while, each spending the silence studying the other.

"Well, you in or not? I ain't got time to sit here making chin music all day."

Will mulled it over a bit longer, then said, "I don't know. Give me some time to think about it. How do I find you? If I want to, that is."

Parker told how to find his headquarters, in a dusty little offshoot valley that cut into the mountains some distance south of Rio Largo.

"I'm warning you, it ain't nothing like living in town. Or the Fishhook. We sleep rough, and the food's so bad it's as likely to empty your gut as fill it."

Will nodded.

"Don't be wasting a lot of time thinking on it. If you're in, haul your butt out there quick-like. There's work to do."

Will nodded.

Parker stood up from the table and hitched up his britches. He turned to leave, stopped, turned back, said "One more thing, Hayes. A whole passel of my hands are toes up under dirt on account of you. Don't you forget that—I ain't about to."

Unblinking, Will looked at Parker for a moment. He did not nod.

He turned his attention back to his coffee.

*****

Three days later, Will reined up his horse on a hillside above Parker's outfit, propped his hands on the saddle horn and studied the layout of the place. He'd followed the rustler's directions to the remote corner of Cane Valley, but rode on beyond the ranch road to approach from the mountains rather than the valley.

Parker hadn't misled him concerning the rough nature of the place. A couple of log cabins, missing most of their chinking and with as many gaps as shingles on the roofs, huddled against the sidehill below him.

Beyond them spread a good-sized corral of cedar posts and pine poles, with four smaller pens attached along two sides. A squeaky windmill turned slowly above the corrals. A wooden pipe lashed to the fence poured a trickle of water into a trough positioned to allow stock in the big corral and two of the smaller pens to water. The overflowing tank and leaky pipe turned a sizeable area of the dusty corrals to mud. Two pens held horses, standing hipshot in the afternoon sun, swishing away flies with their tails. He counted nine horses in the pens, tree others saddled and tied to a hitch rail in front of a log house to the left of the corrals. Five, maybe six men, he thought.

If the house, made of logs like the cabins, was in better repair it was not noticeable. A thin stream of smoke floated out of the chimney. Garbage formed a trail from the back door to a heap sprouting bones, tin cans, whiskey bottles, and who knows what-all kinds of rust and corruption. Will believed he could see the head and horns of a steer in the mess, and imagined he could hear the swarming flies. The buzzing cloud thinned out with distance from the midden, but thickened up again around an outhouse standing at an awkward angle.

Between the front of the house and the corrals a sagging shed stood propped on wood posts barely taller than a man. Underneath was a jumble of boxes and barrels and tarps; saddles hung tethered to the underside of the roof with halters and bridles tangled on pegs driven into the posts.

Up the small valley, a mixed herd of loosely scattered cattle grazed in the brush. Sixty, maybe eighty head, he figured; more if you counted the calves. Down valley, where the small bowl poured out into Cane Valley proper, he noted a guard sitting atop a low ridge, his horse tied to a nearby juniper tree. The man had to have seen him ride past on the wagon road, but his approach over the ridges had not been detected.

Letting his horse blow for a few minutes, Will made a trail of slow switchbacks the rest of the way down the ridge, bottoming out in the angle between the cabins and the house. He stopped in the yard a ways back from the horses at the hitch rail, keeping them between his horse and the front door. The house had no porch; a slice of log standing on end provided a step up or down.

Ratcheting hammers and the metallic levering of a shell into a rifle chamber answered his "Hello the house!"

The barrel of a long gun nosed out a windowpane that once held glass, and two men stepped quickly out of one of the cabins, pistols in hand. The front door opened, and Amos Parker stepped into the vacant space and leaned against the frame.

"Hayes."

"Parker."

"You found the place."

Will did not see that the statement merited a reply.

Parker finally broke the awkward silence. "I take it you're ready to go to work."

"May as well. Ain't got nothing else on at the time."

Another pause.

Will said, "Understand one thing, up front. I'll not rustle Fishhook stock, nor do anything else untoward where that ranch is concerned."

Another pause.

Parker said, "Corral your horse and get settled in, then come back to the house." He thrust his chin toward the log huts. "Unfurl your bedroll in that far cabin. Two men who bunked there ain't needing it no more. I don't have to say why."

With that, he turned into the house and shut the door.

Chapter Eighteen

Without bothering to knock, Will pushed open the front door and walked into the house. The definitive click of a hammer pulled to full cock drew his attention to a dim corner of the room. There sat a man on a wooden chair without a back with a Henry rifle at his shoulder, his thumb sliding off the hammer and finger reaching for the trigger.

"I know you, you sonofabitch. I know just who you are."

Will watched the man snug the rifle tighter to his shoulder, staring down the barrel at the middle of his chest.

"Your first mistake was killing my friends that day on the Fishhook a few years back. Your second mistake was not killing me. Your next mistake—your last—was coming here."

"Put the rifle down! Now," Parker said as he walked into the room, stepped between Will and the rifle, grabbed the barrel, and shoved it upward. "Let go," he said, and jerked the rifle away. "Pull another trick like that, Monte, and you'll be the one looking down the barrel of a gun."

"You know who this is, Amos? Where the hell did he come from?"

"Yes, Monte, I know who this is. He's the new hand around here. And if you'd been doing your job out on watch, you'd know where he came from."

"He didn't come by me. Or I'd of shot the sonofabitch then and there."

"All you need to know is he's here now. And he's staying. Get used to the idea."

"Good hell, Amos, he's the one shot five of our boys when we was rounding up cows over on the Fishhook."

"I know, Monte. And he's the one who shot Mendoza and Earl in town last week."

"Well, what the hell's he doing here?"

"Like I said, he works here now."

Monte stood up, kicking the broken chair over as he did. He grabbed the Henry rifle from Parker, and said, "I don't like it, Amos."

"I don't give a shit."

"He'd best watch hisself, or I'm liable to kill him."

Parker laughed. "Hell, Monte, he could have killed you once, already. And I'm of a mind he could do it again if he took a notion. You're the one who better watch himself. Now, pick up that chair and sit your sorry ass down. We're about to have a meeting. Hayes, you might as well find a seat."

Parker pulled his pistol, opened the front door, leaned out, and fired into the air. Will figured it must be a familiar signal, for the two men in the cabin started for the house, another wandered in from somewhere else in the house, and, through the open door, he could see the man who had replaced Monte on lookout start down the hill toward his horse.

Soon, all the men were assembled, some on crippled chairs, others on the floor with backs to the wall. Will learned the gang had 150 head of cows, calves, bulls, steers, and heifers penned up in a box canyon on the other side of the mountain range. The animals Will had spotted grazing in the brush up behind the house would push the number over 200, enough to satisfy a regular customer down south.

One of the hands, a man they called Blanco, would stay behind. Parker, Will, Monte, and the other three would drive this bunch around the mountains to join the other herd and the two cowboys watching them, and drive the cattle south for delivery.

Given the distance to cover, Parker's was a greasy sack outfit on the trail—with no chuck wagon, the sparse camp equipment traveled on pack horses, meager supplies in bags. A cowboy carried his own possibles tied behind the cantle of his saddle, draped across the fork, or hanging from the horn. The small remuda was hazed along with the cow herd, each hand responsible for roping out his own mounts for the day and for night guard.

Even so, it did not take Will long to realize that driving stolen cattle proved the same in all its particulars as moving any other herd. Same dust. Same trail of excrement. Same endless bawling and ceaseless clacking of dewclaws. Same long days and short nights. Same campfire smoke in your eyes, same sand in the biscuits and gravel in the beans, same alkali in the water.

But he learned, too, that the pay was much better. His share amounted to more than an ordinary cowhand could pocket from years of trail drives, or months of ranch work. That helped compensate for the poor quality of the company the crew offered, and the felt need to keep one eye always on Monte, who mistrusted Will as a matter of course—a favor he returned in kind.

After a few days blowing off steam in a seedy border town, Parker led his crew back to Cane Valley. Will was assigned to accompany Blanco up and down the valley, collecting protection payments from ranchers. Parker's claim that they were happy to pay proved a lie. The ranchers resented their arrival and were glad to see the back of them when they left. With cash hard to come by, parting with a portion of it to satisfy Parker's demands hard pressed even the most frugal and hardworking among them.

But gathering the money was Will's job, and he and Blanco did not ride away from a single ranch without cash in hand, never mind the protests and pleadings, complaints and objections. Most of the ranchers knew Blanco and had dealt with him before. Will was surprised to learn that some knew who he was. Word of his gun-fight in the Rio Largo saloon had spread, along with surprise at word he'd joined up with Parker after gunning two of his men down.

It seemed word of his doings and deeds in Cane Valley had made its way back to Ballard Station and on to the Fishhook. One rancher reported that Jesse Longmore had paid him a visit. He said Longmore rode at the head of a posse in search of Will Hayes, meaning to capture and return him to Ballard Station for trial on charges of the theft from the Fishhook. Or kill him, if it proved more convenient.

Had the rancher any reason to lie, Will would not have believed it. As far removed from reality Longmore had been when he left him, it seemed obvious he had wandered further still. Beyond, apparently, Emma's and Johnny's ability to influence him.

But Will kept at his collections—interrupted once to raid cattle from the Rafter 7, and again to steal from a ranch in the opposite direction called the Bar W, which introduced Will to more new country. When they returned, he learned of another foray into Cane Valley by Longmore, again backed by a posse. He tried to put it out of his mind, asking Parker for more work to keep him occupied.

"You know, Hayes, there ain't no need to keep so busy. If we wanted to work all the time, we'd get regular jobs."

"I know it, Amos. But I can't just sit around here so much. Feels like I'm growing moss."

"Here's something to think about. There's a ranch way down the other side of Rio Largo owned by some fancy-pants from England. Don't believe you've been there yet. Their brand is the Heart Cross. Word is, a couple of weeks ago they brought in a shipment of some fancy breed bulls from England, figuring to improve the bloodlines of their cattle. Looking for more meat.

"Anyway, there's been a lot of talk about these bulls for more'n a year. Seems they've had good success with them other places. Fella I know down on the border, he's all the time dealing with some rich Mexican rancher down in Chihuahua somewheres, and thinks he can get a good price for some of these bulls if we can get our hands on any of 'em."

"Why not just rustle them the usual way? Ride onto his range, gather up a few, and drive them away?" Will said.

"They got lots of fences down on the Heart Cross. That Britisher, he keeps all his best stock, horses and cattle alike, in fenced pastures. That damned barbwire. And he's got a lot of hands riding fence. So it ain't going to be all that easy to get to them critters, and harder still to get out of there with them."

"Let me think on it some. Maybe ride down that way and have a look."

"Fine by me. Give you something to do, anyway. Maybe stop you whining about laying around living the good life."

Will was back within a week, telling Parker he had a plan. He refused the boss any of the details, just said to have a few hands ready and waiting on the road through the mountains to where Parker's hideout canyon was in three weeks' time. Then he disappeared into his cabin, only coming out for meals, and, from time to time, to saddle a horse, ride away, and return after maybe an hour. Questions about what he was up to went unanswered. A few days before the appointed time he packed up some foodstuffs and a thin bedroll and rode away toward the Heart Cross.

A few mornings later, Heart Cross hands checking pastures found gates open and cattle moved from one enclosure to another and hopelessly mixed. After a long day of gathering and cutting and sorting and moving bunches back where they belonged, the cowboys discovered three of the Hereford bulls missing, along with another dozen head of old cows held for shipment to slaughter.

"What do you mean three of my Hereford bulls are missing?" the rancher thundered on hearing the news. "You are supposed to be the foreman here. Why are you not out tracking down the scoundrels who stole them?"

"That's just it, Sir. We couldn't see how anyone stole anything."

"Meaning what?"

"Well, you see, it's like them gates opened theirselves, or maybe got opened by the cows."

"Poppycock!"

"I know it, Sir. But we studied the ground real careful-like, and there wasn't a man track or even a horse track to be found. Nothing but cattle tracks in and out of them gates. We saw where maybe a small bunch moved out to the road, but even then, they was all cow tracks."

"Impossible!"

"Yes, Sir. On the road, it was a hopeless mess. Horses, cattle, wagons going every which way. All the recent tracks was cattle, nothing on top of 'em. We couldn't make no sense of it at all."

The Englishman fumed and fussed, finally fulminated at the sheepish cowboys, "Don't just stand there, you lot! Find my bulls!"

The foreman said, "As you wish. But the truth is, we don't know where to begin, or which way to turn. I'll send some of the men, but don't expect much."

Will, with the stolen stock, was miles away by then, almost to the rendezvous point with Parker. He plodded along and reached the agreed-upon stream crossing well after dark, and the cattle and his mount took a long-needed drink. They had been on the go since well before dawn and here it was well after dark. Will figured they would hole up the rest of the night, then move on the next day to get the bulls to the hidden canyon.

Parker and two other cowboys rode out of the cottonwood trees along the stream as the bulls pawed at the water, drank, then shook their massive heads sending streams of thick water stringing from their snouts.

"Fine looking bunch of cattle you got there, Hayes," Parker said, eyeing the animals by the light of the moon. "Cows look like they're on their last legs, and them bulls ain't hardly got enough legs to walk."

"Well, they started out with more, Amos, but they've walked half a foot off them."

"Damn funny looking critters. Can't see why anyone would want to pay a lot of money for one. What do you plan to do with those sorry cows?"

"I've got no plans for them. Brought them along because I thought they might keep the bulls calm. But there was no need. Those boys are about as docile as an old milk cow."

"Let's get 'em moving, boys. We can't sit here jawing all night. That Englishman's likely to be hot on your trail."

"I don't think so. If things worked out the way I planned, they're still trying to figure out what happened."

Parker tipped his hat back on his head. "Just what is it you planned, kid?"

"I'll tell you later. If you think we need to keep moving, let's move."

Chapter Nineteen

Jesse Longmore sat in the marshal's office in Rio Largo, leaned back in a chair with his feet on the desk, boots, spurs, and all. The deputy on duty, shuffling papers at the other desk, warned him the marshal would not take kindly to such behavior. Longmore ignored him. He studied the wanted posters tacked to the walls and occasionally drew a whiskey flask from the inside pocket of his jacket and took a long pull.

After a time, the marshal came in and hung his hat on a rack standing in the corner near the door. As he edged his way between the desks, he reached out and swatted Longmore's crossed feet, knocking them to the floor and nearly tipping the man off his chair.

"What the—" Longmore started to protest, but the law officer cut him off.

"Don't start with me, Longmore. In this office you'll show some couth or get the hell out."

"You think you can treat me that way, you—"

"I told you to shut up. You might amount to something over in Ballard Station, but in my town you're just another ill-mannered old man who drinks too much. Now, need I ask what the hell you're doing here?"

"Same as last time, John Law. And the time before that. I want Will Hayes and I aim to get him. Now, the question is, you going to help me, or not?"

"I assure you, Longmore, we're always looking to catch Amos Parker and his bunch getting up to no good, including Hayes."

"I take that to mean you ain't found him yet."

"Nope. Had a man out to Parker's place just yesterday. Heart Cross ranch lost some fancy imported herd bulls, so we went out that way looking for them. Parker's bunch has been known to steal cattle now and then."

"Hmmph. Place'll be better off for the loss of them. Texas cattle's always been good enough for this country. Always will be," Longmore said. "So, was Hayes out there? Did you get any word on where the little sonofabitch is holed up?"

"No, he wasn't there. Neither was Parker. Just three or four of his flunkies sittin' around scratchin' their asses. Claimed they didn't know where Parker was. Didn't ask about Hayes."

"Why the hell not?"

"Fact is, Longmore, he's not all that high on my list."

Longmore stood. "Then I guess you won't mind if I go looking for him myself."

"Fine with me. Quicker you and that bunch of fools you've got drinking over in the saloon get out of Rio Largo, the better."

The rancher turned to leave.

"One more thing," the marshal said, stopping him at the door. "You or any of your 'posse' or whatever the hell you call them break any laws, I'll lock you up in a heartbeat. And should you stumble onto Hayes—which is likely the only way you'll find him—you bring him in for trial."

"I wouldn't be putting no trial date on your calendar if I was you. He ain't likely to give up without a fight, and I don't believe he'll survive a fight with me and my men."

*****

By mid-morning, the cattle were well out of Cane Valley. While Parker wanted to move them farther, even to the hidden canyon before stopping, the heavy Hereford bulls were too leg weary to go on. Whatever their advantages over Texas cattle, walking surely wasn't among them.

But with the wagon road long since behind them, Will figured they would be safe enough, so the cowboys moved the small herd into a stand of juniper trees to rest.

The bulls soon found shade and wallowed into the dust. The old cows grazed for a time then followed suit.

All but one of the drovers pulled their saddles and staked the horses out to pick at the bunch grass among the sagebrush, then they, too, plopped down in the shadows of the stubby trees.

Parker corked his canteen after a long drink and said, "So, Hayes, how is it that you're so damn sure there ain't a bunch of Heart Cross cowboys on our tails?"

"I suppose it's possible they are, but I doubt it. They wouldn't know where to start or which way to go."

Parker gnawed on that for a minute but could make no sense of it. "And just why the hell is that?" he said.

Will tipped his saddle over, resting bottom-side up on the ground to dry out, and opened one of the saddle bags. He pulled out a tangle of leather thongs and tossed it toward Parker, who picked it up and studied it.

"What the hell is this? Looks like the hoof off a big ol' cow."

"That's exactly what it is."

"Well what the hell's all this whang leather for? Shoelaces?"

"More or less."

Parker turned the hoof over and over, around and around, trying to make sense of it.

Will said, "See that piece of wood tacked on top of the hoof?"

"Yes."

"What I did was lay that up against my horse's hoof then wrap them thongs around his pastern to hold it there. In my saddlebags, there's one for each leg."

A knowing grin spread across Parker's face. "Well I'll be damned. With these outfits your horse makes cow tracks!"

"That's about the size of it."

Parker's grin turned to laughter. "So this is what you been doin' holed up in that cabin. How'd your horse take to it?"

"Oh, he was a little skittish at first, tried to kick them off, paw them off. But he got used to it. I'd just take him out in the brush and lead him around, then he got so he didn't mind my climbing aboard. He wouldn't win no horse race wearing them things, but he could get around without no problem."

Parker laughed again. "Hell, I can just see them Heart Cross cowboys riding around in circles wondering how it was a cow drove off their cattle!"

"I don't guess it would fool an experienced tracker. At least not for long. But most men wouldn't know the difference. I figure it would make them wonder long enough to give us a good head start, if not keep them off the trail altogether. By the time I got far enough down the road where I figure any tracks would be lost in the jumble, I took them off."

"Pretty good trick, cowboy," Parker laughed. "Looks like just the thing for stealing cattle out of pens. Hell, you might be on to something here."

He threw the hoof back to Will, who wrapped the thongs around it and stuffed it back in the saddlebag where it rode all the way south. They pushed the big bulls as hard as they dared, but it was still a slow trip. The price the Herefords brought from Parker's buyer made it worth it.

Amos gave Will an extra share of the take. "Don't be flappin' your jaws to the others about gettin' this," he said, "but I reckon you earned it this time."

*****

For days, Longmore led his band of vigilantes up and down Cane Valley hunting Will Hayes. No traveler they stopped on the roads admitted seeing him. No rancher claimed to have laid eyes on Will for weeks. The hands at the Heart Cross offered no assistance, saying they did not know if the exiled cowboy had anything to do with the missing Hereford bulls.

Eventually the angry rancher ended up in the gap that led to Amos Parker's small valley. The posse pulled up as one at the sound of a gunshot.

"You best hold up right there," someone yelled from somewhere up the hill.

Longmore studied the terrain, but could see no one.

"State your business!" came the voice again.

"My name is Jesse Longmore. I've come here hunting a man—"

"You've come to the wrong place. There ain't nobody here you're looking for."

"Hmmph. You don't even know who I'm looking for."

"Don't make no difference. Whoever it is, he ain't here. And if he is, he don't want to see you."

Hoofbeats sounded from up the small valley as the bandits holed up at the ranch rode out in response to the gunshot.

The voice came again. "You boys keep your hands empty. I see any one of you reach for a gun, you won't live to feel the steel."

Blanco and two other outlaws rode around the base of the ridge with pistols drawn and reined up in front of Longmore.

"What the hell you want?" Blanco demanded.

"Who am I talking to?" Longmore said.

"That ain't none of your damned business."

"Do you know who I am?"

Blanco leaned over and spit out a stream of tobacco juice. "Don't know. Don't care."

Monte, the guard up the hill, rode out of concealment and into the line, adding another pistol to the arsenal trained on Longmore and his men.

"My name is Jesse Longmore. I run the Fishhook ranch on the other side of the mountain range across the valley."

"I know the place," Blanco said. Then, with a grin, "You raise some mighty fine cattle over there." The three men with him laughed.

"Listen, I ain't got the time nor the inclination to sit here in the sun passing the time of day with a bunch of lowlifes like you. I'm hunting Will Hayes and I'm told he runs with your bunch."

"What if he does?" Blanco said.

"I want him. And I intend to get him."

Blanco said nothing. A horse snorted. Another pawed nervously at the dirt. Saddle leather squeaked with someone's shifting weight.

Finally, "I ain't seen Hayes for a while. Don't know where he is. But last time I saw him, I'm pretty sure he told me he didn't want to talk to you."

Longmore looked from one bandit to the other. "I'll make it worthwhile for any man with any information as to his whereabouts. Like I said, I intend to find him. And I'll do it, with or without your help."

Blanco laughed. "Then you'll do it without us, for certain sure. Ain't a man here who'll tell you a damn thing. Now you best ride on while you still can. Dead men don't make very good hunters."

Longmore looked once again from one man to the other, reading each man's eyes for any hint of weakness. "You boys think about what I said." With that, the rancher wheeled his mount and rode away with the others behind, kicking up a cloud of dust in their wake.

Blanco holstered his revolver and spat another stream of tobacco slobber into the dirt. "Keep a sharp eye on watch, men. If they come back, shoot that bearded sonofabitch. Unless I miss my guess, Amos ain't going to want that man hanging around. Will neither."

Monte rode back up the hill to the watch point, and the other three rode back to the ranch. When his replacement came, he said, "I've worked up a terrible thirst sitting out here in the sun all day. Believe I'll ride into Rio Largo for a drink. Maybe find me some female company while I'm there. Look for me sometime tomorrow. Maybe the next day."

"Blanco might not like that. It leaves us kind of shorthanded."

"To hell with Blanco."

"Amos might not like it, either."

"Amos ain't here."

Monte rode out of the little valley toward Rio Largo. But he had no intention of going to town. At least not yet. Once out of sight of the watchman, he turned in the direction Longmore had taken.

He found them in camp in the cottonwood trees along a small stream winding its way across the Cane Valley seeking the Rio Largo. He stopped in the open some fifty yards away and sat his horse and watched. Soon enough one of the men spotted him and ducked into a Sibley tent. A few minutes later, Longmore walked out toward him.

"Well?" Longmore said after sizing up the man he recognized from earlier.

"Hayes."

"What about him? He there?"

"No. Him and Amos and some others took some cattle to market. But I guess they'll be back soon. No more than a fortnight, I'd say."

"What happens then?"

Monte thought for a minute. "Hard to say. It ain't like Amos keeps us on a regular schedule or anything like that. But lately, before this trip, that is, Hayes was riding with Blanco, collecting money from ranchers. Could be he'll go back to that."

Longmore reached into his pocket and pulled out a flask. After a drink, he offered it to Monte.

"And if he does, he'll be out in the open?"

Monte nodded and handed the flask back to Longmore.

"Can you let me know—tell me when he's back, and if he'll be going out?"

"Might could."

Longmore said he would be back, and said where he would be in two weeks' time to await word. Then he pulled a one-hundred-dollar bank note from a billfold and tore it in two. "Here," he said, handing half to the cowboy. "You'll get the rest when you come back with the information I need."

Monte tucked the bill into a vest pocket.

"Why you doing this?" Longmore said.

"Let's just say I don't have any use for Hayes. There's something between us that goes way back."

Anticipating his newfound wealth, Monte drank more at his favorite saloon in Rio Largo, lost more gambling, and spent more time upstairs taking horizontal refreshments with the women than was his custom. By the time he got back to the ranch two days later he was in no condition to stand guard, even.

Eleven days later, Parker, Will, and the others returned.

Chapter Twenty

Parker's hands each pocketed a share of the take from the sale of the Hereford bulls. "I've never before got so much money for a herd of cattle you could count on one hand," he said. "Them red and white bulls fetched us a pretty penny. Better enjoy it boys, 'cause it ain't likely to happen again anytime soon."

The men sat around the front room of the house passing a whiskey bottle as Amos regaled them with tales of the trip, mostly lies. When he told them about the ruse Will used to rustle the Heart Cross bulls, they thought that a lie, too, until he sent Will for the hooves.

Blanco filled Parker in on the marshal's visit and the later appearance of Jesse Longmore. "The marshal was lookin' for them bulls, but he knew he was walkin' around blind with nothin' to go on." He turned his attention to Will. "Longmore, though, he was lookin' for you."

Later, Blanco took Will aside.

"That old boss of yours, he's got it in for you. He offered us money to give you up. I sent him packin'."

"I'm obliged to you for that, Blanco. Thank you."

"I don't know if this amounts to anything or not. I'll let you decide. After Longmore left, Monte headed for town. He for sure went to town 'cause he came back here stinkin' of sour whiskey and French perfume. That might not be the only place he went, though. It might be nothin' but you might want to keep an eye on him."

"I'll do that. Thanks again."

The next morning, Blanco found Will again.

"How's your backside? You up for some more time in the saddle?"

"Sure enough. What you got in mind?"

Blanco said, "Amos wants me to start out tomorrow to collect from some of the ranches. Says I can take you along if you want to go."

"Beats the hell out of laying around here," Will said. "I'll tell you what, though. Why don't you have some-body else standing by just in case."

"Why's that?"

"I figure we can find out right soon if Monte's up to something. Let the word out that you're going and I'm going with you, and we'll see what happens."

No sooner had the word spread than Monte saddled a horse and rode away. He told Amos he had some busi-ness in town. Will filled Parker in on his suspicions and rode out after Monte. It soon became evident he was not heading for town. Since the cowboy was in no hurry, Will caught up with him in less than an hour.

As soon as he topped a rise and spotted Monte, Will spurred his horse into a dead run. By the time Monte heard him coming, it was too late to do anything but watch with his face hanging out. Will slid his mount to a stop nose to nose with the other horse, which shied away and started fidgeting enough to keep Monte from regaining his composure.

"Where you going, Monte?"

"I don't see as that's any of your damn business."

"Why'd you lie? What are you hiding?"

Monte said nothing. Will rode up beside him and with a backhand swipe, knocked him from the saddle. The empty horse spooked and ran off. Will figured it wouldn't stop until it reached the ranch. But he did not believe Monte would be needing it.

Will dismounted and dropped his reins, knowing his horse would stand.

"Where is he?" Will said as he grabbed Monte by the shirtfront and hoisted him to his feet.

"Who?"

"Longmore."

"I don't know what you're talking about."

Will's fist lashed out and once again Monte was on the ground.

He dragged him up again and said, "Let's try this one more time."

"You go to hell."

And again, Monte hit the ground.

"Get up, you sniveling bastard. I'm tired of picking you up."

Monte crabbed backward to put some distance between them and stood.

"You're taking a roundabout way to town. Makes a man wonder if that's where you're going at all."

Monte said nothing.

"Look, I know you're on your way to see Longmore. You sold me out. So why don't you just tell me where he is."

"You're getting nothing out of me."

Will doubled his fists and started across the space that separated them. But Monte stopped him by going for his gun. Will beat him to the draw so Monte stopped and let his pistol slide back into its holster.

"Spit it out!"

"I already told you, Hayes. I ain't tellin' you anything."

Will stepped forward and whacked Monte's head with the barrel of his Colt. The cowboy's hat absorbed much of the blow, but there was enough momentum to knock him to the ground. The hammer ratcheted back as the barrel swung toward the face of the fallen man.

"Last chance."

Monte swallowed hard. "You goin' to shoot me again?"

"Not unless I have to. But I'll sure as hell do it. Only this time, I'll finish the job."

Again, Monte swallowed, and had trouble doing it. "He's camped in Cedar Canyon."

"Where's that?"

"Fifteen, maybe sixteen miles north. You can't miss it. Just follow Cedar Creek—it'll be the second stream out of the mountains you'll pass—and it'll take you right there."

Monte stood and used both hands to brush the seat of his pants.

Will holstered his pistol. "You've got a long walk ahead of you. You'd best get a move on."

He turned away and started for his horse, then turned back and said, "If I was you, I wouldn't bother going back to Parker's. I don't think you'll be welcome there."

As he turned away again, he heard Monte grab his gun.

Will spun around, dropped to one knee as he drew his pistol, and, before Monte could get a shot off, planted a bullet in the center of his chest. The dead outlaw did not even bounce as he hit the ground.

No plan occurred to Will as he rode toward Cedar Canyon. He crossed Cedar Creek and rather than following it toward the mountain range he continued beyond, turning, instead, into the dry canyon beyond. He followed the bottom of the draw for a ways, then left the floor to angle up the side of the low ridge. When he neared the top, he dismounted and walked to the summit, crouching to stay below the skyline. He crawled over the spine of the ridge, then made his way down to a clump of juniper trees.

From his vantage point, he could see the camp—a Sibley tent, two shelter-half tents, and a makeshift brush lean-to surrounded a ring of boulders where a campfire smoked. Hobbled horses grazed along the creek bank beyond. He counted six men lazing around the camp besides Longmore, who sat on the ground, back against a boulder, hat pulled down over his face. He recognized two of the men from the Fishhook; the others he did not know.

As he squatted in the shade watching the camp and studying the surrounding terrain, Will pulled his Bowie knife from its sheath and mindlessly scraped the blade against his forearm. He looked down and saw a line of greasy dirt piled up by the blade. Good Lord! What am I coming to? He wiped the blade clean against his pants leg and replaced it in its scabbard. Following Longmore's lead, he snuggled back against the trunk of a tree, pulled his hat brim down over his eyes and dozed off. While his plan wasn't fully formed, he believed the night might be a busy one.

The sun was below the ridgeline when Will awakened. Down in the camp, the men had eaten supper and cleanup was underway. Longmore wasn't in sight, but soon came walking out of the willows along the river fastening his pants. He ducked into the Sibley tent, came back out, walked to a pannier hanging from a tree limb, extracted a bottle of whiskey, and went back to the tent.

As darkness fell, one by one the men crawled into bedrolls, whether under shelter tents, the lean-to, or the stars. Expecting no difficulty, they posted no guard. The flames in the fire ring burned down to glowing coals. Soon, the snores of men mingled in the night air with the chirp of crickets and click of locusts.

Will watched the Big Dipper ride its slow circle around the pole star until deep into the night. He walked down the ridge then up the canyon bottom to the campsite, stopped for a moment to listen, then skirted his way around the perimeter until directly behind Longmore's tent. He knelt down as near the tent as was possible without disturbing the canvas. With held breath, he listened for the old man's breathing, and when it came back slow and regular, punctuated by a throaty rattle, he decided Longmore was not only asleep, but passed out from drink.

Drawing the Bowie, he pierced the tent wall near the ground and slowly slit the canvas upward as high as he could reach. Pausing to make sure Longmore slept on undisturbed, he pushed through the slit. The canvas glowed eerily in the moonlight and his eyes soon grew accustomed to the dimness inside the tent.

The old man lay flat on his back atop his bedroll with one arm wrapped around the top his head. Will watched him sleep, pondering what to do. It would be easy to slip the knife between his ribs and be rid of the problem once and for all. But there was Emma. And Johnny. And while he could easily do this to Longmore, he could not do it to them.

So, instead, he cut the buttons off the snoring man's shirt, grabbed Longmore's wide-brimmed hat, and slipped back out the hole. Taking care not to dislodge any rocks, he climbed the hillside, worked his way around and above a rock reef, and perched on top of it to await the day.

*****

The stars faded and the sky grayed and the camp stirred. One of the men rekindled the fire and added a log. Another dumped the dregs of yesterday's coffee and dipped the pot full of fresh water from the stream. Men sat on their bedrolls and scratched and snorted and sniffed and spat.

But the camp awakened with a sense of urgency when a shot rang out.

Before the echo of his pistol shot faded, Will hollered from his perch on the rocks above the camp, "Jesse Longmore!"

Guns came to hand and every eye in the camp glanced in every direction, all eventually coming to rest on Will.

"Sonofabitch!" someone said. "That's Will Hayes!"

"You men put those guns away. I've got no interest in any of you. It's Longmore I want to talk to."

The flap on the Sibley tent rustled and Longmore stumbled through, bleary and tousled. He rubbed his eyes, shook his head, and said to no one in particular, "What the hell's going on?"

Someone answered. "It's Hayes. He wants to talk to you."

"Hayes? Where?"

"He's up there on them rocks."

Longmore squinted in the direction the men pointed, his weak and weary eyes barely able to make out the man perched above, no more than thirty yards away. He swiped a forearm across his mouth and chin, wiping away the drool not trapped in his beard.

"Come down here, you little bastard," Longmore said. "I intend to shoot you down before sunup."

"Take a look at your shirt," Will replied.

Longmore looked down, noticed his shirt was flapping free. He grabbed it, running his fingers up and down the placket in search of fasteners.

"Here!" Will yelled, tossing a handful of buttons to rain down on the befuddled Longmore. "You might want this, too," he said, sailing the Stetson into the air. Longmore watched it glide down, sliding to a stop in the dirt not far from his feet.

Despite the morning chill, sweat beaded on the rancher's forehead and a scarlet flush crept up his neck, around his jaw, and across his cheeks.

"Somebody shoot that sonofabitch!" he bellowed.

Will shot into the air again.

"First gun barrel I see pointed this way, I'll put a bullet in you, Mister Longmore."

The men looked to their boss for direction. He waved them off in frustration.

"All right, Will. Looks like you got the advantage. This time. What is it you want?"

"I want you to leave me alone. Go back to the Fishhook."

"Can't do it, kid. I aim to kill you."

"You've got no cause to do that, Mister Longmore. If you don't let up, I'm going to have to kill you. I don't want to do that."

"You ain't got the guts to kill me. If you did, I'd be dead already. Instead, you torment me," Longmore said as he picked up his hat and swatted the dust off it against his thigh.

Will said, "Just take that as a warning. Like you said, I could've killed you. But I didn't. Next time, things will be different."

"You're damn right they'll be different. Next time, I'll kill *you*."

"Give it up, Mister Longmore. Go home. Leave me be."

"I'll go. For now. But you best watch your back, kid."

Will found cover in the rocks and watched the men pack up and abandon the camp. Missing breakfast wouldn't improve Longmore's mood any, but at least they'd be gone. He shadowed them across Cane Valley and over the divide. But when Longmore and his entourage turned off toward the Fishhook, Will took the opposite direction—toward the Rafter 7.

Chapter Twenty-One

The Longmore family assembled in the front room of the ranch house. As usual, Jesse Longmore burrowed into his favorite chair, whiskey glass and bottle within easy reach. Johnny and Emma shared the settee. Longmore poured a drink, Johnny polished the lenses of his glasses, Emma wadded the tail of her apron in her hands, smoothed it across her lap, crushed it again.

"What is it you want, Pa?" Johnny said.

"More bad news, I'm afraid." He looked at Emma. "It's about that no-account husband of yours."

"What? What is it? Has Will been hurt?"

Longmore tipped his glass, swallowed, then swirled the glass around watching the liquor climb the sides.

"Papa! What is it?"

"He's left Cane Valley. Quit running with that band of thieves and rustlers."

"Well, that's good news," Johnny said.

"I'm afraid not. Seems he's back in this country again—working for Sam Ballard on the Rafter 7."

Johnny hooked his spectacles over his ears. "How do you know that?"

"Heard it in town."

Emma stood. "Saloon talk! That's all it is!"

"No, Emma. Glen at the bank told me. He saw Will ride in with a bunch of Rafter 7 hands, so he asked. Got the word from Ballard himself."

Emma rushed from the room. Johnny folded his bandana and stuffed it in a hind pocket.

"So what do you think it means, Pa?"

"What the hell do you think it means? He's gone over to the other side. At least when he was with Amos Parker, he wasn't working against us. Now, he is."

"I can't believe Will means us any harm."

"Hmmph," Longmore said. "This is Sam Ballard we're talking about. Now that Will's with him, he sure as hell don't mean us any good. He's working for the enemy!"

"And to think he could be here, working for the Fishhook—*would* be here, working for the Fishhook—if you hadn't tried to kill him. All because you're afraid of change."

"Don't you try to lay this off on me, Johnny boy. He didn't have to leave the Fishhook. If he was any kind of man, he'd have stayed here and stood up for himself."

"And if he had, Pa, you'd be planted up there on the hill with Ma, sprouting daisies."

"Maybe. Maybe not. He left. That's the only thing that's changed."

"The hell you say! Everything has changed! Even with Will gone, you've done nothing around here but drink and disrupt the work. That's when you're not wasting time chasing ghosts from hell to breakfast all over the country. Then there's Emma. She's as nervous as a broody hen all the time. This has been harder on her than anyone. She can hardly function anymore. And it's all because of your stinking pride."

Longmore drained his glass. "You may not like the smell of it, son, but my pride is what built this place. The Fishhook. Our holdings in town. All of it. All because of my 'stinking pride.' "

Johnny removed his spectacles and polished the already spotless lenses. "Look on my Works, ye Mighty, and despair!" he said. "Nothing beside remains. Round the decay / Of that colossal Wreck, boundless and bare / The lone and level sands stretch far away."

"What's that gibberish you're spouting?" Longmore said.

"Nothing. Just part of a sonnet. Seemed appropriate."

"You and your damned poems. Why the hell don't you fill that head of yours with something practical?"

*****

Unlike eating arrangements at the Fishhook, hands at the Rafter 7 took their meals at a table in a room in the bunkhouse. It was all one long room, really, with a partial wall and fireplace separating the sleeping quarters from the kitchen and eating room.

Will found this less than satisfactory. Clanging pots and pans awakened him more mornings than not, robbing him of a half hour's sleep. Then there was the stink. The cooking food wasn't so bad, usually, but burnt smells lingered for days and the odor from the haze of rancid grease permeated every pillow, every blanket, every stitch of clothing.

It soon became obvious, as well, that the horror stories he'd heard about a man in the kitchen held true at the Rafter 7. The old man who served as cook, cookie, coosie, pot rustler, dough roller, biscuit shooter, bean master, sop and 'taters, sourdough, hash slinger, kitchen mechanic, or whatever name you attached to him, seemed allergic to soap and water. And it appeared his apron and the clothing beneath it shared his aversion to the cleansing liquid.

The menu seldom varied. Beans were the mainstay, every meal, served up with biscuits so solid they wouldn't sop. Breakfast meant brown and crumbly bacon; supper, beef fried as dark as a latigo strap and just as tender. Occasionally potatoes fried with onions showed up. More rare was the appearance of canned tomatoes. Dessert, if any, consisted of a jug of molasses and another biscuit—if your teeth were still intact after the first one.

Still and all, it was an improvement—if a slight one—over the fare Amos Parker offered.

The company, too, was better. Will always liked the camaraderie of cowboys. A bunkhouse offered conversation, a near-constant card game, sporadic songs and poems and stories, reading material to exchange, and a relaxing atmosphere. And since one of the Rafter 7 hands owned a battered guitar, Will once again felt the ease of fingers on strings.

He was accepted, for the most part, by the hands. There were still few who were around when he killed Caleb Short in Antler Canyon. But no one had liked the man, and considered he had it coming, anyway. The ranch foreman who hired Will, Clint Shipley, was suspicious but opted to give Will a chance. As long as the man worked, it did not matter to him where he came from or why.

Sam Ballard was another story. Why a man who had experienced the animosity between the Fishhook and the Rafter 7 would work for the enemy was beyond him. The cowboy's explanation that he wanted to stay close to an opportunity to reconnect with his estranged wife seemed reasonable enough, but still—he merited watching, for certain. He questioned Will from time to time, trying to ferret out any information about the Fishhook, Jesse Longmore, or his plans, but the young man was not forthcoming. Whether that should be entered in the kid's debit column or asset column, he wasn't sure.

With saddle horses always in demand on the Rafter 7, Will again found himself in the round pen most days, taking the rough off the horses the ranch raised from colts, caught in the wild, or purchased. Late one day, Shipley rode in leading an oversized sorrel stud horse. It stood sixteen hands high on heavy-boned legs, with massive forequarters, a thick neck, and immense head. It seemed gentle enough, but an overgrown mane and tail matted with burrs said he had not been in anyone's saddle string for some time.

Will watched them coming and said, "What's that you got tied to the end of that *mecate*, Clint?"

"This is the finest piece of horseflesh to ever set down a hoof on the Rafter 7. Leastways that was the plan. Years ago, we had a mare here that would work cattle like anybody's dream. Now, most cowboys will shy away from riding a mare but that wasn't the case with this one. Come roundup or branding time, they'd line up to throw a saddle on her. Only problem with that mare was she was kind of scrawny. Strong as an ox, but small enough you couldn't quit wondering if some mossy horn steer might up and drag her plumb off, with you on board."

Will laughed.

"So Sam, Mister Ballard, he bred that mare to a big ol' draft horse he got from a freighting outfit used to be in town. Thought she might throw colts with her quickness and cow smarts, and some of that stud's size. This here's the result."

"Just the one colt?"

"That's all. 'Bout the time this one turned a year old, his mama got locoed. Had to put her down. Anyway, this horse, he's big and he's strong and he's fast and he takes to cattle. But he's crazy as hell. You'd think he's the one got in the loco weed. He'll be going along just fine, then all of a sudden he just loses it. Might shy or go to bucking, might run off, maybe just sull up till you couldn't drag him with a locomotive. Thought maybe you could do something with him."

Clint tossed the lead rope to Will and rode away.

He led the horse into the round corral and pulled the lead rope off the halter. Standing in the center, he watched.

After a while, Will walked toward the horse until it moved, then backed off and did it again. He approached from front and rear and either side. He pressured the horse to turn both ways. Finally, he threaded the *mecate* through the ring on the halter and spent a few minutes rubbing and scratching the stud horse's muzzle, cheeks, and neck.

He led the horse out and tied him to a hitch rail in front of the saddle shed, found the wrangler and asked him to clean up the stallion's mane and tail, telling him to stay to the horse's left as much as possible.

The foreman found Will later in the day and asked about the big sorrel stud. "Think you can do anything with him?"

"Sure. That horse'll do just fine."

"How do you figure? Like I told you, he's known to go nuts for no reason."

"Oh, there's a reason."

Shipley's face went blank. In a moment, "Well, you gonna tell me what the hell it is?"

"That horse ain't got but one eye. He's blind on the right side."

Clint's face stayed blank. In a moment, "Well I'll be damned. That explains a lot. So is he any good for anything that way?

"Depends. If he's as good as you say he is when he's working, he'll make somebody a good horse. You just have to make allowances, is all. I'll work with him for a while. A few wet saddle blankets and he'll be ready for the remuda."

And so Will settled in at the Rafter 7, and the foreman kept him on the winter crew and in the breaking pen working horses. He stayed on the ranch for the most part, only journeying to town on occasion. Even then, he kept to himself, steering clear of company.

On the Fishhook, Emma, too, kept to herself. She burrowed into the bedroom in the house built for her and Will. While the house was finished, it remained unfurnished save the bedroom.

Mealtime found her at the ranch house, helping the cook with preparation and cleanup, but she avoided contact with her father as much as she could. Johnny came over to visit some evenings, but found Emma poor company most of the time.

Longmore spent much of the winter in the ranch house dining room, as it was warmer than the front room he preferred in summer. The cowboys going out to work after breakfast often left him sitting silent at the head of the table, and found him there yet when they stomped the snow off their boots in the dark on the way in for supper. Whether he had moved from that spot they could not say.

As if the rancher did not have enough to trouble his mind, the isolation of Emma and Johnny's ambivalence weighed heavy on his increasingly hoary head.

He took little interest in the ranch. Now and then, as Johnny worked on the books at the desk in the dining room, he would question him about doings at the Fishhook, but paid little attention to the answers. He gave up altogether trying to engage Emma; her desire for conversation less, even, than his.

His only reliable companion visited the ranch regularly, showing up in wooden cases hauled out from Ballard Station. The whiskey didn't stay long; the once-welcome bottles tossed into trash barrels then dumped down a dry wash with everything else that outlived its usefulness on the Fishhook. But, there was always more to come. Longmore could always rely on the whiskey being there.

He only wished he could bank on it being good company.

Chapter Twenty-Two

Spring greened the mountains, signaling time to move cattle to the to the high country. Cowboys drifted in to the Fishhook and Johnny hired his summer crew from among them. The first job would be gathering the herds from the valleys where they wintered, branding the new crop of calves, and parceling out the herds to mountain camps and upland open range.

And, regular as the arrival of the vernal equinox, the same demands of the season activated the Rafter 7.

"You think that one-eyed stud is fit to work cattle?" Clint Shipley asked Will one day.

"Sure enough—as long as whoever mounts him knows to be careful. Treat the horse right, and he'll trust you to be his other eye."

"That's good. We'll put the boss on him. He'll mostly sit in the saddle and watch, so it won't put too much demand on the horse."

"Well, just so's you clue Ballard in on the deal. You sure the old man can handle him?"

Shipley laughed. "Kid, Sam Ballard was topping off rank broncs long before you was even a twinkle in your daddy's eye. He may not ride much anymore, but he sure as hell ain't forgot how."

Saddling-up time on the first day of the spring gather saw cowboys cinching kacks onto furry-looking horses still shedding winter coats. But the sorrel stud gleamed, curried and brushed slick by the wrangler. Will thought he made a fine picture with Ballard's old tobacco-colored, slick-fork, double-rigged saddle perched on his back. The scratched and rope-burned and worn leather told a story of hard work and hard riding that Will read easily.

Sam Ballard hobbled up to the big horse, gave its forehead a good scratch and fiddled with the forelock. "I always thought this horse had what it takes to be a good'n. Clint tells me you figured out why he's so damn ringy."

"Yes sir," Will said. "Just remember he don't see out of that right eye and you'll be fine. Give him a chance to look over where he's going head-on, and he'll get you there. Favor the left side a little, and you can do anything on him you can do with any horse."

"I thank you, son," Ballard said, gathering the reins.

He strained some to get his foot high enough to stab the stirrup, but lifted easily into the saddle. As he rode away, Will noticed the rancher still sat a good seat horseback.

For the next few weeks, branding-fire smoke irritated the cowboys' eyes and the stench of burning hair stung their noses. Every breath brought along a load of dust. Hot irons blistered palms, blood stained skin and clothing, zipping ropes scorched hands and thighs and saddle horns. Hooves scuffed knuckles, hocks bruised ribs, horns scraped away patches of skin.

Branding time meant never enough water, never enough sleep, and too many slick hides at the start of every day. But the cowboys did the job. Occasionally the boss roped and dragged a calf to the fire to keep his hand in, but most of the time Sam Ballard watched. When he wasn't watching the work, he could be seen atop the tall sorrel stud, riding slowly around the day's gather, counting the year's calves, tallying yearlings, and toting up what would ship come fall.

And, no doubt, counting the money it would put in his bank accounts in Ballard Station. At Jesse Longmore's bank—a thought that always creased his forehead and flushed the tips of his ears.

The work done, Ballard and Clint talked over which herds to send where for summer grazing. The foreman went to work lining out the crew for each job.

"Will, you know that Antler Canyon country, don't you?" he said.

"Yes sir. I've ridden 'most every inch of it, one time or another."

"How 'bout you take that bunch they're a-holding out at Jackson Spring and push 'em up Rattle Creek and onto some good grass up them canyons. Split 'em into maybe three bunches, if you will."

"Clint," Ballard said before Will could agree. "A word."

The rancher led his foreman well out of earshot.

"Listen, Clint, I don't think it's a good idea to send the kid that way. Send someone else."

"What's the problem, boss? He's a good hand. He'll get it done. Besides, he knows the country."

"That's just it. He knows Antler Canyon on account of running Fishhook cattle in there. Don't forget he was Longmore's man a hell of a lot longer than he's been ours. Hell, he's still married to the man's daughter."

Shipley's face betrayed no hint of understanding.

"Good hell, man, think about it. He might put our cattle on poor range and save the best grass for Fishhook herds!"

"I don't think he'd do that."

"But you don't know he won't do it. I ain't sure I trust him. Not where Longmore's concerned. He is family, after all."

"Well, you're the boss."

"That I am. And it ain't like we ain't got other good men for the job. Hell, I think I'll ride along with that herd myself. Been a few years since I seen Antler Canyon."

"Suit yourself, Mister Ballard."

Clint ambled back over to where the men waited. "Change of plans, Will. You ride out past the south hay meadow and take those men and the cows they're holding on up to Black Mesa."

Will looked puzzled, but did not question the orders.

*****

Along about that same time, Jesse Longmore took a notion to take to the saddle himself. With the branding well in hand and men enough to finish the job, he buttonholed Johnny and arranged a ride to Antler Canyon to check grazing conditions and decide how many cattle to put where.

Riding down a branch canyon, Johnny spotted a haze of dust in the main gorge below.

"Look at that, Pa."

"Hmmph. That much dust ain't from no wind. You don't suppose that sonofabitch Sam Ballard's got cows over here already, do you?"

"Can't say. Must be, come to think of it. Like you said, something's stirring up that dust and it's unlikely anybody else would try to put a herd in here."

"Well, we'll find out soon enough," the old man said.

By the time they bottomed out at Rattle Creek, the herd had passed. The Longmore men turned upstream and spurred their horses into a trot, watching the drag riders push the tail end of the herd around a bend. Bringing up the rear, just far enough back and to the left of the cattle to miss the worst of the dust, rode Sam Ballard.

"Look!" Longmore said. "There's that sonofabitch Ballard, himself!"

The rancher tossed aside the whiskey flask he'd been sipping from, put the spurs to his horse, and took off on a beeline across the broad streambed toward his nemesis.

Johnny hollered, "Pa! Hold up there—what the hell are you doing?"

If Longmore heard, he paid no attention.

Maybe it was the noise of the cattle in the canyon that kept Ballard and his big sorrel horse from hearing the approach. But Longmore rushed out of nowhere right into the stud's blind spot, undetected. When he sensed an unknown presence, the powerful stallion shied, darted sideways to the left, lost his footing, and went down. The screaming horse mashed Ballard's left leg in the fall, but clawed its way upright without inflicting further damage.

Looking down on Ballard, lying helpless in the dirt, Longmore spurred his mount forward. The horse, reluctant to step on the fallen man, stomped backward, jumped sideways, reared up, came back to earth, under constant pressure from Longmore's spurs and quirt to trample Ballard.

"Pa!" Johnny hollered, riding into the melee in an attempt to stop him. "Damn it! Back off!"

The drag riders following the Rafter 7 herd were aware of the fracas and one of them peeled off and rode toward the fight.

Ballard's pistol was in hand by now and he fired off a shot, missing Longmore and further upsetting the panicked horse. His next shot shattered Longmore's collar bone. A third bullet followed, this one slamming into the old man's breastbone, laying waste to his heart and turning his chest into a soggy wad of mashed muscle and broken bone and gushing blood.

Pulling his pistol at the sound of gunfire, the Rafter 7 cowboy, approaching at a lope, snapped off a shot that, against all odds, burned a hole through Johnny Longmore's skull and turned his extraordinary brain into a useless glob of gore.

*****

Back in her room at the Fishhook, Emma Longmore Hayes sat on the edge of her unmade bed and wadded her apron tail, then smoothed it across her thighs with trembling hands, then bunched it up again as a tear made its slow way down a pale cheek to drip off her jaw onto the damp clump of fabric in her lap.

Chapter Twenty-Three

Nearly a month passed before Will made it back to the ranch. He and his cowboys pushed the herd to summer grazing lands atop Black Mesa and scattered them through the high-country meadows where plentiful grass was available as well as water in streams and ponds. Four men stayed behind in pairs to ride herd on the cattle, occupying isolated line shacks to be supplied periodically by camp tenders sent out from the ranch.

Clint Shipley met him at the Rafter 7 the moment he rode in.

"Will, come with me up to the house. The old man wants a word."

"Sure enough, Clint. Soon as I tend to my horse."

"Leave it. The wrangler'll take care of it."

Will tried not to trip over his jaw as they made their way to the ranch house. Leaving a horse untended, or leaving the job to another, violated every tenet of cowboy etiquette. Whatever awaited him at the house must be important.

Clint led Will to the back door, through the kitchen, down a hallway, and into a front room where sat Sam

Ballard, buttressed up by pillows with his left leg propped on the arm of the settee.

"Sit, Will, please," he said, gesturing toward a Windsor chair within his line of sight. "I've got news for you, and I fear it's not good."

"I'll stand, Sir, if you don't mind."

Ballard waded into the tale of the attack in Antler Canyon. Before a gun was fired, Will was seated in the chair, white-knuckled hands gripping the arms.

"I don't have any idea what got into old Longmore. But he was damn sure determined to tromple me to death. Weren't a thing I could do but shoot him. It's like he was crazy, out of his head."

Will's voice abandoned him.

Ballard said, "It pains me to say it, kid, but I don't feel bad at all about killing Jesse Longmore. It was him or me, simple as that."

He paused for a moment, studying Will, before continuing.

"Johnny, now, that's a whole 'nother thing," he said.

"Johnny? What about Johnny?"

"He was in the middle of it, trying to stop the old man. One of my cowboys—it don't matter which one, so don't ask—was coming to bail me out. He didn't know what was going on, just that I was in some kind of a jackpot, and he took a shot. He couldn't have done it if

227

he tried, but that bullet hit Johnny in the head and killed him before he had time to fall off his horse."

Ballard paused.

"I'm awful sorry about that, Will. But I don't see as how it could have turned out any different in the circumstances. Law looked into it and said the same thing. Ruled the killing of the old man justified, and the death of Johnny Longmore an unfortunate accident."

He waited for a response from Will, but there was none.

"I reckon you'll be wanting to get back to the Fishhook. Take your pick of horses from the saddle string. Clint's got your wages up through the end of the month. It ain't much, but I hope it helps some."

After roping out and saddling a horse, Will found his voice just before leaving.

"One question, Clint," he said. "Why didn't somebody come for me?"

"We would have, Will. We offered to send a man right away. But Emma, she said not to. We thought it best to honor her wishes."

All the way to the Fishhook, Will worried over that one. That Emma shunned him made no sense, unless her father had finally succeeded in poisoning her against him. But he did not believe Johnny would stand by and see that happen.

Still, something had Emma upset where he was concerned. And he intended to find out what, and why.

He was not long finding out. He had no sooner ridden into the yard at Fishhook headquarters when Emma stepped onto the porch of the house he should be living in; a house he was seeing finished for the first time.

"How dare you!" she shouted at Will. "How dare you come here! Get out! Get out now!"

For the second time in as many days, Will's voice abandoned him. He could only sit and watch as Emma, wringing her hands in her apron, turned her back on him and went into the house.

Getting out was the last thing he intended to do, so he unsaddled and turned his tired mount into the horse pasture and hauled his bedroll to the bunkhouse. He was surprised to find the outfits of so many cowboys there—most of them should be gone by now, out at the line camps drifting the herds on their summer ranges. Tonight, he would find out why they were here, and not there.

In the meantime, he needed answers of a different sort so he crossed the yard to the ranch house to talk to the cook.

"Wilson Hayes, as I live and breathe!" she said when he darkened the door of her kitchen. She abandoned her batch of biscuit dough, slapped the flour from her hands and threw them around his neck.

"Thank God you're here. This place has been at a standstill ever since . . . Well, you know," she said, releasing her hold and mopping tears with her apron. "Thank God you're here!"

"Emma seems to feel different about that."

"Oh, Will, that girl has been beside herself since you left. Her heart's been badly broken. And now with Mister Longmore and Johnny killed . . . "

"What's that got to do with me?"

"She thinks you were tied up in it, Will. She thinks you had some part in those killings."

"That can't be! I wasn't anywhere near the place— hell, I was way out on Black Mesa, or on the way there. I didn't even know it happened till day before yesterday! I had nothing to do with it."

"I know that. The sheriff knows it. But the girl won't listen to sense. Even Mister Ballard and that foreman of his said so, but it just don't seem to get through to her. Only thing I can think of is that Mister Longmore—God rest his soul—caused enough doubt about you that the shock of it all put the idea in her mind."

Will thought it over for a few minutes.

Finally, "Thank you, ma'am. I don't get it, but I see what you mean. I guess I might as well be on my way.

Maybe I can get back on at the Rafter 7. Maybe I oughta just quit the country altogether."

The cook set into slicing bread and cold roast beef, sawing away like she was felling a tree.

"Oh, no, Will! You mustn't!" she said. "You can't! Emma will come to her senses sooner or later. Besides that, the Fishhook needs you. Like I said, this place is at a standstill. With no one to tell them what to do, those fool cowboys don't know what to do. You can't leave, Will—you've got to set this place to rights."

"Well, I don't know . . . "

"Well I do. You've got to stay," she said as she stacked beef on bread and bread on beef. "And don't worry about Emma. She'll be over here soon to help with supper and I'll convince her the Fishhook needs you, even if she thinks she doesn't. Meantime, you best lay low until supper time. Here," she said, handing him the thick sandwich. "You look a mite peckish. This'll hold you over until then."

Will went out the back door and followed the path behind the house up to the spring. He sat on the log he and Emma had so often occupied. The trees were green with fresh leaves, the birds in full-throated song, the spring water sparkled in the sunlight. But, somehow, none of it registered with Will. The calm he usually found there was missing.

231

When the Fishhook hands started drifting into the bunkhouse late in the afternoon, they found Will there to greet them. He questioned them about the state of things on the ranch and found out the cook wasn't far from wrong in her assessment.

Johnny had taken back the ranch foreman's duties when Will left, so, with his death, and that of the rancher, no one on the Fishhook felt in a position to assume authority, and Emma was in no condition to make decisions. The cowboys who remained thought it best to maintain the status quo and hold the cow herds in the lowlands since no one could agree on how many cattle to move where.

"You know, boys, them cattle are going to need that feed come fall and winter. That's why we move them to the mountains in summer."

"Well of course we know it, Will! We ain't stupid," one of the cowboys said. "But there's a difference between knowing why and knowing how. Hell, we damn near go to our guns every time we try to work it out. Ever'body's got different ideas and none of them's the same."

Will gathered reports from the hands on the location of the herds. He noted the number of cowboys available and gathered information about their knowledge of the outlying camps and distant ranges.

"Let's go to supper," Will finally said. "Cook's probably wondering what's become of us. By morning, I'll have it all worked out so roll up your sougans and be ready to ride. There still somebody here taking care of the stores?"

"Yeah, ol' Tommy O'Shannon's still around. But there ain't much left in the storeroom. No one's ordered supplies since Johnny went and got himself killed."

Will lined out one of the cowboys to work with O'Shannon to put together camp outfits in the night. "Get on it right after supper."

The evening meal came off without incident. The first thing he noticed was how much he had missed the chuck at the Fishhook. Next thing he noticed was the absence of Emma. She confined herself to the kitchen throughout the meal and the cleanup to avoid contact with Will.

After supper, as Will sat at the Longmore desk figuring out how and where to distribute the Fishhook herds and hands, the cook came in with fresh coffee.

"I've convinced Emma she needs you—well, that the ranch needs you. She's not happy about it, but she'll accept your presence here so long as you steer clear of her. It's not much, but it's a start."

"I guess that means I won't be living in our house."

The cook laughed. "Believe me, Will boy, you wouldn't want to. That house is nothing but an empty shell. Fire's only been laid in one fireplace in that house since the roof went on. But you don't belong in the bunkhouse, so you'd best stay here at the house. Take your pick of rooms—except my own, of course," she said with a wink.

Will sorted out the summer range arrangements then started looking through the desk, opening ledger and account books. The columns and rows of numbers made no more sense to him than a swarm of bees around a honey tree. There was a payroll book, listing the names of Fishhook hands over the years and payments to them, with occasional deductions for items from the company store. There were receipt books for payments from cattle buyers, books of checks for various Longmore enterprises, account books related to the town businesses, and so much other evidence of his newfound and unwanted responsibilities that his stomach churned.

In the quiet of the night, he wandered the house. It almost seemed he'd never left, so little had changed. The room he'd shared with Emma was the logical choice for him to bunk in, but that did not seem right, somehow. Longmore's old room, with the old man's imprint smothering every inch, lacked appeal.

That left Johnny's room. Will had visited the room, of course, but only briefly. He looked around, impressed, but not surprised, with the tidiness of the place. But it was the books that captivated him. They covered two entire walls of the room, filling floor-to-ceiling shelves. The bindings displayed countless colors, the books in sizes from short to tall, thick to thin. There must be some rhyme and reason to their arrangement, but Will could not see it.

He pulled a book from a shelf, a slender volume with marbled covers and cloth binding. He thumbed the pages, recognizing what was within as poetry. He found the title page and read, *Household Poems* by Henry W. Longfellow. Will balanced the spine in his palm and the book fell open to a poem titled "A Psalm of Life." In the margin next to one of the stanzas was an X in light pencil.

Johnny's voice rang in his ears as he read, "In the world's broad field of battle, / in the bivouac of Life / Be not like dumb, driven cattle! / Be a hero in the strife!"

Chapter Twenty-Four

Hat in hand, Will stood on the porch of Emma's house, wiping nothing off one boot and then the other on the rag rug in front of the door. After his second knock, just a moment before the third, she opened the door. She said nothing, only eyed him warily.

"Emma, we've got to talk."

"I can't imagine why. There's nothing you can say that I want to hear."

"You don't know that, if I ain't said it yet."

No reply.

"It ain't us I want to talk about Emma, much as I'd like to. We need to talk about the ranch."

She laughed, but without mirth. "The ranch. Well isn't that rich, Will. Papa always said the ranch is what you wanted. Now I guess you've got it."

Will could hardly speak. "Emma," he said. "Emma. You know that ain't so. I know that's what your Pa thought, but it ain't so. And you know it."

She stared.

"Let's not get into that now," Will said. "There's things to be done. Things we've got to decide."

She stared. Just before Will was ready to walk away, she stepped aside and said, "Well, I guess you may as well come in, then."

Will's boots echoed on the bare floor, ricocheted off the bare walls, and bounced off the bare ceiling.

"I'd offer you a chair, but, as you see, I don't have one."

Emma sat on the fireplace's hearthstone and wadded the front of her apron in her hands. Will squatted and leaned against a wall.

"So what are we going to do, Emma?"

"About what?"

"Like I said. This ranch."

"I don't know thing one about the ranch. Papa never, ever, said anything at all about the Fishhook, other than supper-table talk. And I missed most of that helping out in the kitchen. Johnny, he offered to teach me the books," she said, lifting her apron to dab at her eyes. "But I never got around to letting him. What about you, Will? You were the foreman."

"That's different. I can take care of the cattle and hire the hands and such. I reckon I could even get the cattle to market and get a fair price, come to that. But I cracked open some of them account books in the desk, and I couldn't make hide nor hair out of any of it."

Will sat the rest of the way down, stretching his legs flat on the floor.

"Then there's laying in supplies, dealing with the payroll. And those businesses in town your Pa owned—I don't even know what all they are, let alone what needs to be done about them."

"Don't ask me. I couldn't help you if I wanted to."

Will shook his head. "Something's got be done, Emma. This ranch ain't going to run itself."

Emma crushed and wadded the apron in her lap as she tried to think. "I just don't know," she finally said. "The only thing I can think of is to talk to the bank in Ballard Station. Go see Glen. I know that's who Papa dealt with lately at the bank. Maybe he can help."

"Sounds good to me. Worth a try, anyhow. Will you come with me?"

"No."

"Aw, c'mon, Emma. The Fishhook is yours. All that stuff in town, too. It's all yours. You ought to be in on it. I sure can't be making decisions for you—not the way you're feeling about me."

"You're going to have to, Will. I just can't deal with it right now."

*****

Before breakfast, Will came to the kitchen looking for his wife.

"The buckboard's all hitched up, Emma. Why don't you come to town with me?"

"No, Will, I won't."

"C'mon, Emma. If you're worried about being alone with me, Tommy O'Shannon's coming along to pick up supplies."

"I know. He was in here a while ago getting a list from cook. Like I told you, I just can't deal with it all right now."

"Somebody's got to deal with it. And it's your ranch."

Emma said nothing.

Will put on his hat and said, "We'll be pulling out right after breakfast if you change your mind."

With the ledgers and account books in the wagon, packed in one of the many empty whiskey crates stacked behind the ranch house, Will and Tommy rattled their way to Ballard Station. O'Shannon's voice accompanied every creaky turn of the wheels. His history with the Fishhook was a long one, starting out as a cowboy until too old and stove up, as horse wrangler for a time until the limited physical demands of that job became too great, then working as swamper and chore boy and keeping the company stores and supplies in order.

He regaled Will with tales of Jesse Longmore in his younger days, when he'd been a hand that everyone respected. "Jesse, he was a ranahan if ever there was one. Horse sense and cow sense both, he had. A mite rough, but he got the job done. Expected the same of every man who rode for him.

"The Fishhook was still a ragtag outfit when I showed up. But Jesse, he determined to make something of himself and let nothing stand in the way. Nor nobody. He rode roughshod over the homesteaders and nesters who came along, he did. Those he couldn't pay off he ran off. Bought up neighboring spreads by hook or by crook. No matter how much he got, he always wanted more. Like he couldn't resist it. Took hold of him and wouldn't let go, just like the whiskey did.

"Before he fell into the whiskey barrel, he was tough and determined; still and all, you could always figure him out. But then when he got to drinking so much, all bets were off. It pained me to see it, I'll tell you. Watching that man waste away was a hard thing. And now he's gone."

Will asked about the children—Johnny, and Emma.

Tommy started that story with the late Missus Longmore. To hear him tell it, the sun rose and set on the woman. She was smart and beautiful and tough enough to withstand the force of Longmore. The rough edges came off the ranch, if not her husband—although, according to Tommy, she smoothed him out considerably as well. The people who worked for Longmore, even those who worked against him, got fair treatment while she lived. Her financial smarts first solidified the family holdings then extended them.

The children only added to her determination. She wanted them to have everything—not just a successful ranching empire, but all the advantages money could provide in the larger world. Longmore believed she coddled young Johnny too much, keeping him at his studies when he thought the boy ought to be at work on the ranch. But, along with his mother's smarts, Johnny inherited his father's physical gifts and made a good hand without trying too hard or caring much about it. Had his mother lived, O'Shannon believed Johnny would have left the Fishhook to attend a college, and maybe live a different kind of life in a city.

Emma came along later, so did not benefit as much from her mother's influence. She started life as a rough and tumble tomboy, riding before she could walk and preferring the company of cowboys to dolls or school-books or anything else. But, after the wagon accident that caused her mother's death, Longmore all but locked her away in a misguided effort to keep her safe. She had something of her mother's strong will, but, Tommy believed, much of it was willed out of her, or at least suppressed, by Longmore's smothering protectiveness.

"I wish you could have known Missus Longmore. Sure, and I wish you could have known Jesse before the drink got him. You'd have liked him—and I think he'd have liked you, then. It was but a husk of the man that you met. Sad, it was. I knew Jesse Longmore as long as I've known any man, and never did I see one slip away as he did. His will. His strength. His smarts. His judgment. All washed away in a sea of whiskey." Tommy pulled a hanky from his pocket and mopped his eyes before they could overflow.

Will stepped off the buckboard in front of the bank and reached over the sideboard to heft out the box of books, arranging with Tommy to rendezvous at the Elkhorn Saloon when the work was finished. He hauled the whiskey box into the bank and plopped it on the counter in front of a barred window.

"Can I help you?" the startled clerk asked from his cage.

"I need to see someone named Glen."

"One moment, please."

The clerk used a key tethered to his vest like a watch fob to open the door that let him out of the enclosure that held the vault and cash drawer, and locked it behind him. Across the small lobby were two offices, walled in with wood on the bottom and glass panes on top to allow the occupants to watch activity in the bank. The clerk knocked at the door of the smaller room and the man sitting inside behind a desk looked up and waved him in. The sign on the door read Glen Olson, Vice President.

Will watched the clerk and the man he assumed to be Olson talk, look at him, then talk some more. As the clerk turned to leave, the vice president stood and walked around the desk, tugging the lapels of the coat of his business suit.

"Mister Olson will see you now," the clerk said, with a nod of his head toward the office door.

Will lugged the box with him. The man met him at the door and automatically extended an arm for a handshake. Will looked at Olson, looked at the extended hand, looked down at the box he carried, looked back at Olson.

"Oh, my goodness," Olson said. "I am sorry. Come in, please. I see you are in no position to be shaking hands. Please, take a seat."

The banker grimaced when the whiskey box lit on his tidy desk with a clump. Will reached across for the delayed handshake, then sat in one of the matched pair of upholstered chairs facing the desk. He looked around the office, noting that while the furnishings and fixtures were fancier than he was accustomed to, they were far from ostentatious. Olson, in his vest and suit coat and necktie, looked to be maybe thirty-five years old, but it could be his thinning hair and high forehead added years that weren't there. He compensated for the tonsorial sparseness up top with muttonchop whiskers below.

He sat, unbuttoned his suit coat, tugged the tails of his vest over his paunch, and said, "I don't believe I have had the pleasure."

"My name is Wilson Hayes."

Contempt flashed across the banker's face, but Olson subdued it in an instant, for, he realized, this common-looking cowboy across from him was, in some sense, his employer. He could not let pent-up jealousy—for he once had designs on the young Emma Longmore—endanger his position at the bank owned by the late Jesse Longmore, and now, he assumed, by Emma and this, her husband.

"Ah, yes, Mister Hayes. I know, of course, who you are. It is a pleasure, finally, to meet you. How may I be of service?"

Will reached out and pushed the box toward Olson. "This stuff. I don't know a thing about it. I looked it all over and it don't make a lick of sense to me."

One by one, Olson took the books from the box, opened each, glanced through it, and set it aside. Most went into one pile on the corner of the desk, he stacked two big green-backed ledger books in the center.

"These, we won't concern ourselves with at present," Olson said of the stack on the corner. "They are, of course, important. But, less so than these. These are the operating ledgers for the Fishhook," he said, separating the wide books and opening them across the desk.

"Basic double-entry bookkeeping is what you have here, Mister Hayes. This ledger lists the ranch's income and assets, this one records the expenses and liabilities."

"I'm with you, so far. At least the part about income and expenses."

"Good. Now, it all comes down to debits and credits. Every financial transaction is both a debit and a credit, and is entered in the appropriate ledger as such. Debit the assets and credit the expenses with a sale, for instance, or debit the expenses and credit the assets with a purchase. That way, it all adds up and the books balance."

Olson could see he had lost Will somewhere along the way. For the next hour, he walked Will through bookkeeping one step at a time, using Fishhook ledger entries as examples, tracking transactions from one account to another, showing how it all equaled out on the bottom line, assets and income balanced by expenses and liabilities.

"My head's swimming, Mister Olson," Will said. "It just don't make sense to me. Especially this balancing business. Seems to me you don't want things to balance out—you want to come out ahead on income side."

The banker thought it over for a minute, decided to let it rest for the time being. "Let's not worry about it for now. As for these other things . . . "

For another hour, Glen Olson led Wilson Hayes through the Longmore family's many holdings. The Fishhook, of course. The bank, and shared ownership of another bank elsewhere. The mercantile. Other town businesses and real estate, rentals and partnerships. He explained the cash on hand, investments in stocks and bonds, and funds on deposit in banks in Salt Lake City, Denver, Kansas City, St. Louis, Chicago, and New York.

"Hell's bells, Mister Olson, I never imagined it was all so complicated. Or that there was so much of it. I can see I'm in way over my head here."

Olson pursed his lips and tapped the fingernails of one hand on the desktop. "What about Emma? She could help."

"I'm afraid she ain't interested in this or much of anything else just now. She may come out of it, but it'll take a while. It hit her pretty hard when her Pa ran me off. Then when him and Johnny got killed, well, that was her whole family gone, just like that. And she's taken a notion that I was tied up in the killings somehow, so she wants no part of me."

Will paused to gather his thoughts.

"If I could just keep this all from falling apart till we figure out what to do—that's all I want for now. Once Emma comes around, then we can decide on the future."

The banker stood, tugged the tails of his vest, fastened a button on the suit coat, and pulled the lapels into place. He walked past Will and stared through the window glass into the bank proper.

"Since I've been here in Ballard Station," he said, "Johnny has been keeping the books. He was a smart fellow, and had a head for it. But before that, before Johnny grew up enough to do it, we took care of everything here at the bank. Mister Longmore, he didn't care for the details, you see. He knew, better than most, how to make money, but he had no head for figures and details drove him to distraction."

He turned, placed a hand on Will's shoulder. "We can do the same for you. For the time being—or for as long as you like. You concentrate on running the ranch, and we'll deal with the money. Just save all your receipts, bills of sale, and write down everything that comes in or goes out."

Will stood, plopped his hat on his head with a bit of a grin, and extended his hand. "I sure do thank you, Mister Olson."

Olson grasped the handshake and said, "Please, call me Glen. And don't thank me—this is, after all, your bank. We'll put up a sign and sell sausages if that's what you want us to do."

Will walked out the office door and found Tommy O'Shannon slouched on a sofa in the lobby, fast asleep and snoring softly.

"Tommy!" Will said, jostling his shoulder. "Wake up! What are you doing here? I thought we were going to meet up at the saloon."

Knuckling the sleep out of both eyes, Tommy shook his head to clear the cobwebs and said, "I stayed there long as I could, Will. Drank all the beer I could hold without embarrassing myself. Thought I'd may as well wait here."

"Hell, Tommy, I never realized how late it was. I'm awful sorry. Let's get some supper and get back to the ranch. We'll be late getting there."

"I hope you won't mind stopping along the way now and again," the old man said. "I ain't drained off all I took in yet. Gotta keep things balanced, you know."

Chapter Twenty-Five

Before the year was out, Will Hayes had settled into his role as master of the Fishhook and all the Longmore holdings. He built a new livery stable and wagon yard in Ballard Station, erected storefronts on vacant properties and rented the space to merchants and artisans, and expanded the shipping pens at the rail yard.

And that, he believed was just the beginning. He expanded the ranching operations as well, and intended to enlarge the empire.

The Fishhook herds were thriving, and cattle markets were strong. A controlled breeding program for ranch horses improved the saddle stock, and demand for the quality mounts throughout the region brought additional income. He brought in a few Hereford bulls and a bunch of brood cows and started a purebred herd he imagined would pay off one day.

"Glen, how is our cash situation?" he asked the banker one day. His relationship with Glen Olson had solidified since the two men started working together managing the family enterprises. Not only was Olson a good money manager, he had a good head for business that Will recognized and came to rely on. Between his aggressive intentions and Olson's financial acumen, the partnership proved a profitable one.

"We're in fine shape, Will. What do you have in mind?"

"I'm thinking we could use more rangeland. With cattle prices the way they are, running more cows seems to make sense."

Olson mulled it over for a moment. "As I said, money is no problem. But land—now, that's another matter. Between you and Sam Ballard, you already control most of the best range in the valley. And the few other places worth owning, well, you know as well as I do that those ranchers aren't inclined to part with their holdings. So, you must have something up your sleeve."

"You know, Glen, there's some mighty fine range over in Cane Valley. I've been all over most of that country, and on the far side of the valley there are some good streams comin' out of the mountains that water a lot of country. Good graze, and plenty of hay meadows for winter feed if you need it."

"Sounds good. But how would you manage it? In the valley here, and in town, you can keep a pretty close eye on things."

"True enough. But it ain't all that far, if it comes to it. Train'll take you to Rio Largo quick enough. Anyhow, here's what I been thinkin' about. Sam Ballard's got a man on the Rafter 7 name of Clint Shipley. He's foreman out there, but from my time workin' for him I know he does a lot more than that for Ballard. Pretty steady man, in my estimation. If we could put together a few of them small ranches over there into a good-size spread, we might could get Shipley to run the place for us—maybe even make him a partner."

"I know Clint. I agree with your estimation of him. If you can get him he would be a good man to have. But I would advise against a partnership—pay him whatever wage you have to, even share the profits, but don't relinquish control."

"Good point. I guess we can tie that calf once we get it roped. I'll talk to Emma then take a ride over there and have a look around one of these days."

While the ardor she once felt for Will had not returned, Emma had, after a time, made her peace with him and their marriage. The house built for them sat empty, as they decided it more practical to live in the main ranch house. They gutted Longmore's old room and completely refurbished and refurnished it so it bore no resemblance or held any remembrance of its previous occupant. While she was at it, Emma redid the front room and, according to cook's recommendations, added conveniences to the kitchen. Emma's old room needed only minor adjustments to ready it for the baby on the way.

As for their intended home, Emma suggested they find a family man to handle day-to-day operations on the Fishhook once Will's other responsibilities grew beyond his ability to give the ranch the attention it deserved. She thought it would be good to have other children on the place, and a nice home would help attract the right kind of people. Will concurred, but told himself it would be a good long time, if ever, before he would be willing to relinquish his duties on the Fishhook. At least not in any way that would weaken his control.

"Emma, what would you think of gettin' more cattle? Me and Glen, we talked it over and think it might be the thing to do."

"Good heavens, Will, how many cows do we need? As it is, you can hardly take a walk around here without wiping their droppings off your shoes."

Will laughed. "With the market the way it is, it's a shame not to have more yearlings to ship," he said. "But you're right about havin' room for them. We'd have to have more land."

"I don't know where you're going to find it. Between Papa and Sam Ballard, everything hereabouts is spoken for."

"We're thinkin' Cane Valley. There's some mighty pretty country over there, and I think we can buy out some of those ranchers and put together a nice outfit. Of course, we'd have to hire someone to run it, but we figure we can do that."

"Sounds like you and Glen have it all worked out."

"No, Emma, it ain't like that. We just talked it over, is all. I've give it a good deal of thought, though, and I'm for it. What do you think?"

"Does it matter, Will? Do you and Glen care what I think?"

"Sure we do. Leastways I do. Whether Glen cares or not don't matter. He'll do what he's told."

"That's Glen, all right. Sometimes I think he'd make you a better wife than I do."

"Now, Emma, don't you be gettin' down on Glen. He ain't no ball of fire, that's for sure, but he's forgot more about dealin' with money than I'll ever know. Besides, he's been loyal to us and his advice is always good. Fact that he's tame as an old milk cow is just so much the better, to my way of thinkin'—less likely to be stickin' his fingers in the pie, that way."

"I suppose you're right, Will. I just worry that you're getting greedy like Papa did. He thought he was doing it for the family, but it was just to satisfy his lust for power. Don't be that way, Will."

"Not a chance, Emma. So, what do you say about my takin' a trip to Cane Valley?"

"Go ahead, if you—and Glen—think it best."

*****

The last time Will left the Fishhook for Cane Valley, he slipped out the back door and took an out-of-the-way horseback route over the mountains. This time, saddle in hand instead of on a horse, he boarded a passenger coach in Ballard Station with a ticket for Rio Largo.

As soon as he stepped off the train, he headed for the livery stable and bargained for a likely looking saddle horse. A brief stop at a grocer's shop to stuff his saddle-bags with camp grub, and he rode off along the river road into the expanse of the valley. The creeks and streams out of the mountains offered the only respite from the aridity of Cane Valley. Even the land along the river had nothing to offer, as the Rio Largo flowed in a shallow and rocky gorge for most of its run through the valley.

Three or four miles out of town he left the road and angled off toward the mountains, his destination a canyon that poured a spring-fed stream, called Cotton-wood Creek, into the valley. The wagon road would have taken him to a lane that served the ranches along the watercourse, but his plan was to start at the upstream homestead and work his way downstream.

Beginner's luck was with Will. The ranch at the can-yon's mouth was an old homestead still operated by the original owner, who was also the first settler on that watershed. Ray Barlow and his wife, Allie, were getting up in age and thinking about living out their years back in Iowa, their home country before moving west. Their one child, a daughter, was long since married and moved away to California and had no interest in the ranch, so an offer on the place was welcome.

The old rancher spent the next day showing Will around the place. The Box-B was a prosperous ranch, but Barlow made no attempt to oversell it. In fact, he pointed out a number of places where improvements were needed that he had never got around to making. Will questioned him about the number of cattle the ranch could support, free range for summer grazing, water rights, and other details of the operation.

After supper, Will and Ray sat at the kitchen table coming to terms, then drafted and signed a bill of sale, agreeing to meet later on at the courthouse in Rio Largo to officially record the transaction.

He was now owner of the Box-B ranch and its herd of cattle—a foothold in Cane Valley and the first step in his plan to spread the Fishhook empire.

The reception at his next stop wasn't nearly as satisfying.

Downstream from the Barlow place, the Diamond Bar ranch spread across the valley from its limited frontage on Cottonwood Creek. With restricted access to the stream, the Diamond Bar's range started in the lush creek-bottom meadows but soon dried out in the brush away from the stream.

Where Ray and Allie Barlow prospered, the occupant of the Diamond Bar scratched and scrounged for every penny. He envied the Box-B's access to the water, guaranteed by priority rights, and resented that it consigned him to a tenuous and limited existence. When Barlow dammed up most of the stream flow to flood hay meadows, it left barely enough water for Diamond Bar stock and further parched the land. The result was an uncomfortable coexistence, punctuated by frequent arguments and occasional threats.

Will sat horseback and listened to a long and angry tirade on the subject from the owner of the Diamond Bar, found resetting posts at pole corrals near the Rio Largo road. "You know, Mister, you can make all those problems go away if you sell the place to me," Will said.

"To hell with you. You come prancing in here with your pockets full of money thinking I'll give up on all the years of work I've put into this place just to please you. Well, pard, it ain't gonna happen. I ain't old and give-out like Ray Barlow. I'm bound to make a go of the Diamond Bar, and if that means having you for a neighbor, well, I guess that's just one more pain in the ass I'll have to put up with."

"Suit yourself," Will said. "But we'll be burning our brand on the Box-B herd before long, and I think you'll find that Fishhook cattle drink a hell of a lot more water than Ray's ever did."

The man whipped up the shovel he leaned on, pointed the blade at Will and stepped toward him—but he stopped short at the sight of a pistol barrel looking back at him.

"You sonofabitch," he said.

"That's no way to talk to your neighbor," Will said, sliding the revolver back into the holster on his hip. "A man who can't get along with his neighbors ought to think about moving on. You think on it—and when you've made up your mind, we'll talk business."

*****

Will followed essentially the same plan as he followed each stream. He made a few deals, but his success was limited, much as he expected. Once the Fishhook was established here, it would become easier to wield his influence and acquire the properties they wanted most, fill in critical pieces as they could, and pick off the holdouts one by one over time.

One way or another, sooner or later, the land he wanted would be his.

At the upper reaches of the valley, the Rio Largo forked. The main branch entered the valley from a gap it cut through the rugged mountains from its origins at a lake in the neighboring valley. But the branch that gave this valley its name, Cane Creek, had its headwaters in a crystal spring tucked into the end of a steep-walled box canyon in the corner of the valley. Cane Canyon was too small to support a sizeable operation, but it was home to Cane Creek ranch, a homestead of similar vintage to the Box-B.

Will rode into the canyon not knowing what to expect and was immediately taken with the beauty of the place. It reminded him of the spring in the grove at Fishhook headquarters writ large. Cane Creek meandered along the canyon floor, shaded by cottonwoods and lined with willows. Thick grass carpeted the rest of the canyon bottom, except where the occasional clump of trees stood, mixtures of aspen and pines. Will sensed the temperature had dropped a good five degrees since entering the canyon, where the walls limited the effects of the sun, and water and shade further moderated the heat.

A half mile or so into the canyon, he came upon a cowboy in pursuit of a steer. The rider handily threw a loop around the critter's horns, spurred his horse on past the steer, dropped his slack around its hip then hurried off at an angle, tripping and tumbling the steer. Will watched the cowboy bail out of the saddle and follow the taut lariat to the stunned steer while yanking a short length of rope from his waistband, which he used to bind together one front and both hind legs of the animal while the well-trained horse kept the lariat tight.

Riding closer, Will ground tied his horse and walked over to the downed steer. "Lend you a hand, cowboy?" he said to the young man—no more than twenty years old, by Will's estimate.

The cowboy looked him over, said, "Sure. You look like a man who knows his way around a cow. This steer, he's got lumpy jaw. Must have got a thorn with his feed or something. Help me turn him over."

Once the steer was rolled, Will knelt with one knee on its neck and the other on its ribs, and grabbed the shank of the untied foreleg and bent it back to keep it from thrashing around. The young cowboy walked to his horse and came back with a corked bottle from his saddlebags. Pulling a jackknife from his pocket, he held the steer's muzzle to the ground with one hand while slicing across the abscess with the knife blade.

"Looks like you got it about right," Will said. "Thing was so tight it was about to pop."

With both hands, the cowboy worked around the lump, squeezing blood and stinking yellow pus from the wound. Once all the gunk was out and the lump deflated, he shook and uncorked the bottle, spread the incision, and doused the hole with the liquid. From the smell, Will recognized it as carbolic acid.

"We'll see if that takes. I'll keep an eye on him. If it comes back worse and he gets to where he can't eat, he'll end up in the kitchen," the cowboy said as he wiped his hands back and forth on the grass.

Will pulled slack in the lariat and pulled it off the steer's horns then untied the pigging string from its legs. He stood, helped the steer up by lifting its tail, then swatted it on the hip with his hat for good measure. It ran off, shaking its head. Within a matter of minutes, it would forget the whole affair.

"C'mon over here," the cowboy said, coiling his lasso rope as he led his horse the short distance to Cane Creek. Will followed. Will and the cowboy washed their hands in the clear stream, and the young man offered one, still dripping, for a handshake. "Ira Wright," he said.

"Will Hayes. Pleased to make your acquaintance."

The men sat in the shade of trees along the stream and talked for more than an hour.

"This place was homesteaded by my granddad," Ira said. "But my dad, he didn't stick. He went for the mines. Started at the coal mine down the valley, then went for hard-rock mines. Made a pile, first running a pick and shovel, then working his way up till he was running the mines. Moved all over the place, from one mining town to another, always going for a bigger share of the profits.

"Me, I liked this place, so I spent as much time here as the folks would let me. When granddad died last year, he left the place to me in his will, along with more money than anyone knew he had. So me and the wife, I guess this is our home now."

The ranch was big enough to provide a living but not much more, he said, but with the ranch free and clear and his granddad's money, he was pretty well fixed. Still, he ran the Cane Creek ranch with an eye to turning a profit, so Ira mollycoddled the small herd to get the most out of them. But when it came to a choice of doing something to make more money or doing things "right," Ira favored the latter.

Will broached the idea of a sale, but Ira declined to discuss it. "I love this place. And I love cowboying. Fact that it's small enough I can take care of it pretty much on my own makes it about the ideal situation, far as I'm concerned."

Asked about the possibility of going to work for the Fishhook as cow boss in Cane Valley, or some other situation, he politely refused that idea as well. "If you understood my position here—and I think you do—you'd understand the appeal of doing as I damn well please, not having to answer to nothing or nobody."

"I can see it, all right," Will said. "But I'm a selfish man and can see where you'd be good for the Fishhook. So you'll have to excuse my asking. And expect that I'll ask again. And be warned—most of the time, I get what I want."

The young cowboy laughed, got to his feet, and dusted off the seat of his pants. "Come on up to the house for dinner, why don't you. It's just another mile or so up the canyon. You'll see the rest of the place and meet Betty."

"Thanks, but not today. I got some business to wrap up in Rio Largo, then I need to get back over the mountains to the Fishhook. See what's become of the place since I been gone," Will said as he swung into the saddle. "You haven't seen the last of me, Ira Wright."

"I sure hope not, Will. You're welcome here anytime."

Once out in Cane Valley proper, Will spurred his horse into a long trot on the road to Rio Largo. He topped a rise and rode up on two men sitting horseback in the middle of the road, waiting.

"Amos," Will said. "Blanco."

Chapter Twenty-Six

Amos Parker sat his horse as if he hadn't a care in the world, hands stacked on the saddle horn. Blanco looked a little less sure of the situation, his right hand resting on the butt of his holstered revolver. Will stopped with the horse's muzzles nearly touching, Blanco to his right and Parker to the left, no more than a yard between them.

"Been a while, Hayes," Parker said.

"That it has, Amos."

"Not long enough," Blanco said.

Will offered no response.

"So what have you been up to," Parker said, "now that you've left off killing my men?"

"Keepin' busy. Runnin' the Fishhook. One thing and another."

Amos sat. Blanco fidgeted. Even his horse was nervous, snorting and pawing at the road. After a long minute, Parker said, "Word is you're moving in on the ranchers here."

Will let that sit for a moment, then said, "I'm buying a few ranches, if that's what you mean. May be buying more."

"Now, Will, you know we don't allow that sort of thing in Cane Valley."

"What sort of thing is that?"

"Big outfits ridin' roughshod over the smaller ranches. I get paid to prevent that sort of thing."

Will laughed. "So you're still runnin' that shakedown operation? And you, Blanco, I guess that means you're still puttin' the arm on the ranchers you're supposed to be 'protecting.'"

Blanco glared at Will but did not utter a word.

"I've made a fair offer on every place that's interested me. Those that have sold to me are satisfied."

"Sure," Parker said. "But what about the others? The ones that don't want to sell?"

"Oh, I reckon they'll come around, sooner or later."

"You mean after you're starved them out, or cut off their water?"

Will said, "If it comes to that."

"It won't. I'll see to it."

"This don't concern you none, Amos. Oh, I can see how you'll miss out on this racket you've been runnin' all these years. That's small potatoes compared to what I intend to do in this valley. You're a resourceful fellow. You'll come up with somethin' else. But be warned—it won't be rustlin' Fishhook cattle. I didn't let you get away with it before, and you sure as hell won't get away with it here."

Parker arched his back and rotated his shoulders, as if loosening up for some anticipated activity. Blanco's gun hand twitched, his fingers tapped the grip of his pistol.

"You're forcing me into an uncomfortable position, Will. I hoped it wouldn't come to this. I always kind of liked you—"

Will drove his spurs into the belly of his horse, surprising the animal and, save himself, every other thing that drew breath in that place. The frightened horse reared slightly and lunged forward, between the other horses, knocking them aside.

At the same time, Will drew his Colt and lashed out at Blanco, landing the barrel on the side of his head and knocking him off his horse.

Parker tried to control his panicked horse and pull his pistol at the same time, not having much luck with either. He jerked the horse's head around and pulled down on Will, but before he could shoot, a bullet in the belly doubled him over, then a second in the head straightened him back up as it blew the back of his head out in a bloody spray. His eyes glassed over in an instant as his horse wheeled, spinning him off into the dust.

Will turned his attention to Blanco, on his knees on the wagon road, shaking his head to clear it and lifting his gun from its holster. Calming his horse, Will waited until the gun cleared leather and Blanco made a move in his direction, then he blew his chin and jaw apart with the third bullet to smoke his gun barrel, and followed it up with a fourth shot that shredded the outlaw's heart and lungs.

Blanco tipped over slowly and the last breath he drew was forced from his useless lungs by the impact of hitting the hard-packed road.

*****

The hitch rail in front of the marshal's office in Rio Largo was Will's first stop after the bloody encounter on the road. The sun was low in the sky and most other offices were locked up for the night, but the window showed a burning light inside and prompted him to stop. He walked through the door to find the marshal at his desk, busy with paperwork.

"Evening, Marshal. Remember me?"

"I sure do, Wilson Hayes. Seems like every time you show up around here it means more dead bodies to deal with."

"I'm afraid that's the case again."

"Who the hell did you kill this time?"

"Amos Parker. And one of the men that runs with him—the one they call Blanco."

"Well I'll be damned," the marshal said. "We've been trying to corner Parker for years. How'd you manage it?"

"Didn't have to. He cornered me. Tracked down my whereabouts, I guess, and met me on the road. It seemed clear enough them two intended to kill me. Instead, I got lucky."

The marshal laughed, "You are one lucky sonofa-bitch, Hayes. Maybe the luckiest man I ever met."

Will explained in detail how the fight started, how it ended, and everything in between. He told the marshal where to find the bodies. He'd had no desire to spend the afternoon tracking down their runaway saddle horses to haul the bodies to town, so, other than dragging them out of the way of anyone who might happen along the road, he left them lying.

"I don't see any need for me to ride clear the hell out there. Probably won't find anything to dispute what you're telling me. I'll send the coffin monger out with his wagon to fetch his latest customers. Probably just sittin' down to dinner about now, but he'll be back in time for breakfast if he don't dawdle."

The mention of food sounded pretty good to Will. He'd enjoyed a few home-cooked meals at some of the ranches he'd visited, but most of what he'd eaten of late had been dried or canned and cold. A hot supper at his favorite Rio Largo hash house would sit well, and a long night in a hotel bed would be a welcome change from a bedroll on the ground.

After supper, he stopped by the hotel across the street from the railroad depot, rented a room, and ordered up a hot bath, which he expected would be ready by the time he arranged board for his horse at the livery where he bought it. He would have it kept for future use, for his visits to Cane Valley would, for a time, likely merit having a mount ready at hand.

Come morning, Will kept folks scurrying at the courthouse getting the paperwork in order for transferring the deeds to the ranches now in the Fishhook fold, then he visited the bank and telegraph office to arrange the transfer of funds. He made it clear at both the bank and the courthouse that from now on, he would be a man to reckon with in Cane Valley.

After dinner, he met Ray Barlow and the other two ranchers he'd made deals with at the courthouse to sign the necessary stacks of papers, then sent the ranchers on their way with bank drafts in hand and smiles on their faces. Part of the deal required the sellers to continue operating the ranches until the Fishhook could bring in its own man to take over.

Will's next job was recruiting Clint Shipley for just that job, and he intended to get right to it.

Before nightfall, he stepped off the train in Ballard Station, slung his saddle over his shoulder, and headed for the hotel.

Next stop, the Elkhorn Saloon. With luck, someone from the Rafter 7 would be there to carry a message to Shipley. If not, it would be easy enough to recruit one of the town hangabouts for the job.

Come morning, Glen Olson and Will spent hours together in the bank, figuring out how to most efficiently integrate the Cane Valley ranches into Fishhook financial operations. After dinner, Will took up residence at a back table at the Elkhorn, anticipating a meeting with Clint Shipley. He nursed his beer for a considerable time past the appointed hour and ordered another.

"Sorry I'm late, Will," Shipley said when he finally walked through the batwing doors and made his way to the table. "Had a few things going on at the ranch I couldn't leave undone. Got here as soon as I could."

"Sit down, Clint. Have a beer," Will said, signaling the bartender to draw one. "Glad you could make it. I didn't give you much notice."

"Nor explanation. What is it you need to see me about?"

Shipley's beer landed on the table, and Will waited while he drained off a long swallow. "Damn, that's good. Now, why am I here?"

"How are things at the Rafter 7?"

"About as usual. Why? You take a sudden interest in the competition?"

"No, it ain't that. My interest is in you."

"How's that?"

"The Fishhook is expanding, Clint. We've bought up a few small ranches over in Cane Valley. Together, they make good-sized outfit. But we intend to buy more, try to grow some more, consolidate our holdings there."

"Sounds like you're getting ambitious, Will. Must be something in the water out there on the Fishhook. Sure as hell got into old Jesse's system. Looks like you've caught the same bug."

Will ignored the implication. "Do you know that country, Clint?"

"Cane Valley? No, not really. I been through there a time or two, buying cattle and what not, but not enough to say I know it. Why?"

"I'd like you to head up our operations over there."

"Me? Why me?"

"We need a good man, Clint. One who knows the cattle business. Knows how to handle men. Knows how to run a ranch from the bottom up. I can't think of anyone better than you."

Shipley sipped his beer in silence for a few minutes.

"You've sure as hell caught me by surprise. Truth is, I've never thought about any such thing. I been on the Rafter 7 with Sam Ballard so long it ain't never occurred to me to be anyplace else or work for anyone else."

Will sipped his beer for a few minutes, giving Shipley time to rearrange his mind and make room for the idea. Then, "We'd make it worth your while, Clint. Give you a freer hand than old Sam does. You'd be pretty much on your own over there."

Another pause, more sipping.

"What's the pay?"

Will sensed Clint was at least entertaining the possibility. "I don't know what Sam's paying you, but we'll better it. And we'll cut you in for a share of all the profits that come out of Cane Valley."

"You make a mighty persuasive offer, Will."

"Let me warn you, Clint, that it won't be no Sunday school picnic. You'll earn it. One of the outfits we bought, the Box B, is in prime condition. Another one's pretty good, but there's one that's in sorry shape. Corrals and pens and buildings were cobbled together in the beginning and ain't had much in the way of repair since.

Some of the range is worn down to dirt. But the place has good water and I think it'll come back with a little care."

"What about the cows?"

"Same deal. Two of the ranches have good herds, looks like they've sold off old cows about when they ought to, and kept good heifers for replacements. The ramshackle outfit—well, it's about like you'd expect. Too many cattle for the grass they've got, so none of 'em's in real good shape. Even at that, it looks like they've sold off most of the young stuff for years, and they're still carryin' cows so old they don't calve any-more."

Shipley walked over to the bar and brought back a beer for each of them. When he sat back down, Will said, "The cows will be the least of your problems. Some of those ranchers over there resented my showin' up. A few were downright hostile. If you take on the job, you won't be any too popular. And it's likely to get worse when we keep buyin' places. Especially from those who ain't inclined to sell right off."

"I figure I can deal with that. Went through it with Sam, when him and Jesse Longmore was buyin' up everything in sight around here. Sooner or later, most folks get used to the idea. Or, they don't. Either way, you have to keep shovin' grass into the cattle 'cause that's all that really matters."

Will laughed.

Clint leaned his elbows on the table, tipped his hat back with a forefinger, and furrowed his brow. Will let him think.

"What about cowboys? They got any good hands over there?"

"We'll need to hire some. The Box-B's got a pretty good crew. The other place, maybe one or two hands worth keeping. That rundown ranch, it's just the rancher and his boys there—still kids, really. They won't stick around. Wouldn't want them to. Too many bad habits."

Clint leaned back and pulled his hat brim down. Reached out for his glass and drained the beer. "Let me think about it, Will. When do you need to know?"

"The sooner the better—but take what time you need." Will finished his beer. "What about Sam?"

"Oh, he'll be mad as hell if I quit. But I won't worry about that. He'd sure as hell get rid of me in a hurry if he thought it to his advantage."

"Go see Glen over at the bank when you want to talk money. Send word out to the Fishhook when you're ready to sign on."

Clint stood and leaned across the table to shake hands, thought better of it, and withdrew the offer.

Will knitted his eyebrows.

"Too early for that, I guess," Clint said. Ought not be shakin' hands till there's reason for it."

Deciding it was still early enough to make the Fishhook in time for bed, Will put together a sandwich from the Elkhorn's flyblown free lunch counter, fetched his horse from the fancy new livery stable he'd put up, and started up the road.

Chapter Twenty-Seven

Will woke up alone in the morning. He was not accustomed to seeing the sun filtering through the bedroom window upon arising, but he had got into the Fishhook late after a long ride home from Ballard Station.

Breakfast was long since gone when he made it to the kitchen, but cook had kept the gravy warm, and while she fried bacon he split a pair of biscuits and smothered them in the gravy. Emma, heavy with child, sat in the kitchen fanning herself with a tin plate.

After a second mug of blistering coffee, Will headed out to the yard to see what his hands had been up to in his absence. Most of the cowboys were out at the Fishhook's line camps loose herding the cattle on summer ranges, but there was still activity at headquarters with preparations getting under way for fall roundup.

If Will's reading of the weather was right, that would come around in a month or so—maybe sooner if they needed some of the hands to work roundups in Cane Valley.

The camp cook hired for the fall roundup had the chuckwagon in pieces. He would check the running gear for wear, tighten the spokes and felloes in the wheels, lubricate the hubs and axles, work with the blacksmith to reset the iron tires, replace broken boards in the wagon box, patch up the chuck box, and otherwise get the kitchen conveyance in perfect working order.

A couple of cowboys worked the round corral, taking the rough off horses to add to the remuda for the fall gather. Tommy O'Shannon had already ordered roundup supplies and had set his hand to helping out repairing saddles and harnesses. Will was pleased to see the work carried on in his absence.

But it was the cow herds he was most interested in. He brought in a fresh horse from the saddle string—one the breakers told him was green and needed some saddle time—tied on his bedroll and grub sack and hit the trail.

At Antler Canyon, his first stop, Fishhook herds were spread into the hills up three of the side canyons branching off Rattle Creek. He had a good idea from past experience which canyons they would be in by now, and guessed right. A short ride up each drainage showed him what he needed to know—cows strong and healthy, calves showing good gain over the summer, yearlings so fat they were slick. It looked like another big deposit in the Fishhook bank accounts come shipping time.

Lem Garrett was the man in charge of the canyon herds, and Will found him in camp at the mouth of the third of the canyons Fishhook cattle occupied.

"How's it goin', Lem?"

"Can't complain, Will."

"Cattle look like they're gettin' plenty to eat."

Garrett nodded. "Plenty of feed in these mountains this year, all right."

"Any problems?"

"Not to speak of. If any cows have wandered off, it's been too few to matter. Had a mountain lion sniffin' around for a while, but one of the boys shot him before he got any calves—at least that we know of."

"How about Sam Ballard's men? They give you any trouble?"

"Not a bit. Ain't hardly seen any of 'em. Ain't caught a one of 'em burnin' a Rafter 7 brand on any of our long-eared calves, neither. Not a one."

"Well, that's a change, all right. Wish I could believe it would last."

"Doubt it will. I think they're buffaloed after killin' Jesse and Johnny. But they'll forget it before next summer, I suspect. Maverickin's a hard habit to break."

Will filled Lem in on the land and cattle he had acquired in Cane Valley and warned him they may round up early here to free some hands for fall works there, bid him goodbye, and rode on to inspect other herds.

Conditions were much the same everywhere—calves showing good growth, cows well fed, cowboys keeping an eye out for and branding slicks born late or missed in the spring, doctoring up cattle that took sick, keeping an eye out for rustlers and other varmints, and otherwise enjoying the best part of the cowboy life.

When Will got back to Fishhook headquarters he found a letter from Clint Shipley waiting for him.

> Will—
>
> Your offer is too good to pass up, so I wont. I told Sam and he did not take it well. Got mad as h--- to tell you the truth. It did not help that 4 of his best hands quit, said they worked for me and not for him. You said we would need men so I put them on the payroll. They are all good men. Olson at the bank says you wont mind. We are here in town redy to go when you say so.
>
> Yours,
> Clint Shipley

That, Will decided, was reason enough to get back to Ballard Station. He looked in on Emma—looking like she should have had the baby long ago—hit up cook for a quick meal, saddled a fresh horse, and got back on the road.

He got to town in time to share supper with Clint and the four cowboys that followed him off the Rafter 7. He sketched a rough map of Cane Valley, showing the path of the Rio Largo, the location of the town of the same name, the run of the valley road, the streams flowing out of the mountain range, the whereabouts of the ranches now part of the Fishhook, and the places he intended to add to the ranch.

"Looks like you oughta be able to do that soon enough," Shipley said. Tapping his finger at points on the map, he said, "You control the water here and here, and that means you can choke off these ranches here and here. They get thirsty enough, they'll sell. Or shut down."

Will said, "If it comes to it. I hope it won't. But we'll get that land before we're through."

Then it was off to the Elkhorn Saloon, where Will stood his new hands to several rounds of drinks, told them to be at the station with their saddles and bedrolls in time for the morning train to Rio Largo, and headed for the hotel.

Glancing into the hotel bar as he headed for the staircase, he saw Sam Ballard in a quiet corner with a well-used whiskey bottle in front of him. It reminded him of the many times he had seen Jesse Longmore in that same place. Will detoured into the bar and walked over to Sam's table.

"Evenin', Sam," he said. "What brings you to town?"

Ballard glared at him from under bushy eyebrows and turned up the corners of his mouth in what could not, under any circumstances, be called a sincere smile.

"Do not be daft, Willy boy. You know damn well why I am here. Fall works almost upon us and I find myself in the position of having to hire more cowboys than usual—all because you stole my men, you little sonofabitch."

"Your men? Hell, Sam, you remember that big war they fought a while back? The side that said you can't own a man won."

"That is as it may be. But there is no call for you to be poaching my men just to feed your greed."

Will laughed. "I guess you'd know about that, all right. Between you and Jesse Longmore, I've had a pretty good education in lust and gluttony and other such sins."

"You will learn it is a young man's game. I don't know that I have the stomach for it anymore."

"I guess there's plenty I could learn from you, Sam. Look, I went after Clint, all right. Them other men, that wasn't my doin's. Let me buy you a drink."

"Already got a drink. Get a glass and sit down and I will pour you one."

Ballard had a big head start on Will in the intoxication department and by the time they finished the bottle he was nearly incoherent. Sensing an advantage, Will ordered up another bottle of the bar's best and kept Ballard's glass topped up.

The old man harangued Will with many and longstanding complaints against Longmore. Mostly, the fact that he had been displaced as top dog in these parts when Longmore proved more ruthless in their race to empire. He claimed to be a man who liked power, but said Longmore took all the fun out of it.

"Why don't you get out of it, if you don't like it anymore?" Will said.

"Damned if I know. I wouldn't know how, I guess."

Will poured him another drink. "How 'bout I buy you out?"

Ballard laughed without mirth. Emptied his glass. Will refilled it.

"Don't be daft. I wouldn't sell a wind-broke nag to you. You are nothing more than an extension of Jesse Longmore."

Will refilled Ballard's glass. "C'mon, Sam. You ain't gettin' any younger. You might as well spend what years you got left enjoyin' life."

Ballard poured down another drink, belched, said, "What the hell do you care whether I enjoy life or not, boy?" His eyes were heavy.

Will poured Ballard's glass full again. "Don't, really. I care about gettin' more land, more cattle. More of everything. Buyin' the Rafter 7 would save me a lot of time and trouble."

Ballard belched, wiped his mouth with his sleeve. "I would sooner give it away," he said, suppressing another belch.

"Have another drink," Will said, topping off the old man's glass. "You a gamblin' man, Sam?"

"Was. There was a time I would risk everything I had on the turn of a card. I've become more cautious as I've aged."

"Lost your nerve, more likely."

"Like hell."

"Yep, Sam, I believe you have. One thing about old Jesse, he stayed tough right to the end."

The whiskey flush on Ballard's face deepened. "Just what is it you are saying, boy?"

"Oh, I didn't mean anything by it, Sam. Just that Jesse Longmore died goin' after what he wanted. He fought right up to the end. Risked everything and died like a man. To my way of thinkin' that's a hell of a lot better than playin' it safe and livin' like an old woman."

Slapping the palms of both hands to the tabletop, Ballard pushed himself upright. Too drunk to stand, he staggered and fell back into his chair. The whiskey bottle wobbled but stayed upright, his empty glass tumbled and rolled around its rim.

"You impertinent little bastard," he said. He tipped his glass upright again, and Will refilled it. Ballard drained the glass. "You know nothing about risk. Everything you have is yours by marriage. All given to you. You live in Jesse Longmore's shadow. And, as much as I hated the old reprobate, I don't believe you're worthy to stand there."

Will signaled the bartender and asked for another bottle and a deck of cards. When they arrived, he refilled Ballard's glass, although he was barely able to lift it, then opened the deck and shuffled the cards.

"Tell you what, Sam. Let's see just how much nerve you've got. One hand of poker. Five-card stud. Fishhook against the Rafter 7. Just the ranch, you understand. This don't include my holdings in Cane Valley or here in town. That oughta make the stakes about even—even tips it in your favor, I'd say, since the Fishhook's a bigger operation than yours."

Ballard drained off his drink, swirled the glass around in the wet rings it left on the table. He stopped when Will tapped it with the neck of the bottle and refilled it.

"Why would I risk it, Willy boy?"

"Oh, I don't know, Sam. Maybe just to prove to yourself that you're still as tough as old Longmore was—if ever you were."

"Why would you risk it?"

"I don't see that there's any risk. Looks to me like you ain't got a hair on your ass, Sam—you're nothin' but an old woman. At the very least, I walk away from here knowin' that."

Will paused, took a drink. "And you know, Sam, things like that have a way of gettin' around."

The drink Sam was taking just then did not make it to his already sloshing stomach. Instead, he spewed it across the tabletop in a fit of anger. "You sonofabitch," he said through clenched teeth. "Deal the cards."

"Now, don't be hasty. I don't want to push you into anything."

"I said, deal the cards."

"All right, Sam, all right. Just hold your horses." Will signaled the barkeep, told him to fetch a pen and paper. When he brought them back from the hotel desk, Will told him to write out the terms of the wager and to sign as a witness.

"Oh, Mister Hayes, I don't know about that."

"Listen, do you like your job here?

"Yes sir, Mister Hayes. Of course."

"And you know I own this place."

"Yes, sir."

"And that means you work for me."

"Yes, sir."

"So, you best do what you're damn well told."

"But—"

"But what?

"Mister Ballard, sir—he's pretty drunk."

Ballard said, "Do as he says. I am not some old woman. I do not need you watching out for me. Write it up."

The bartender pulled up a chair and wrote down the terms of the bet. Ballard scrawled a signature. Will signed. The bartender added his signature as witness.

Will said, "Now go lock that in the hotel safe. We wouldn't want anyone destroying the evidence if he loses his nerve."

"Just deal the cards," Ballard said. "We will see who loses his nerve."

Will shuffled the deck and slid it across the table for Longmore's cut. As he lifted the deck to deal, he spied the four of diamonds on the bottom and dealt it as Ballard's hole card. He dealt himself a hole card from the top of the deck, followed by an up card for each—king of spades for Ballard, nine of diamonds for himself. Will peeked at his hole card, the six of hearts.

The king of hearts turned up next for Ballard, the ace of clubs landed on Will's hand.

"It's not looking so good for you, Will."

"It ain't over yet."

He dealt Ballard the queen of spades, himself the six of diamonds he had seen on the bottom of the deck. Ballard took another look at his hole card and Will edged the next card off the top of the deck and saw it was the six of spades.

"Queen looks pretty good with my kings," Ballard said. "You have nothing showing."

As luck—or what passed for luck in a crooked game—would have it, the six of clubs was on the bottom of the deck. There was no way he could lose. If there ever had been.

He dealt the spade to Ballard. "Ha! Looks like I have your six, boy. Not that it would help much against my kings."

Ballard's eyes widened when the six of clubs landed on Will's hand, but not for long. "Pair of sixes," he said. "Looks like my kings win."

"Hold on a minute, Sam. We still got hole cards to show."

Ballard turned up his four. "No help there," he said. "But I don't need it, unless you have the other six under there." He grinned. "And with three of them already on the table, I don't see that happening."

The flush left the old man's face when Will turned up the six of hearts.

"Sorry, Sam. Three of a kind. You lose."

The heels of Ballard's fists hit the table, this time upsetting the nearly empty bottle and both glasses.

"You sonofabitch! You must have cheated!"

This time, Will grinned. "You saw the whole thing, Sam. Every card. Don't try to welch on me now, or you're more of an old woman than I thought."

Before long, the sun came up over Ballard Station. By the time it did, a quiet, private card game in the otherwise empty hotel bar was already the talk of the town. And it was common knowledge that Sam Ballard had been too drunk to be in his right mind. And that Wilson Hayes had poured the drinks that made him that way. And that Will had lured the drunken man into the game. And that there was every possibility—but no evidence—that the game was fixed.

When the train for Rio Largo pulled out that morning, the new owner of the Rafter 7 was aboard. The former owner was still in bed at the time. But he awakened later, cleaned out his sizeable accounts at the bank, and, later that day, boarded a train headed the opposite direction and was never again seen or heard from in the town that bears his name.

Chapter Twenty-Eight

Wilson Hayes and Clint Shipley and the former Rafter 7 cowboys who accompanied them rode toward the Fishhook holdings in Cane Valley.

"Tell me how you did it, Will," Shipley said.

"Hell, it don't make no never mind. Sam drank too much and let his pride get in the way."

"I didn't think the old man would ever give up on the Rafter 7. Let alone gamble it away on a poker hand."

"Like I said, he had too much to drink."

"But how 'bout you, Will? You could have lost the Fishhook."

"Clint, now that you're part of the Fishhook, it's important that you understand how I do business. I'll say this only once—I never gamble."

Will turned off the valley road to lead the group up Cottonwood Creek toward the Box-B. As they rode past the Diamond Bar house and yards, the owner left whatever work he was doing and stepped out of the barn to watch them pass. He offered no greeting and Will's reply was the same.

"I take it you're not too popular with that one," Shipley said.

"Nope," Will said. "He didn't much want to talk to me before. It don't look like he's changed his mind. He'll come around, though. He'll have to."

They toured the Box-B then pitched camp near the house and enjoyed a fine supper whipped up by Allie Barlow on short notice. Will and Clint and Ray talked business late into the night and come morning, rather than ride back downstream to the Rio Largo road, the Fishhook party took a cross-country route to the other outfits Clint would have charge of. Another long day of touring and another long night of campfire talk, and Will left it to Clint and his cowboys to decide how and where to go to work.

Will thought to pay a visit to Ira Wright and his Cane Creek ranch. Maybe, given the passage of time and time to consider, the young cowboy would be more amenable to some kind of relationship.

The narrow canyon was as handsome as Will remembered it—lush meadows lining the clear stream with its cover of cottonwood trees; patches of pines and aspens and scrub oak here and there on the canyon floor and clinging to steep canyon walls wherever rock outcrops and cliffs gave way to enough soil to support growth. He rode well beyond the place where he and Ira doctored the steer and noticed that, if anything, Cane Canyon grew more beautiful the farther into it you rode.

The gorge narrowed as he neared the box end. The trees thickened and Will could see a well-shaded log house tucked into the corner of the canyon. Next to it, Cane Creek originated in a spring that flowed out of the base of the canyon's rock wall. A half circle of piled rocks temporarily dammed the stream, creating a pool that tumbled over the rocks and into the streambed. Sunlight filtered through the trees, dappling the house, the ground, the water. The beauty was breathtaking.

Will did not even notice. All his attention was on the woman.

Knee deep in the pond, she dipped a cloth, raised it to her neck and squeezed out the water, which flowed over her porcelain skin. Stacked haphazardly atop her head, a mass of glistening auburn hair dripped thick tendrils over her shoulders and face. She continued laving water over her sculpted body, which glowed where sunstruck.

Will sat entranced.

Somehow sensing she was being watched, the woman froze, except for dark eyes which darted back and forth, seeking out the intruder. She saw Will and instinctively tried to cover her nakedness. Realizing it was too late, she dropped her arms in resignation, eyes locked on Will's. Then, turning, she walked out of the pond, gathered up and pulled a shift over her head. It clung to her wet skin, concealing no more than the water had. It was followed by a cotton-print housedress and some semblance of modesty was again hers.

"You must be Betty," Will said, when finally he could speak.

The woman let her hair down, tipped her head back, and shook the chestnut locks behind her shoulders. "I am," she said. "You might as well ride on in."

Will skirted the pond and tied his horse to a hitch rail beside the house then seated himself on the edge of the low porch. He said, "Is Ira around?"

"Who shall I say has come to call?"

"I'm sorry. We ain't been introduced," Will managed to say. "My name is Wilson Hayes."

"Oh, yes," she said to the red-faced intruder. "Ira mentioned your name. Something about helping him doctor a cow. Says you're bound to be a big man in Cane Valley."

"Yes, ma'am—about the doctoring, I mean."

"But not the other?"

"Maybe. Most likely. That's my plan, and I usually get what I want."

"Well, Mister Hayes, I'm afraid Ira is away just now. Went to town on business yesterday. Don't expect him until tomorrow. He's negotiating with buyers for the cattle that will be ready to ship soon."

"I'm sorry I missed him. I'll have to try again."

"That you will, Mister Hayes."

"Please, call me Will. I don't suppose a man could get a cup of coffee before ridin' on?"

Betty stepped onto the porch and opened the door. "Come on in."

Inside, in the soft, dim light of the house, the woman—as if such a thing were possible—looked even more beautiful to Will. She carried two mugs to the table where he sat then brought a coffee pot from the stove. Her nearness as she filled his mug overwhelmed Will and he grasped her wrist.

"Betty," he said. "I'm sorry to be so forward, but I swear you are the most beautiful woman I have ever seen."

She pulled her arm loose. "You've seen more than you've any right to, Mister Hayes—Will. And you know I am a married woman. Behave yourself."

"I'm sorry," he said, and occupied his hands with the coffee mug.

She sat opposite him at the table and they exchanged small talk. Had you asked him, Will could not have said what they talked about.

When the mugs were empty, Betty carried them to the sink. As she worked the pump to rinse them, Will walked up behind her, put his arms around her waist, and buried his face in her hair.

"Will—"

"I'm sorry, Betty," he said, pressing tighter against her. "I can't help it. I must have you."

Betty was not what you would call willing. But finding herself alone at an isolated ranch with a man who had lost all sense of propriety, knew no restraint, and was accustomed to having his way, she saw no alternative but to give him what he wanted.

Come morning, they were better acquainted than two married people not married to each other ought to be.

When he mounted up to ride away, Betty said, "I'll tell Ira you came by."

Will laughed. "You do that, Missus Wright. I'll be back."

He did not encounter Ira on his way out of Cane Canyon, or on the road to Rio Largo. Most likely, the Cane Creek rancher passed by while Will was checking in at one of the Fishhook properties to learn what Clint and the cowboys had planned. He spent another night discussing the Cane Valley situation with his foreman and agreed to a course of action for the ranches.

Will made it back to Rio Largo in time to stable his horse, have a meal, and board the afternoon train to Ballard Station. Glen Olson was working late at the bank, and answered Will's knock at the door.

"Come in Will. How are things in Cane Valley?"

He listened quietly while Will filled him on progress and plans. Then it was his turn.

"What about this business with Sam Ballard?"

"What about it?" Will said. "He signed the Rafter 7 over to me. The paper's locked up in the hotel safe. Soon as I get time, I'll have it recorded at the courthouse."

"I know that, Will. Sam left town the same day you did. Stuffed every penny he had on deposit here in a carpetbag, got on the train with an open ticket, and left for parts unknown. Before he did, he gave me an earful. As much as said you cheated him."

"It was a poker game, Glen. One hand. Winner take all. He watched every card dealt."

"According to Sam, you got him so drunk he couldn't see straight."

"I didn't get him drunk. He poured every single one of them drinks down his own throat. All I did was fill the glass. It ain't my job to watch out for him. If he wants to get drunk and gamble away his ranch, I'm glad to help him do it."

"Well, your stock in this town has dropped, Will. Folks aren't too happy with the situation."

"To hell with them. It ain't none of their business. What, did Sam raise a big stink all over town?"

"No. I think he was too embarrassed. And hung over. But, word gets around. The bartender over at the hotel, he didn't exactly verify Sam's story—but he didn't exactly deny it, either."

"All in all, Glen, I'd have to say I don't give a shit. Folks can think what they want."

"They can. And they will. Right now, they think it's a bad idea to let one man—you—have so much power and control."

"Let! What the hell do you mean, 'let'? Nobody 'let' me do any of it. I wanted to do it, and I did it. They didn't let me, and they won't keep me from doing whatever the hell I take a notion to do."

"That's just the trouble, Will. They know you can do whatever you please. It scares them. If you want my advice, you'll walk softly for a while. Give them time to calm down.

"We'll see," Will said as he put on his hat and got up to leave. "I'm goin' to the hotel."

"By the way, Will, that reminds me. Emma's there."

"Emma? Why?"

"I guess the baby's getting close, so she came into town to be near the doctor."

"I guess I better get over there. She won't be happy if I miss anything."

"No hurry, Will. I didn't mean to imply it was happening right now. I think you've got a few days."

"Still, if I don't show an interest I'm liable to catch hell."

And catch hell he did. No sooner did he open the door than Emma lit into him.

"Wilson Hayes! Leave this instant! I do not care for your company."

"Emma! What's wrong?"

"Don't you feign innocence with me. The news is all over town about your fleecing poor old Sam Ballard."

"Poor old Sam Ballard! Good hell, Emma, the man's been an enemy of the Longmores since before you were born. Never has a kind word about him ever been said by any member of your family. 'Poor old Sam Ballard' my ass!"

Emma pulled the bedcovers up to her chin. "Watch your language. You're not out riding with your cowboys now. For a change, I might add."

"You know I've got responsibilities. Someone's got to look after the Fishhook."

"Yes, I know. And 'someone' has to be in Cane Valley all the time to look out for the Fishhook. And now 'someone' will have to spend time on the Rafter 7 looking out for the Fishhook, because it's part of your empire now, too. What it means is that 'someone' won't have time for his family—which is what this baby will make us. As if you cared."

Will did not know what to say.

Emma talked on. "Tell me something, Will. Is there no end to your grasp? How many ways can you divide yourself up?"

"I'm awful sorry, Emma. Someone's got to tend to business."

"Hire someone. Heaven knows you can afford it."

"Runnin' a ranch is a big job. Not just anyone can do it."

"Oh, I see. Not only are you the big man around here, you're the only one with a big enough brain?"

"That ain't what I meant. I guess what I mean is, others can't do it right."

"Nonsense. What you mean is they can't do it to suit you. Not only that, if someone else does it, that means you can't pretend to be all knowing and all powerful. Folks might realize that the great Wilson Hayes is just an ordinary man. A lowborn Texan, at that."

Will stood silent for a time, leaning against the wall of the hotel room and fiddling with his hat. Finally, "I'm awful sorry, Emma. Soon as I get things runnin' smooth over in Cane Valley and get things sorted out at the Rafter 7, I'll stay home for a while. Maybe we'll take a trip, like we did after our wedding—even take the kid, if you want."

"Don't make promises you have no intention of keeping, Will. It will not go in your favor. I'll believe you are interested in something other than greed and power when I see evidence of it. Not until."

"All right, Emma. Sounds like I better get myself my own room."

"Look at me, Will!" Emma said, patting the bedclothes where they tented over her distended belly. "Did you really think, even for a moment, there was room for you in this bed?"

Will turned and left, arranged for a room, then headed for the Elkhorn Saloon. He picked up a beer and a bottle of whiskey and a glass at the bar, and found a table in the far corner. Just now, he did not care for company. And had he been attentive to the other patrons in the saloon, he would have noticed that no one cared for his company, either.

After draining the beer, he put together a plate from the stale food at the free lunch counter. A boiled egg, limp dill pickle, crust of dry bread, hunk of oily cheese, and slice of fusty ham didn't make much of a meal, but it was all he was likely to get at this hour.

Several drinks later, he corked the bottle and carried it back to the hotel.

He awakened hours later feeling the effects of both the food and the whiskey. Splashing his face with tepid water from the wash basin cleared his eyes some, but not his head. Leaning on arms propped on the windowsill, he watched Ballard Station come to life. When the bank clerk turned the key in the front door, he pulled on his boots, put on his hat, and walked gently down the stairs.

The newly arrived daytime man at the hotel desk was tidying up and arranging things to his satisfaction when Will asked him to open the safe and fetch the Sam Ballard paper. Then he pounded on the door of the bank until, finally, the clerk peeked from behind the window shade then fell all over himself getting the door open.

"Yes, Mister Hayes. Sorry. I didn't know it was you. How can I be of assistance?"

He thrust the paper into the clerk's hands. "Here. Give this to Glen when he shows up. Tell him I said to take it to the courthouse and make it official. I was going to do it, but I think I'd best get out to the Rafter 7 and make sure the place hasn't fallen apart."

Chapter Twenty-Nine

Rather than follow the road to the Rafter 7, Will left the track not far from town and headed into the hills, thinking to get a fresh look at some of his newly acquired land and cattle on the way to headquarters. While the grass had lost its green and cured to yellow-gold, there was plenty of it in the low country, which bode well for winter feed.

He started encountering cows as he climbed higher, and they looked to be in fine shape. It was evident that Sam hadn't been as careful about culling as he was on the Fishhook, as there were too many cows without calves at their sides. He'd see to that soon enough—those cows would find themselves in railroad cars after the fall gather.

As he rode down a ridge and out of a thicket of junipers, Will heard something zip past above his head, crackling the air as it went. He heard the report of the rifle as his spurs found the horse's belly and Will reined it hard into another cluster of trees. Once concealed, in one motion he swung out of the saddle, drew his rifle from its scabbard, dropped the reins, and scrambled for thicker cover.

A faint wisp of smoke floated in the still air above a rock outcrop on the opposite ridge. Further examination revealed a dun horse standing in a nearby clump of boulders. Its ears were sharp, its eyes on him. The reins dangled, which meant that mount, like his, was ground tied. That told Will the sniper had probably not been laying for him—how could he have been, when no one knew he was coming?—but had seen him ride over the ridge and taken the opportunity. The why of it was another question.

Will watched carefully, looking for the shooter to reveal himself. After a moment, he detected a slight movement and soon made it out as the shift of a rifle barrel. If the barrel was moving, it was not fixed on him—maybe the rifleman lost sight of him in the mad dash through the juniper trees. He levered a shell into the chamber and sighted in on the gun barrel protruding from the rocks. He knew he could not hit what he could not see, but a near miss—if it was near enough—might flush the gunman from his nest.

He squeezed off a shot and saw the flash of a spark as it hit rock and pinged off into the dirt. As he hoped, the sniper jumped up and sidestepped toward his horse, pumping lead into the hillside as fast as he could jack the lever on his rifle. Will realized his opponent had no idea where he was. That gave him time to draw a bead on the panicked shooter. His aim proved true. The bullet staggered the man and the shirtfront that showed in the V of his vest bloomed scarlet. He sat down against the steep hillside, then leaned into it as his legs straightened and he slid, slowly, a couple of yards down the slope piling dirt with his spurred boot heels as he went. The dun horse, Will noticed, hadn't moved an inch though all the commotion.

Retrieving his own horse, Will fed two cartridges from his saddlebags into the rifle to replace the ones he had fired and slid it into its sheath, checked his cinch, then mounted up and made his way to the base of the ridge and started up the opposite side of the canyon on a switchback route that would take him to the dead man.

The dun horse was a mite disturbed by the smell of blood, yet stood still but for its trembling. Will led it to a spot on the steep hillside just below its downed rider. He hefted the dead weight and flopped it over the saddle. A pigging string from the cowboy's saddlebags, cut in two, served as a tether to secure the man's wrists to one stirrup and his ankles to the other.

Will decided to abandon his tour and rode off on a more direct route toward Rafter 7 headquarters, the bloody load in tow.

He rode into the yard and found Harry Dalton, the Rafter 7's cow boss and *segundo* to Clint Shipley, leaning against a heavy corner post on a corral as if holding it up. Will pulled up in front of him and tossed the dead cowboy's hat at him. "Recognize that?" he said.

"Sure," Dalton said, nodding toward the body. "His."

"Who is he?"

"Who was he, looks like you mean. Billy Camden was his name. Showed up here not long after you left. Didn't have two pennies to rub together. Wasn't much of a cowboy. But, the old man gave him a chance."

"Why would he bushwhack me?"

"Well, Billy was kind of a hothead. No one around here is too happy with what you done to—what happened with Mister Ballard. Billy, though, he took it personal. He really liked the old man. Guess he saw a chance at payback and took it."

"You say others are unhappy. Any more of them likely to try to shoot me?"

"Don't think so."

"Good. It'll save me havin' to kill them."

"That's welcome news, Will. Seems like you've cost us enough men already."

Will shifted in the saddle. "Tell me, Harry, how's things goin' around here?"

"Well as can be expected, I suppose. We're a little at loose ends. But, with the cows out on grass, things kind of take care of themselves. 'Course that'll change in a few weeks when we need more hands for fall roundup."

"One more question, Harry. Think you could handle Shipley's old job?"

"Foreman? I reckon so. I been around here long enough to know how things work."

"I can pretty much guarantee things won't work that way anymore. Will that be a problem?"

"I reckon not. I been takin' orders long enough to know how to do that, too. You just tell me how you want things done, I'll see it gets done."

"Sounds good." Will dismounted and handed the dun horse's lead rope to the foreman. "Get rid of this and meet me in the bunkhouse. That filthy old man still the cook around here?"

"That he is."

"I'll see if I can get him to fix me something to eat."

"Good luck," Dalton said and led the laden horse away.

Will rousted the cook out of a wad of biscuit dough and told him to rustle up anything he could in a hurry. By the time leftover beefsteak, scrambled eggs, reheated beans, and cold biscuits hit the table, Dalton had tended to the dun horse and set the chore boy to digging a grave.

"Grab a plate," Will said.

"No thanks. Ain't been that long since breakfast."

"Long time since supper, though," Will managed to say between the bites he shoveled in. "And a damn sorry supper it was."

After doing away with enough of the food to take the edge off his appetite, Will told Dalton of his plans for the upcoming roundup.

"Take what hands you've got and start to gather out of Antler Canyon. The Fishhook hands and your men can team up, seein's as how we don't need to keep the herds separate once we brand the Rafter 7 cattle. There ought to be enough riders for that, anyway. I'll send orders with you for the Fishhook cow boss so he'll know.

"I've got to go to Cane Valley and get things goin' over there. I'll see if I can find some cowboys in Rio Largo to send over, and maybe I can flush some out of the saloon in Ballard Station when I get back. By that time, you ought to be about done in the Canyon and we'll figure out what to do next."

By the time Will made it to the old Box-B headquarters in Cane Valley, Clint Shipley had most of a crew assembled and preparations for the gather there were well underway, with supplies laid in, a chuckwagon outfitted, a remuda assembled, and Fishhook branding irons forged. Fall works here in Cane Valley, as at the Rafter 7, would involve stamping the Fishhook brand on all the acquired stock.

Clint had his hands divided into two crews to work the hills and canyons, but did not believe any of his men would serve to head up the second crew. Will told him to ride to Cane Canyon and offer Ira Wright whatever it took to recruit him for a few weeks' work.

It took some talking, but Clint convinced Ira to come to work for a while, with the guarantee that once the Fishhook work was handled, he could take as many cowboys as he needed to cut out and move the cattle he had sold on contract to the railroad pens at Rio Largo.

Will sat in the shade of a juniper tree, his horse hitched out of sight in a dry wash, and watched Shipley and Wright ride out of Cane Canyon. As soon as the dust settled, he pulled his cinch tight, mounted up, and rode toward the log house at the head of Cane Creek.

Afterward, tangled in bedclothes and out of breath, Betty told Will they had to stop. "It's not right," she said. "You're married. I'm married. And, God knows, I love Ira. I don't even know why I'm doing this."

"Does it matter? Maybe it's wrong—but somehow, it's right. I don't know how the hell that works. But no matter, there ain't no way I can do without you. I only wish I could have you all the time."

Betty rolled closer to him. "I can't see how that can happen. But you're here now."

Will stayed the night and rode out in the morning for Rio Largo, the train, and Ballard Station. He was probably a father by now and thought it best to try to make peace with Emma.

Come sunrise, with six itinerant saddle tramps he had gathered up along the way, Will rode out to Antler Canyon and delivered the cowboys. There was already a sizeable herd of Rafter 7 cattle assembled, and branding fires flamed bright. The smoke and sharp odor of burning hair drifted heavy in the air, the bawling of confused cattle echoed through the hills, and Rattle Creek ran thick with mud stirred up by milling hooves. The new hands pitched in, speeding up the process of burning the J-shaped Fishhook brand on the Rafter 7 herd.

Will rode deeper into the canyon to check on the gather of the Fishhook cattle and found what he guessed must be two-thirds of their number loose herded on the canyon floor, awaiting the others the cowboys were still pushing downhill from the many prongs of Antler Canyon.

Already, the sun was low enough that its rays did not penetrate the depths of the canyon, but there would still be an hour or two of faded daylight. Will rode back down to the branding fires, pulled down his lariat and started in to roping and dragging cattle to the hands on the ground crew. When loss of light halted the work, he helped push the cut of branded cattle a ways down canyon to avoid mixing.

He unsaddled in the dark, gave his horse to the night-hawk to run with the remuda, and lined up at the chuck-wagon for a hot supper and some scalding coffee and settled in to spend the night. Morning—and Emma—would come soon enough.

"What do you mean she moved out?" Will asked the cook at the Fishhook ranch house.

"She didn't say why. When she came back from town with the baby—a handsome boy, by the way—she packed up her things and had Tommy tote the baby bed over to the new house."

"Sonofabitch!" Will said. "Pardon the language, ma'am, but I don't know what else to say."

He stomped out of the house and across the yard to the house built for him, but in which he had never slept a night—unless you count the time old Longmore tried to kill him and he huddled in the cold within the unfinished walls. Without stopping to knock or wipe his feet, Will flung the front door open, banging it on its hinges. "Emma!"

The shout brought his wife into the front room, face gone pale. She wiped her hands on her apron and shushed Will, said, "You'll wake the baby!"

"I don't give a damn. What I—"

"That's certainly the truth. You don't give a damn about the baby, or me, or anything else but your damned empire."

"That ain't what I meant. What I was sayin' is, why the hell are you livin' here again?"

"Because this is the only place on this ranch that doesn't stink of you. I don't know what the future holds, Will, but for now you're to stay clear of me. If ever you decide to put aside your pride and conceit and be satisfied with owning less than everything, we'll talk."

"This got anything to do with Sam Ballard?"

"Sam Ballard, those folks over in Cane Valley—all of it. Word gets around, Will. You can't expect to ride roughshod over people to get what you want and expect people to like it. Half the people in Ballard Station are scared of what you might do—far as they know, you could turn them out any minute."

"What the hell, Emma! Don't you see I'm doing this for us? For you, and that baby boy in there?"

Emma laughed. "Oh, Will—you sound just like Papa. He always liked to pretend there was some highfalutin reason for his avarice, but it was nothing but lust for power. And you're no different. I don't know how you came to be the man you are, but you're sure not the man I married."

Will stared at her, his mouth opening and closing in an attempt to find words.

"By the way," Emma said, "his name is John. And I hope he grows up to be more like my brother than his father. Now, get out."

Chapter Thirty

Winter seemed colder than usual to Will. He divided his time between Fishhook headquarters, the old Rafter 7, and what was once the Box-B in Cane Valley. He rode into the Box-B late one evening and sat down with Clint Shipley.

"You know, Clint, about that herd of purebred Herefords we're runnin' on the old Fishhook?"

"Heard tell of 'em, but I ain't seen 'em. Ain't seen too many of those fancy cattle anywhere, to tell you the truth. Why?"

"There's more and more of them showin' up around the country, and from what I read in the papers, some ranches are havin' good luck usin' them red and white critters as herd bulls. I'm thinkin' demand is likely to go up. So, what I'm wantin' to do is to start up a purebred herd here. Between the two bunches, we oughta could raise enough bulls to make it worthwhile."

"If you say so, boss. Where we gonna come up with breedin' stock?"

"Denver. From what I hear, there are a few established herds around there. That, and they're shipping in more and more Herefords and runnin' them through the sale yards up that way. I'm thinkin' Ira Wright might be sufferin' from cabin fever in that canyon of his and would maybe welcome a chance to get out. See if you can hire him to make a buying trip for us. The man's got a good eye for breeding stock and I believe he'd do us right."

"Whyn't you go yourself, boss?"

"I got more than I can do already. Besides, it's colder than hell in that Colorado high country. There's plenty enough winter for me, right here."

When Shipley rode out in the morning to recruit Ira Wright for the job, Will rode the opposite direction and took a room in Rio Largo. A couple of afternoons later, he watched out the window as Ira boarded the train. The smoke of the departed locomotive was still visible when he led his horse out of the livery stable and headed up the valley road toward Cane Canyon.

He stayed a week with Betty in the log house, and the only time either of them went outdoors was to visit the backhouse or fill the wood box.

Later in the winter, he contrived another outing for Ira, this time delivering a shipment of saddle horses to a buyer down on the border, for further shipment somewhere in Mexico. That trip kept Will at the Cane Creek ranch for most of another week.

As he and Betty lay abed the afternoon he planned to leave, she sat up, flung her auburn mane behind her back with a flick of her head and said, "Will, I'm not sure—but pretty sure—that I am with child."

Will yawned and stretched, and wove his fingers behind his head. "I imagine Ira will be pleased."

"No, Will, he won't."

"Why ever not?"

"He's tried to get me in the family way ever since we married. But we gave up long ago thinking it would ever happen. We knew one or the other of us isn't working properly in the reproduction department. It's pretty obvious, now, that it's Ira."

"Damn."

"I don't know what to do."

"Come away with me, Betty. Leave Ira and come with me."

"You've already got a wife, Will. Besides, I couldn't leave Ira. I still love the man—despite all this."

"But what about him? What'll he do? If you're right, he ain't gonna be too happy with the news."

"I don't know. I'll have to think on it some more. Though, heaven knows, thinking about it hasn't done gotten me anywhere so far. He might turn me out. And I wouldn't blame him if he did."

"I sure as hell would blame him, Betty. Any man that would let you out of his grasp ain't worth spit. And that includes me—which is why I'll always stick with you, no matter what. And I hope to hell we find a way to be together."

He rode back to the Box-B in a snowstorm in the gloaming, bundled up against a stiff wind. And so he did not notice, as he rode past the Diamond Bar, the owner watching him through a window. Nor was he aware that the man took a rifle from the rack, pulled on a coat, and left the house.

The first hint he had that something was amiss was hearing—and feeling—the thwack of a bullet slamming into his horse's flesh. The crack of the rifle followed instantly. The animal staggered but once and folded up, hitting the snowy ground and rolling to the side, pinning Will's leg.

Lying still despite the pain, he watched the horse struggle to draw a few last breaths, shudder, and still. In the silences between gusts of wind, he heard approaching footsteps squeaking through the cold snow. He could not see past the dead horse to locate his attacker. Carefully, he pulled his pistol but kept his hand and arm under his body. Twice, the footsteps stopped, waited, then slowly walked on. Will imagined the man, both hands on his rifle, watching him for any movement. He made sure there was nothing to see.

The third time he stopped, Will knew the Diamond Bar rancher was no more than ten feet away, separated only by the horse that lay cooling between them.

With a roar like a wounded bear, Will rolled onto his back, swung his revolver into line and blew a hole in his attacker's throat, drilling through an artery and releasing an arc of blood that looked black in the dim light, steaming as it splashed to the snow. The man dropped the rifle and grabbed at this neck and blood welled between his fingers then poured out his mouth as if someone turned a valve somewhere. The surprise in his eyes dimmed as he fell to his knees then tipped over unhindered, face first into the snow.

It took more than an hour of lying in the cold snow for Will to finally wiggle his way out from under his fallen mount. He worked his leg this way then that, pushed his other leg against the saddle for leverage, sat up and lay down and sat up and lay down again, each time gaining a fraction of an inch toward freedom.

When finally he pulled free, his clothing was soaked through from head to toe, and, if feeling was any indication, through and through. There was not an inch of his body that wasn't chilled. Will untied the tie strings securing his saddlebags, slung them over his shoulder, and hobbled off toward the Box-B.

He staggered into the bunkhouse, that being the first occupied building he came to, well before daylight. The bleary-eyed cowboys awakened by the ruckus of his entry carried him to the ranch house and rousted Clint Shipley from a dead sleep. He, in turn, awakened the cook.

They stripped Will to the skin and rubbed him down with towels to get his circulation going, poured whiskey down a throat almost too weak to swallow, and followed it with coffee as soon as the pot boiled. He spent three days and nights on a pallet on the floor next to the kitchen cook stove, with one of the hands assigned to keep it stoked through the night. The men who did so wondered, each in his turn, how a man under so much cover and so close to a stove hot enough to glow red could shiver so.

The storm turned out to be the last of the season, and the snow that hadn't blown away in the wind soon melted off. Will lingered at the Box-B for weeks. Even after he was up and around, he did not drift too far from the stove in a futile attempt to melt the ice in his veins. Soon, with calves on the ground all over the valley, it would be time to think about heating the branding irons.

"Clint," Will said one evening as they sat sipping coffee at the kitchen table. "I need your help with something. It's an unpleasant job—worse than that—but it's got to be done."

"Tell me about it."

Will hesitated, rotating his coffee mug in his hands. "What I'm about to say ain't to go no farther than you."

Clint nodded.

"It's Ira Wright. I've got myself crosswise where he's concerned."

"You're talking about you and his wife, ain't you?"

Will's eyebrows shot up.

"It ain't nearly the secret you think it is, Will. I suspected it long before I knew it. I know some of the hands wouldn't be surprised to hear it, either."

"Who else?

"I don't think it goes beyond here."

"I may as well tell you the whole of it then. She's gonna have a baby. And it seems she and Ira haven't been able to get that job done on their own. So, once it becomes obvious, it's gonna mean trouble for Betty."

"I can see that, all right."

Will said, "Here's what I want to do."

For the next several nights, Will and Clint rode through the Fishhook herd and cut out a few cows with their calves and confined them in a pen in an out-of-the-way canyon. Then, for good measure, they gathered some from the herds of smaller ranchers in the area. Once they had about twenty pairs assembled, they kindled a fire and used a running iron to burn the CC brand of the Cane Creek ranch on the hides of the calves and whittled their ears with the proper marks for Ira Wright's cattle.

They drove the small herd into Cane Canyon and ran them in among Ira's cattle.

"All right, Clint, there's that done. Now, I'll go into town for the law. You take a couple of hands and call on these ranchers. Tell them you've got it on good authority that Ira Wright has been swinging a wide loop. Once you get them onto his place—well, things ought to take care of themselves."

"I don't like it, Will."

"I don't either. Ira's a good man. But I'm backed into a corner here and don't see any way out of it, but this."

Clint ducked his head and took a big breath.

"You with me on this, Clint?"

"I guess so. But I don't like it."

*****

Will and the marshal from Rio Largo rode into Cane Canyon the next afternoon. The day was a pleasant one, but, still, Will rode bundled in a heavy coat. Nothing seemed amiss as they followed the creek up the gorge. Soon enough, they came across cattle grazing in the meadows, seeking out fresh green shoots from among last year's grass.

"Look here," Will said, pointing out a calf newly branded CC sucking a cow with a Fishhook brand. A few other mismatched pairs showed as they rode through the scattered herd.

"That sure don't look right," the marshal said. "I'd have never thought it of Ira."

"Neither did I. I guess tucked back here in this canyon, he figures he's safe. Kind of off the beaten path."

"I guess. Could be."

A little farther on, a saddled horse grazed among the cattle, dragging bridle reins.

"That don't look right, either," the marshal said.

They rode toward the horse, in the direction of the creek. The marshal pulled up so suddenly his horse fought its head.

"Sonofabitch!" he said. "Look at that."

Ira Wright dangled from the limb of a tall cottonwood tree, twisting slowly in the gentle spring breeze.

"I'll be damned," Will said.

"Looks like you ain't the only one suspected his calves don't suck the right cows."

Will rode over to the hanged man and pulled loose a sheet of paper hanging on a button of his vest.

"What's it say?"

"Cow Thief," Will read. "T-h-e-e-f, they spelled it."

The marshal rode up and Will handed him the paper. "Why don't you go fetch his horse."

Will opened his jack knife, stood up on his saddle seat and sliced through the taut lariat. All that was left of Ira Wright fell to the ground with a thump like a side of beef hitting a butcher block.

Chapter Thirty-One

It took two days, but Betty Wright shoveled out a grave for Ira.

The marshal and Will offered to do it, but she ordered them out of Cane Canyon with a vehemence that surprised the lawman. Her pique was especially directed at Hayes, but the marshal had no idea why.

When they rode up to the ranch house with her husband slung over the saddle facedown, the lawman explained what happened, and why. Betty collapsed, sobbing on her knees on the porch. But she was soon on her feet, eyes dried and shooting fire that seemed to burn holes through Will. She did not know how or why but was certain he was, one way or another, responsible for Ira's death.

Once she refilled the fresh grave beside Ira's grandparents in the family plot under the trees behind the house, she waded naked into the pond to wash off the soil and sweat and stink. She hitched the team to the buckboard and drove it up next to the porch. She hauled her empty trunk out of the house and hefted it into the wagon then carried out and packed her belongings there, afraid she would not have been able to load the trunk alone if full. With her few other goods loaded, she shut the door, lifted the endgate, and lurched away with a snap of the lines on the rumps of the horses.

And so Betty Wright left Cane Creek ranch forever, leaving the gates open as she drove out of the canyon.

*****

Will sat alone in the ranch house dining room at the Fishhook. The stove ticked and wheezed with heat, but still he huddled against the cold. He nursed a tumbler of whiskey, disappointed in its inability to warm him from within. Autumn was barely upon them and already he was chilled to the core; a chill no warmth could penetrate.

By now, he figured, he was a father twice over.

His son, living no more than a stone's throw away, did not know him. And the boy's mother was determined to keep it that way. Emma was already making overtures about leaving him and moving to town—and not Ballard Station—to provide John better opportunities.

He did not know anything of the child he fathered with Betty—if it lived, if it was boy or girl, where it lived, how its mother fared.

He craved the advent of fall works. Once the round-ups—here, on the old Rafter 7, in Cane Valley—occupied his mind, perhaps he could quit worrying so much about things he could not control. More and more, it seemed, the things he could not control controlled him.

Refilling the glass, Will slid it aside, propped his elbows on the table, and buried his face in his hands. Heaving a sigh, he flopped back in the chair. Blinking burning, tired, eyes, he looked around the dining room and settled his gaze on his dusty old guitar propped in the corner, broken strings twisted and coiled around splintered, shattered wood.

*****

No one knew what became of Clint Shipley.

All they knew is that he rode out one morning and did not come back. They knew he had not quit the country, for his saddled horse trotted into the old Box-B ranch that evening dangling broken bridle reins.

If he suffered an accident, they could find no evidence of it. They rode far and wide, day after day, but found no broken man, no lifeless body, no indication at all of what happened or where it happened.

But had someone, anyone, been standing on the Rio Largo bridge, or on the railroad span across the river as it left town, he might have seen Clint Shipley drift past, slowly rolling in the current. This far downstream from his entry into the waterway, there would be no crimson tendrils drifting and dissipating in his wake for his blood would long since have clotted or drained from his body.

And so, one would have to fish Clint's corpse out of the stream and see the bullet hole between his shoulder blades, its edges burned black, to understand the cause of his demise.

*****

Wilson Hayes thrashed around, arranging and rearranging the heavy bedclothes.

No matter how deep he piled the quilts and blankets and robes or how red the woodstove glowed or how high the flames roared in the fireplace he could not ward off the chill that emanated from his bones.

He thought of all the power and possessions he had worked so hard to have and to hold. More of everything than any other man in the territory—any three men, four men, for that matter. More land. More cattle to graze the land. More horses to work the cattle. More cowboys working for wages riding the horses and tending the cattle. More wagons, more cow camps, more shipping pens. More buying. More selling. More money. More banks to hold it.

More and more and more, he thought, and still more.

And yet it was not enough.
Not enough to keep a man warm in his own bed.

About the Author

Winner of four Western Writers of America Spur Awards and a Spur Award finalist on six other occasions, Rod Miller writes fiction, poetry, and history about the American West. A lifelong Westerner raised in a cowboy family, Miller is a former rodeo contestant, worked in radio and television production, and is a retired advertising agency copywriter and creative director. Miller's award-winning poetry and short stories have appeared in numerous anthologies, and several magazines have carried his byline.

Find the author online at:
writerRodMiller.com,
writerRodMiller.blogspot.com,
RawhideRobinson.com.

Coming Soon!

ROD MILLER
FATHER UNTO MANY SONS

Is Lee Pate a man of principle or a misguided dreamer? Troubled by the institution of slavery, he uproots his family— wife, Sarah, and sons, Richard, Melvin, and Abel—without notice and heads west. Lee sends his sons back to Tennessee on a quest that will change the relationship between the brothers forever. In Fort Smith, the Pate family meets the Lewises, a Mormon family fleeing persecution in Missouri. Together, they follow a barely explored trail to the Mexican Province of New Mexico. The travelers face many difficulties, but family struggles prove the most formidable obstacle. Testing the strength of family ties. . .

For more information
visit: www.SpeakingVolumes.us